KT-459-902

FACELESS MORTALS

by

Bob Cook

Dales Large Print Books
Long Preston, North Yorkshire,
BD23 4ND, England.

British Library Cataloguing in Publication Data.

Cook, Bob
    Faceless mortals.

    A catalogue record of this book is
    available from the British Library

    ISBN   1-84262-010-X pbk

COVENTRY CITY LIBRARIES
3. 4. 07

First published in Great Britain by Victor Gollancz Ltd., 1988

Copyright © Bob Cook, 1988

The moral right of the author has been asserted

Published in Large Print 2000 by arrangement with
Sheil Land Associates Ltd.

All Rights reserved. No part of this publication may be
reproduced, stored in a retrieval system, or transmitted in any
form or by any means, electronic, mechanical, photocopying,
recording or otherwise without the prior permission of the
Copyright owner.

Dales Large Print is an imprint of Library Magna Books Ltd.

Printed and bound in Great Britain by
T.J. (International) Ltd., Cornwall, PL28 8RW

3 8002 01381 7707

CITY OF ... SALE

STO

ADV.

FACELESS MORTALS

When Herbie Feigl, teacher at an obscure English prep-school, goes missing in Yugoslavia he is branded a spy. Michael Wyman, ex-MI6, begins to investigate – could Feigl really be a KGB agent? Is he still alive?

As he travels around Europe Wyman realises that others are on his trail: the CIA, the KGB, the President of a neutral state – they are all seeking Feigl. The Superpowers stalk Wyman as he draws nearer to the dark secret which could have devastating consequences if revealed.

FACELESS MORTALS

To my foreign informant
in recognition of his courage
in the face of savage
political oppression

A civil servant is like a faceless mortal riding like a flea on the back of the dog, Legislation.

Anonymous

Your public servants serve you right.

Adlai Stevenson

PROLOGUE

Frank Schofield was still alive. It was generally agreed that he had no right to be. He was too old, too fat, and too bibulous. Most importantly, he was retired. Old journalists do not fade away: they die of cirrhosis, or tachycardia, or plain dilapidation. For some reason, retirement hastens the process.

But Frank Schofield defied the rules. Each evening the ancient American would haul his swollen, nicotine-stained carcass up the stairs of Rome's Foreign Press Club and into the bar, as he had done for nearly fifty years. There he would hold court, dispensing anecdotes and advice, and tormenting the barman with his execrable Italian.

Tonight was no different, except that Schofield arrived a little earlier than usual, and there were no other journalists around. The pack were away in Milan, covering a scandal involving an industrialist, a bishop, and a modelling agency. 'Sounds fascinating,' Frank had yawned. 'Tell me about it later.'

Yet he would not be alone this evening. An old friend had made an appointment to see him, and though he did not know the purpose of the visit, he suspected it would be more than just a social call.

His friend arrived at half-past eight: a portly, bespectacled Englishman with thinning white hair and an air of tweedy tattiness. Schofield grinned affably and shook his hand.

'Evening, Mike,' he said. 'You well?'

'As ever, Frank.'

Professor Michael Wyman taught Philosophy at the University of Rome. He had only been there a couple of years: formerly, he worked for the British Foreign Office, but had left under peculiar circumstances. His friendship with Schofield dated back some twenty-five years, when Wyman had been posted to the British Embassy in Rome.

Like most of his profession, Schofield had little time for academics, but Wyman was an honourable exception. The Englishman was an unusual character, who collected interesting experiences the way other people acquire postage stamps.

'What are we drinking this evening?' Wyman asked.

Schofield shrugged.

'Depends on what kind of evening it's going to be. At the moment it's Scotch, but I'm broad-minded.'

Wyman placed a folder of documents down on the bar, and smiled apologetically at the American.

'It may well be a long session,' he said.

'OK,' Schofield said. 'In that case, grappa. It gives good mileage.'

They ordered two glasses of the spirit, and sat down at a table. Schofield studied Wyman's folder with interest.

'What exactly have you got here?' he inquired.

'A story, I think.'

Schofield frowned sternly.

'In case you've forgotten,' he said, 'I'm out to grass. Nowadays I don't write stories. I just listen to them.'

'I know,' Wyman said. 'But I'd be grateful if you considered this one. I want it printed rather urgently. No, don't pull a face: even by your own exacting standards, this is extraordinary stuff. Quite explosive, in fact.'

'They always are.'

'No, they seldom are, but this is in that league. I dare say someone would pay handsomely for it, and you're welcome to

13

anything they're offering.'

'You're too kind,' Schofield laughed. 'Trouble is, I wasn't planning to make a spectacular comeback.'

'Think of it as a supplement to your pension,' Wyman suggested.

Schofield chuckled and took a sip of grappa.

'Tenacious bastard, aren't you?' he said.

Wyman nodded solemnly.

'That's right.'

Schofield leaned back in his seat and lit a cigarette. After a long pause, he sighed regretfully, like a man ignoring his better judgment.

'OK,' he said. 'Impress me.'

SUMMER

Here comes Summer, the violent season!

Guillaume Apollinaire *Zone*

SUMMER

Here comes Summer, the violent season.

Guillaume Apollinaire *Zone*

ONE

'You're a bunch of limp pricks,' General Zhdanov said charitably.

'Yes General,' Kuleshov said.

'Useless,' Zhdanov grunted.

'I'm sorry General.'

'Tell me how it happened.'

'He simply vanished. We tracked him down to a resort in Yugoslavia–'

'Don't give me that shit,' Zhdanov broke in. 'He takes his summer holiday there every year. There was no "tracking down" involved: you knew damned well he'd be going there again. So don't try to excuse your stupidity with mythical feats of detective work.'

'I beg your pardon, General,' Kuleshov said. 'We knew he was going to Yugoslavia, so we sent Rudenko there to keep an eye on him. By the time Rudenko arrived he'd disappeared.'

'Indeed,' Zhdanov snorted. He got to his feet and stomped impatiently around the office. The General was well into his seventh decade, but he still had the build of a heavyweight wrestler. In contrast, Kuleshov was frail and scrawny. The General did terrible things to his blood-pressure.

'Yes,' Kuleshov said uneasily. 'He took a walk one afternoon along the lake and didn't return. By the time Rudenko arrived, the police had taken charge. There were search-parties looking for him in the forest, and a team of divers dragging the lake.'

'But nobody found the body,' Zhdanov grinned.

'That is so,' Kuleshov admitted. 'The woods are very dense. It's probably just a matter of time.'

'Bollocks,' said the General.

Kuleshov took a deep breath. Like all bureaucrats, he hated and feared plain speech. Unfortunately, the old man understood this very well, and took a savage delight in bombarding Kuleshov's defences with a battery of expletives.

'Bollocks,' the General repeated. 'How do you know he didn't just sneak out of the country? It can't be more than twenty miles to the Austrian border.'

'It's possible, but Rudenko thinks it unlikely. He checked at the hotel: they still had all the man's belongings, including passport and cash.'

'That means nothing,' Zhdanov said. 'He might have been carrying false papers.'

'Maybe,' Kuleshov agreed. 'But all the locals seemed to think he met with some kind of accident.'

'Perhaps that's what they were supposed to think,' Zhdanov said heavily. He shook his head in disgust and stepped over to the window.

In the square below, the Moscow evening rush hour had already begun. Commuters swarmed across the pavements, jostling and barging their way into the Metro station, while grimy cars and battered taxis sped the more affluent citizens away to homes in the outer suburbs. In the middle of it all stood the statue of Zhdanov's great predecessor, Dzerzhinsky, gazing thoughtfully into space, oblivious of the noisy stampede. Of course, it wasn't called the KGB when Dzerzhinsky founded it: in those days it was known as the CHEKA. There was no difference, Zhdanov thought; the old man was surrounded by useless fools, just like me.

'The fact is,' Zhdanov said, 'he should have been tailed all the way from England to Yugoslavia. Shouldn't he?'

He turned round and stared grimly at Kuleshov.

19

'Perhaps,' Kuleshov conceded. 'But we did piece together his itinerary. He spent a couple of days in Vienna–'

'Exactly,' Zhdanov said. 'Vienna! Hardly a coincidence, is it? But you don't know what he was up to, do you?'

'Not yet,' Kuleshov said lamely. 'But Rudenko–'

'Fuck Rudenko. And fuck you, too. That man should have been tailed all the way. But you treated this like just another routine job, and fouled it up. You people make me spew.'

Kuleshov tried to think of something re-assuring to say, but nothing sprang to mind.

'You still don't think he was important, do you?' Zhdanov said. 'You're still not convinced. That's why you've made such a stinking mess of all this, isn't it?'

'I must confess, General, we do have our doubts. We're talking about a man whose hypothetical knowledge has hypothetical bearing on a hypothetical project. It's all a little–'

The General was not gifted with much patience. Suddenly, he lost what little he had. He walked up to Kuleshov and bawled into his face.

'This isn't a fucking seminar, you pillock!

I'm not interested in your poxy opinions, and I never asked for them. All I want is that you do as you're told. Otherwise, I'll chew your balls off. Right?'

From a range of four inches, Kuleshov got an interesting view of the General's features. They were pitted, leathery, and suffused with blood vessels. Tufts of grey hair sprouted in unexpected places. Matters were not helped by the General's breath, whose aroma was an unhappy compound of vodka, tobacco and onions. Kuleshov decided that the General improved with distance. He wiped the spittle from his face and tried to recover his composure.

'What does the General require?' he asked stiffly.

'Find him,' Zhdanov said. 'No ifs, no buts, no *hypotheses.*'

'And then?'

'Then speak to me. Make it a top priority, Kuleshov. And follow up any leads, however trivial.'

Kuleshov nodded reluctantly.

'Yes, General. What if they find a body? In Yugoslavia, I mean.'

'They won't,' Zhdanov said. 'I guarantee it.'

TWO

In summer, Rome gets unbearably hot. Most of its citizens have the good sense to leave the city for the coasts and mountains. Those who remain usually sleep between noon and four o'clock, when the sun and the petrol fumes conspire to turn Rome into a vast stone oven. Outside these torrid hours the city is fairly manageable, provided one moves slowly, with no ambition to achieve anything. Perhaps the most prudent course of action is to sit beneath an awning outside a bar, and do nothing more strenuous than drink coffee. On a Tuesday morning in late July, Professor Michael Wyman did precisely that.

He was enjoying the summer vacation, and spending much of it outside his favourite bar in the Piazza della Rotonda. Fifty feet away, a crowd of tourists was milling about the Pantheon, the astonishing domed temple built two thousand years ago and still functioning as a church. Wyman was reading his *Daily Telegraph* contentedly, puffing his cigarette and slurping at his espresso, when his wife sat down at his table.

'I thought I'd find you here,' she said.

'Hello, Margaret,' Wyman said, without looking up. 'I see Max Gebhard won the Australian elections.'

'Really?' Margaret said, with little enthusiasm.

'Yes. I think he'll make a good President. He's a sensible chap, by all accounts.'

'Is that so?'

'Quite intelligent too. He's written some interesting books on political theory. Of course, I don't agree with all he says, but it makes a nice change to have a thinking politician.'

Margaret shook her head and smiled at her husband.

'Michael, aren't you going to ask me why I'm here?'

'Oh. Yes,' Wyman muttered absently. 'What's up?'

'There's a mysterious letter for you from England,' Margaret said. 'It's marked "urgent", so I decided to bring it over to you.'

'And satisfy your curiosity?' Wyman suggested.

'And have a nice stroll. Signora Malfi offered to look after Cathy for the morning, so you can buy me lunch as well.'

'Indeed,' Wyman said drily. He took the envelope and opened it. The letterhead bore a coat of arms. 'St Lucian's Preparatory School, Sussex. That's where Herbie Feigl teaches. What on earth...?'

He read the letter and glanced up at his wife.

'Did I ever tell you about a friend of mine called Herbert Feigl?'

Margaret shook her head.

'Not surprising really,' Wyman said. 'I don't know him particularly well. But we've remained on speaking terms for over thirty years, which is more than can be said for most people he's known. I suppose that makes me one of his closer friends. That must be why they've written to me.'

'What's happened?'

'Herbie's disappeared. Each year he goes on holiday to a lake resort in Yugoslavia, somewhere in the Julian Alps. He goes on long walks in the mountains. This time he went out and didn't return.'

'Is he dead?'

'They don't know,' Wyman said. 'Apparently he left the hotel one afternoon and strolled in the woods beside the lake. They didn't realise he was missing until a couple of days later, and the police then searched the area. They even sent divers into the lake, but nothing was found.'

'Good heavens!' Margaret exclaimed. 'So why have they written to you?'

'Herbie's school learned about this a day or two later. They want to know if I've heard from Herbie recently. I suppose they're wondering if this wasn't an accident.'

'Suicide, you mean?'

'Perhaps,' Wyman said. 'Or simply a deliberate disappearance.'

Margaret blinked in astonishment.

'Are you serious?' she said. 'What kind of person is this Herbie?'

'He's rather odd,' Wyman grinned. 'An unhappy little chap, with a long catalogue of personality disorders.'

'And how did you know him?'

'A year after I took my PhD, the College made me interview the Philosophy candidates. It's a rotten job; not only do you have to assess a lot of spotty schoolboys, but you're pestered by their housemasters as well. Every day I took half a dozen phone calls from these characters, each of whom vowed that his lad would be the next

Wittgenstein. Some of them even came up to see me. That's how I met Herbie.'

'He was teaching Maths in a public school somewhere, and his headmaster browbeat him into visiting me. He obviously didn't want to do it, and I felt rather sorry for him. For some reason, we got on fairly well.'

'I thought you said he taught at a prep school,' Margaret said.

'He does,' Wyman said. 'The public school eventually sacked him, and no other secondary school would have him. The only place he could find was a grotty little preparatory school in Sussex, teaching elementary algebra to a herd of unwashed nine-year-olds. He's been there ever since.'

'He sounds a bit of a mess,' Margaret observed.

Wyman nodded and lit another cigarette.

'That's a fair description,' he said. 'His wife died about ten years ago, which didn't help. His colleagues detest him, and his pupils are all terrified of him. He's actually quite harmless, and he can be quite charming if he feels like it. Unfortunately, he seldom feels like it. He never took a degree, and remains convinced that people look down on him for it. He does a spectacular line in sarcasm, is prone to depression, and regularly loses his temper, with volcanic results. Care for a coffee?'

Wyman ordered two more espressos and smiled at Margaret's expression of horror.

'In fairness, I should add that he was always impeccably polite towards me. He was extremely loyal to his school, and loved showing me round the place. As far as I could see, it was just another tatty little exam factory, but Herbie thought the world of it. The eye of the beholder, I suppose.'

'What was his background?' Margaret asked.

'Jewish,' Wyman said. 'His family fled Germany in the thirties, when he was a boy. He served in the British army during the war; firstly in artillery, and later in army intelligence. After the war he went into teaching. That's the lot, or so I thought.'

'What do you mean?'

'This letter ends on a curious note,' Wyman said. 'Listen to this: "You may have come across the scurrilous article in the Sunday press suggesting that Mr Feigl was involved in espionage activities for the Yugo-slav government. Please rest assured that we have written to the newspaper concerned, protesting in the strongest terms about this absurd and offensive defamation."

The waiter arrived with the coffee.

'*Grazie,*' Wyman said. 'Darling, would you mind if I went to England for a few days?'

'Of course not,' Margaret said. She picked up the letter and read it. 'But you don't really think–?'

'I've no idea,' Wyman said flatly.

'But someone like this Herbie ... such an inadequate.'

'Yes,' Wyman nodded. 'They often are. They're often small, unhappy men with emigré backgrounds. The trouble with Herbie isn't that he's an unlikely candidate: it's that he's too good to be true.'

THREE

'You're looking good, Mr President,' Bradwell said. 'That's twelve miles already.'

'Twelve, huh?' panted the President. 'I'll stop at twenty. You know, George, I swear this thing gets easier every day.'

'A good sign,' Bradwell observed. 'Means you're getting fitter all the time.'

The static bicycle in the White House basement was the President's unofficial virility gauge. The official gauge, his wife, had long ago ceased to provide the President with his nightly appraisal, so the Chief of Staff, George Bradwell, had introduced this daily substitute. Each day, two assistants would help the middle-aged President into a tracksuit and on to the bicycle, where he could gyrate himself into a happy, sweaty delusion of second youth.

Of course, Bradwell was taking no chances. On advice from the President's doctor, The Chief of Staff had set a team of mechanics to work on the bicycle. Unbeknown to the President, the pedals and chain were now made of the lightest alloy, the gears were more sympathetic to his advancing years, and for every mile he pedalled the tachometer registered three.

The President was delighted by his new-found athletic prowess, and could not resist the urge to display it to his staff. All private meetings were now held in the basement, including those of his closest advisers. They sat in a respectful semicircle around the President's exercise bicycle, as the National Security Adviser drew their attention to the subject at hand.

'This could indicate a problem. On the other hand it might not. The debrief wasn't very specific. There's no mention of Waltz, but of course there needn't be. This agent, what's his name, Bulgakov, certainly didn't know.'

'He wouldn't,' said the CIA Director. 'It wasn't his department. This is just gossip he picked up at the London *rezidentura*. Question is, how seriously do we take it?'

The President grinned and continued to pedal.

'Hell, I feel great,' he said. 'You know, I think I might try for thirty miles.'

'Careful, sir,' Bradwell said anxiously. 'You don't want to get carried away there.'

'I can't get carried away,' the President grinned. 'It's a static bike.'

'What are the possibilities?' asked the Secretary of State.

'Our best scenario,' said the CIA Director, 'is that the Russians know nothing, and this is just a blind.'

'Very funny, Mr President,' Bradwell said, with a dutiful laugh.

'And the worst?'

'They've heard, or guessed, and this story indicates the start of a campaign.'

'I think I'll try jogging,' said the President.

'I'd stay with the bike for the time being,' Bradwell advised.

'What sort of campaign? Personal? Military?'

'It sounds personal,' said the CIA Director. 'At least, that's what the debrief suggests.'

The National Security Adviser waved a sheaf of paper.

'It's too vague,' he said. 'This could mean anything.'

'Sure,' said the CIA Director. 'It needs clarification.'

'What about a military response?' asked the Secretary of State. 'What's the likelihood of that?'

'A healthy mind in a healthy body, George,' said the President. 'That's my motto. Should be yours too.'

'We have to consider it,' said the CIA Director. 'What's the Pentagon view, Bud?'

General Cremona pensively scratched his crew-cut scalp.

'Waltz would certainly have significant ramifications for the geopolitical overview in that sphere of operations, gentlemen. I guess we can't rule out the possibility of a pre-emptive strategic initiative, maybe involving a meaningful upgrading of the tactical precursors, in an anticipatory context.'

'That's – that's your view, is it, Bud?' gasped the Secretary of State.

'How about weight lifting?' said the President. 'Never too old to pump iron.'

'It's a viable scenario,' Cremona said.

'I'd leave out the weights too,' Bradwell shuddered. 'Could be a little excessive.'

'Like I said, we need clarification. Maybe we can get some more out of this Bulgakov guy.'

'Who debriefed him?'

'Edwards, with help from Rawls.'

'A rowing machine,' the President suggested.

'Why not?' Bradwell said. 'We could easily fix one of those – I mean, fix one up for you.'

'Didn't Rawls handle Bulgakov's defection?'

'Yeah, he pulled Bulgakov in from Rome. He seems to like the guy. Maybe if we sent Rawls back to Bulgakov one more time'

'Good idea. Do we tell Rawls the whole story?'

'Do we need to?'

'Twenty miles,' the President announced, breathing heavily. 'You know, George, I think I'll take your advice and stop there. Can't waste all my energy, can I?'

The two assistants helped the President down from his bicycle.

'Good work, Mr President,' Bradwell said.

'Of course,' said the President, breathing in gulps. 'I could have done another ten if I wanted. Twenty, maybe. But these guys need my full attention now.'

'OK, that settles it,' said the CIA Director. 'I'll send Rawls down to Bulgakov, and we'll take it from there.'

They got to their feet and turned to the President.

'Thank you for your help, Mr President,' said the Secretary of State.

The President slumped back in his chair and wiped a towel across his forehead.

'Pleasure, boys,' he panted genially. 'Any time.'

FOUR

Wyman drew up his car on the roadside and consulted his map.

'Another mile,' he muttered. 'Good.'

The map suggested a busy main road, but this was little more than a country lane, winding through soft green farmland and fuscous patches of forest. It was a warm day, and the sky looked vast and pure. At such times, Wyman reflected, and in such places, one almost forgets that England is usually a sallow little country, tarnished by rain and gloom.

He drove on until a rusting sign came into view: 'St Lucian's Preparatory School for Boys. Certified as Efficient by the Department of Education and Science.' He turned off the road, and drove for a quarter of a mile along a gravel path. Eventually he came to a peeling Edwardian house, hemmed in by a cluster of newer outbuildings. As he got out of the car, Wyman was greeted by a tall, cadaverous man in his early fifties.

'Professor Wyman? I'm Nicholas Wright.'

'How do you do,' Wyman smiled. 'As a matter of fact, we've met before. Many years ago, when your father was headmaster. I believe you were in the Navy at the time.'

'Of course,' Wright said. 'I'd forgotten. That must have been at least fifteen years ago.'

'Nearer twenty, I think, when there was just one house. All these buildings have appeared since then.'

'Yes. We've expanded a bit since I took over. I've tried to keep change to a minimum, but some things can't be helped. New facilities are required, staff come and go … Mr Feigl was our longest-serving master, you know. A terrible business.'

'Was?' Wyman said. 'Does that mean you now assume the worst?'

'I have to,' Wright sighed. 'The Foreign Office organised another search-party, you know, and it came to nothing. They've officially abandoned the case, and told us to presume that Mr Feigl has perished.'

'That's terrible,' Wyman said.

'Indeed,' Wright said. 'And not helped by the activities of the Sunday press. Have you seen the article?'

'No. Do you still have it?'

'It's in my office,' Wright said. 'If you'd like

to follow me...'

As they went inside, Wyman's nostrils were assailed by a peculiar blend of disinfectant, floor polish and chalk, sharpened with a liberal infusion of sweaty socks. Even after fifty years, the smell revived some of Wyman's worst memories.

He was shown into the headmaster's office, where Wright poured out two cups of instant coffee.

'The housekeeper normally deals with this,' Wright said apologetically, as he passed a cup to Wyman. 'I hope it's drinkable.'

Wyman took a sip of the coffee, and managed a pained smile.

'It's fine,' he lied.

Wright opened his desk drawer and took out the offending newspaper article, which he gave to Wyman.

'As you can see, it was written by someone called Eddie Fulton. I tried to speak to Mr Fulton on the phone, but he wasn't available, which hardly surprises me. Apparently he is a freelance contributor. His article is most offensive.'

Wyman nodded sympathetically.

'I see what you mean. "A long-term Yugoslav secret agent has finally broken cover"...

"Posing as a second-rate teacher in an undistinguished private school"… "Trained by the British in the last war, he changed sides and worked for the Communists"… "An unknown school in the middle of nowhere was an excellent cover, but not good enough to escape exposure"… Not very flattering about Herbie, are they?'

'Oh. I suppose not,' Wright said. 'But I'm incensed by what they've said about the school. "Undistinguished", indeed. "Unknown". No doubt we are unknown to the readers of that sort of paper, but it's still an insulting description.'

Wyman gave the headmaster a surprised blink.

'Yes,' he said.

'Of course, I've written to the editor. For some reason, he hasn't replied. Just the sort of bad manners one expects from the popular press. The local newspaper is extremely courteous, you know. They reply to all our correspondence and return all our phone calls. And when *they* wrote about Mr Feigl's disappearance, there were no unpleasant remarks about the school.'

'I'm sure there weren't,' Wyman gasped. 'Do you have that article, by any chance?'

'Of course,' Wright said, as he took a

second newspaper out of the drawer. 'As you can see, it's a sensible, well-balanced report. Very *professional*, don't you think? I complimented the editor at the Rotarians' dinner last week–'

'Quite so,' Wyman broke in. 'And I take it you provided them with Herbie's career details?'

'Of course.'

'Did Herbie ever talk about his time in army intelligence?'

'No,' Wright said. 'It was simply mentioned in his curriculum vitae. The local paper was good enough to keep to what I gave them, without having to spice up the tale with nasty references to this school.'

'And with sensational tales about Herbie's life,' Wyman observed. 'Where do you suppose they got this spying idea from?'

'I haven't the foggiest. I suggest you ask the editor of that newspaper, though you'll probably have no more luck than I did. You know, I even invited him here, to see the school for himself. I pointed out that, far from being "undistinguished", we have superb standards. Our kitchens have passed all inspections – except for one a few years back, and the pest-control people soon put that right – and we offer the best–'

'I'm sure of it,' Wyman said hastily. 'It's most – unfortunate. And I'm sure you're equally bothered by the allegations about Herbie.'

'But of course,' Wright said. He settled back in his chair and smiled ruefully. 'I'm sorry, Professor, you must think I care about nothing except the school. Obviously, I'm appalled by this … this fantasy about Mr Feigl. We all are.'

'Herbie's colleagues are also distressed?'

'Why naturally,' Wright said. 'The article implies our recruitment policy is so lax that we employ spies and criminals. It hardly reflects well on the rest of the staff, does it?'

'No,' Wyman croaked. 'I suppose it doesn't. May I ask how the other masters felt about Herbie? In general, I mean.'

Wright looked closely at his coffee-cup.

'Mr Feigl was a senior master,' he said carefully. 'He had a very distinctive personal style, and he made a deep impression on our community. I am sure he will be missed by all those who were close to him.'

With some effort, Wyman succeeded in turning a laugh into a cough.

'Of course, Professor, that isn't all,' Wright said solemnly. 'When we read this article, the same thought crossed all our minds.

Even if we ignore the sensationalism, the defamation and the distortions, we are still left with one question unanswered.'

Wyman nodded eagerly.

'Absolutely,' he said.

'And,' Wright continued, 'I think you'll agree it's the most important question of all: what on earth will the parents think?'

FIVE

Edgar Rawls got out of his car and nodded approvingly at his surroundings. They had been carefully chosen. Tucked away in a suburb of Los Angeles, the house was partially hidden by tall conifers, but still gave its occupant an excellent view of the driveway. There were no obvious symptoms of paranoia, such as closed-circuit TV cameras or an electronic gateway, but Rawls had little doubt that his arrival had been noted.

Rawls took his time, to make certain he was recognised. He was not entirely sure of the occupant's frame of mind, and disliked the idea of being hit by a hastily fired bullet. He took off his tinted spectacles, wiped them with his handkerchief and put them back on. With an affected fastidiousness, he folded away his jacket and ran a comb through his hair. In the wing mirror, he could see the first flecks of grey were coming through: not too bad for forty-five, he supposed. He locked the car, walked slowly up the drive and rang the doorbell.

The door was opened by a short, fair-haired man, also in his forties. His face was adorned with a beard, sunglasses, and a hostile grimace.

'Hi,' Rawls smiled. 'Mind if I come in?'

'I mind,' said the other man. 'Get out.'

'I like the beard,' Rawls said. 'Suits you.'

'You're not supposed to be here. We agreed.'

'Nice house,' Rawls said.

The other man took a deep breath.

'It would be even nicer,' he said, 'if you were a thousand miles away from it. Good-bye Rawls.'

'I won't be long,' Rawls said.

'You won't,' the other man agreed. 'You're going now.'

'Sorry,' Rawls insisted. 'We have to talk.'

'I've talked enough. Now I want some peace.'

'You'll get it, after we're through.'

The other man nodded unhappily and let Rawls in.

'This way,' he said, leading Rawls to an upstairs room at the rear of the house. It was expensively furnished, though devoid of any character, as though someone else had bought the fittings on the owner's behalf, without knowing his preferences. They had played safe, and not just in matters of taste. The window panes had a slightly bluish tint: bullet-proof, Rawls guessed. He sat down in an armchair and grinned affably at his reluctant host.

'Well,' he said, 'aren't you going to offer me some coffee or something?'

'No, I'm not. What do you want?'

Rawls threw up his hands in exasperation. 'Listen Bulgakov, this wasn't my idea, OK? I don't know why they want this. My orders are, quote, to seek detailed clarification of page eighteen of appendix four, unquote.'

'Appendix four of what?' Bulgakov asked.

'Your debrief, buddy. Now can I have some coffee, please?'

Bulgakov left the room and slammed the door behind him. Rawls grinned and settled back in his armchair.

'Black, no sugar,' he called out.

Bulgakov returned a few minutes later with two cups of coffee.

'I told them everything,' he muttered. 'Absolutely everything. We agreed at Langley that I was to be left alone. No more of these afterthoughts.'

'Tell that to Langley,' Rawls said. 'I'm just

following orders. Look, I'm sure they wouldn't be doing this if there wasn't a good reason. And you can't complain: you've got a new name, a new house, and a fat bank account. What more do you want?'

'Privacy,' Bulgakov said. 'I want to be safe, and that means being left alone.'

'What are you worried about, for Christ's sake?'

'You don't understand, do you?' Bulgakov sighed. 'When a new man joins the KGB, Rawls, they don't just teach him how to use guns and decrypters. They show him films of people being killed. They aren't clean deaths, either. They use systematic torture, very refined.'

'Who are the victims?'

'Traitors. Defectors. The message is simple: we repay loyalty. If you're caught, we'll do our best to get you home. But if you betray us, this is what we'll do to you. It's very effective, Rawls. I was shown those films twenty years ago, and I still have night-mares about them.'

'The reprisal squads,' Rawls nodded. 'I thought that was just propaganda.'

'No,' Bulgakov said. 'I know the man who runs it. His name is Drebednev. He handles people like me, defectors from the First

Directorate. We get special treatment if we're caught, and it's our deaths that are recorded on film.'

'That probably makes you the only man in California who doesn't want to be in the movies,' Rawls grinned. 'Don't worry Bulgakov. You may not have noticed yet, but LA isn't exactly crawling with *shavkis.*'

Bulgakov permitted himself a wry smile.

'I'm sorry, Rawls. But don't make a habit of this.'

He lit a cigarette and blew out a long stream of smoke.

'They never gave me the pleasure of reading my own debrief,' he said. 'So you'll have to tell me about appendix four, page eighteen.'

'Pleasure,' Rawls said. 'Milo Lalic. Remember him?'

'The Croatian: sure. What's the problem? I told you all I knew.'

'Tell me again. It's important.'

'Very well,' Bulgakov shrugged. 'He's one of Nadysev's people.'

'Nadysev?'

'Nadysev at the London *rezidentura*. He keeps an eye on emigré organisations. One of the pleasanter sinecures.'

'Latvians, Lithuanians, and so on.'

'That's right. Sure, thirty years ago they were a headache. But nowadays – well, who cares about a lot of flag-waving geriatrics? No, Nadysev has an easy job with them. His only real work is dealing with the Yugoslavs.'

'Makes sense,' Rawls said. 'Your ex-employers still get kind of upset about Yugoslavia, don't they? The one that got away.'

'They never forgave Tito for breaking with us. And on the principle that the enemy of my enemy is my friend, we encourage the Yugoslav emigré groups: these idiots who still hanker after a free Kosovo, or a republic of Bosnia. We give them money, printing presses, the usual thing. Milo Lalic is involved with a number of those groups, and he liaises with Nadysev.'

'How does it work?'

'Lalic gets a request for funds from, say, the Croatian Liberation Campaign. He takes it to Nadysev, who gives him the cash. In return, Lalic gives him the latest on the inner workings of the organisation in question, the forthcoming press campaign, the infighting, and so on. Lalic takes his percentage from the handout, and he gets a little extra from Nadysev for his trouble.

'Of course, we all thought Nadysev was a

bit of a joke. He wasn't exactly producing white-hot intelligence, but then, what did Moscow expect?

'Then one day he turned up at the embassy after a meeting with Lalic, looking very pleased with himself. I think he'd been drinking. "You think I'm just a dilettante, don't you?" he said. "Well, you'll see." Of course, we asked him what he'd found. "Gold," he said. "Twenty-four carat gold. Lalic has a source you'd all give a year's wages for. He's beautiful."

'We poured a few brandies down his throat and asked him to explain what he meant. "It's the best kept secret in Europe," he said, "and I found it. Oh, it's been rumoured for some time. But now there's proof. You wait and see." He staggered away, and we thought no more of it. It sounded just like another piece of Nadysev bullshit.'

'What changed your mind?'

'Two days later, a man called Kuleshov turned up at the embassy and went straight to Nadysev's office. If you check your files, you'll see that Kuleshov is one of General Zhdanov's flunkeys at Dzerzhinsky Square. He's a grey man in a grey suit, but he has no dealings with the Nadysevs of this world.'

'What did he want?'

'I don't know,' Bulgakov said, 'but he frightened the wits out of poor Nadysev. The office door stayed shut for three hours. At the end of it, Kuleshov left, smiling sweetly and behaving as if they'd just been chatting about the weather. But Nadysev was white as a sheet, and trembling. They say Stalin used to have that effect on people.'

'So this Kuleshov's a mean motherfucker?'

'That's the strange thing: he isn't. He's a diffident little paper-pusher. If it were General Zhdanov, I'd have understood. The old man can be quite an ogre if he feels like it. But Kuleshov's just a clerk.'

'But he scared Nadysev,' Rawls said.

'He terrified him. Nadysev wouldn't talk about it to anyone.'

'What's your conclusion?'

Bulgakov shrugged.

'I suppose Nadysev must have really found something important. I've no idea what. Kuleshov presumably warned him to be more discreet; no more careless talk among the others. I'm guessing, of course.'

'Of course,' Rawls said. He put down his coffee-cup and frowned in concentration.

'Is this what your people want?' Bulgakov asked.

'Maybe.'

'So what needs clarifying?'

'Why do you think Nadysev was ordered to say nothing to the rest of you?'

'Simple,' Bulgakov said. 'We asked Nadysev what happened, but he refused to discuss it. We asked him if it was anything to do with his bragging the previous night, and he walked out. He'd obviously been gagged.'

'Is that normal in the KGB?' Rawls asked. 'Is security so tight that you can't talk about your job with your closest colleagues?'

Bulgakov stubbed out his cigarette and nodded.

'I see your point,' he said. 'It is unusual.'

'Also,' Rawls went on, 'I'm puzzled by this guy Kuleshov. You say he's a clerk, a paper-pusher. He wouldn't frighten anyone. But he scared Nadysev shitless. So maybe he was bringing a message from someone who *could* scare him, someone with real muscle.'

'Who would that be?'

'You said Kuleshov was Zhdanov's flunkey. You also said Zhdanov can get mean. Sounds like Kuleshov gave Nadysev a quick burst of his master's voice.'

Bulgakov blinked in surprise.

'Extraordinary,' he said. 'And that's what's troubling your superiors, isn't it? Why is the head of the KGB interested in a nobody like Nadysev? And why does he send Kuleshov all the way from Moscow to tear a strip off him? Why not do it through the London *rezident?*'

'You tell me,' Rawls said.

Bulgakov shook his head.

'I'm sorry, I've no idea. Whatever the explanation, it was kept hidden from everyone else in London.'

'So what's "the best kept secret in Europe"? Any ideas?'

'None.'

'And why should Nadysev discover it?'

'Ask Nadysev,' Bulgakov said facetiously.

'I'd love to,' Rawls said calmly. 'But Nadysev isn't around any more. Two months after you defected, Nadysev was sent back home.'

'Moscow?'

'Irkutsk,' Rawls said. 'Out of harm's way. So let's go through this once more, shall we?'

SIX

The docklands of east London never quite recovered from the pounding they took from Hitler's bombers. To this day, the area is still defined by crumbling buildings and senseless patches of wasteland; overgrown pavements and lunar roads barge their way through clusters of grimy, gutted houses. It might have stayed this way for another forty years, had not property prices and computer technology conspired to lure in new residents. The financial institutions are now slithering into the East End, with their push-button oracles and besuited boors. The newspaper industry has also staggered in, and shiny new complexes are replacing the grubby old sweatshops of Fleet Street. Camp followers have also arrived: prefabricated pubs and pretentious wine bars have arisen, like pustules, overnight.

Wyman stepped into one of these new oases at midday. It was empty, save for one pubescent girl behind the bar.

'Good afternoon,' Wyman said uneasily. 'A

glass of the house claret, please.'

The girl read a list and frowned.

'I'm sorry,' she said. 'We don't do that one.'

'I beg your pardon?' Wyman said.

'We haven't got it. Here, look at the card.'

Wyman examined the list and looked up at the girl.

'But according to this you have eight different Bordeauxs,' he said mildly.

'That's right, but it doesn't say claret, does it? So you'll have to have Bordeaux instead. It's just as nice, really.'

'Yes,' Wyman said solemnly. 'I'm sure it is. Very well, the house St Emilion please.'

Wyman paid for the drink and went to a corner table. As soon as he sat down, he regretted leaving the bar. The furniture was made of white-painted tubular steel, shaped to cause maximum discomfort to its users. It had doubtless won several design awards. Wyman tentatively sipped his wine, and found his worst fears confirmed. He toyed with the idea of complaining, but thought better of it: the girl at the bar would not relish a debate on the finer points of oenology. If this is the new London, Wyman thought, thank God I live in Rome.

A few minutes later, a man stepped into

the bar and went up to Wyman's table.

'Professor Wyman? I'm Eddie Fulton.'

Wyman stood up and shook his hand.

'How do you do, Mr Fulton,' Wyman said. 'Thank you for seeing me at such short notice. I hope I haven't inconvenienced you.'

'Not at all,' Fulton said. 'Drink?'

Wyman looked at his glass and scowled.

'I think I'll try their Scotch,' he said.

'I should have warned you,' Fulton grinned. 'You could probably run a car engine on that stuff.'

As the barmaid poured out their drinks, Wyman looked over his new acquaintance. Fulton was a solidly built man somewhere in his late thirties. His physique was half-way along the journey from youthful muscle to middle-aged sag, though Fulton displayed little interest in his own appearance. His hair was dishevelled, and needed a cut. His blue polyester suit was in its death throes, and clashed somewhat with his yellow shirt, lilac tie and scuffed brown shoes. He goes well with the wine, Wyman thought.

'Right Professor,' Fulton said as he returned with the drinks. 'What can I do for you?'

Wyman produced a newspaper clipping from his wallet and passed it across the table.

'I believe you wrote this story, Mr Fulton.'

'Call me Eddie,' Fulton said. 'Yes, that's my piece. What about it?'

'I was a friend of the gentleman in question,' Wyman said, 'and I'm rather intrigued by your allegation. I knew Herbie for over thirty years, you see. If he was a spy, he kept the fact extremely well hidden.'

'Well he would, wouldn't he?' Fulton laughed. 'Isn't that what spying's all about?'

'I suppose so,' Wyman nodded. 'And I take it you're convinced he was a spy.'

Fulton lit a cigarette and leaned back in his chair.

'I stand by my story, if that's what you mean.'

'No,' Wyman smiled, 'that's not exactly what I mean. Are you personally convinced that Herbie was working for the Yugoslav authorities?'

'It seems very likely, doesn't it?' Fulton said. 'If he really died in an accident, why haven't they found the body? Answer: he didn't really die. So why did he disappear?'

'A good question,' Wyman said. 'But why should this be the answer? It's one thing to say his disappearance is suspicious, but quite another to conclude that he was a spy. Further evidence is required, surely?'

'Right,' Fulton agreed. 'It's there in my article. Feigl was in army intelligence during the war, and that's where he learned the trade.'

'Indeed,' Wyman said. 'But as I recall, army intelligence had little connection with the main intelligence bodies. It had more to do with collecting straightforward military information than performing sophisticated feats of espionage. Most of its people were ordinary officers who happened to speak foreign languages. Of course, I could be wrong. I know very little about these matters.'

'You're a philosopher, aren't you?' Fulton said.

'That's right. I teach at Rome University.'

'Is this story what's brought you to London?'

'As I said, Herbie was my friend.'

'And you're trying to clear his name?'

'I'm trying to establish the truth,' Wyman said. 'And I'm still unsure why you think he was a spy. The evidence in your article is, if you'll forgive me, circumstantial. Herbie was a schoolmaster in Sussex, and I fail to see what use he might have been to the Yugoslav government, or any other. What was he doing? Whom did he spy on?'

'You're right,' Fulton said cheerfully. 'You don't know much about spying, Professor. Agents aren't just men in trench coats with microfilm cameras. They can be ordinary people in boring jobs, and they don't just gather information. They can collect it from other agents and pass it on.'

'So Herbie was a kind of middleman?' Wyman said. 'Most intriguing. Though it still sounds rather speculative.'

'Not convinced?'

'Regrettably, no.'

Fulton shrugged.

'I'm sorry, Professor. But I stand by the article.'

'No doubt,' Wyman said. 'But you do agree that if offers no proof that Herbie was a spy.'

Eddie tilted his head back and blew a few smoke rings.

'I'm not a lawyer, Professor, or a philosopher like yourself. I'm not obliged to produce the sort of rigorous proof you're probably accustomed to.'

'Of course not,' Wyman smiled. 'If you were, it would make for very dull newspapers. But if you're convinced Herbie was a spy, you must have information not mentioned in the article.'

'I must have,' Fulton agreed.

'And I suppose you're not at liberty to disclose it?'

'Oh, Professor...' Fulton said, in mock reproof.

'The vows of silence, and all that.'

'We have to protect our sources.'

'Of course you do,' Wyman laughed. 'Well, Eddie, I think that tells me everything I need to know. Thank you very much.'

He stood up and put on his jacket.

'Still not persuaded?' Fulton asked.

'About Herbie? I've no idea whether or not he was a spy. But I'm now certain of one thing: you haven't either.'

Fulton's eyebrows lifted inquiringly.

'Why is that?'

'A week before your story was published, Herbie's local newspaper reported his disappearance. It told the facts of the case, and gave a potted history of Herbie's career, including his spell in army intelligence.'

'So?'

Wyman put his hands in his pockets and gazed thoughtfully down at the table.

'We're in the middle of summer,' Wyman

mused, 'which is always a lean period for news stories. It's known as the "silly season", I believe. The politicians are all on holiday, so journalists have to settle for trivial items of news, which they stretch beyond recognition.

'If I were a cynical man, I should think you had found that story in the local press, and embellished it with your own lurid speculation. After all, you offered no facts about Herbie beyond those in the original article. Your story is highly defamatory, of course, but what does that matter? If Herbie is dead he can't sue you, can he?'

'I suppose not,' Fulton grinned. 'I hadn't thought of it that way.'

'I'm sure you hadn't,' Wyman said. 'Philosophers are a jaded crew. Thanks for the drink, Eddie.'

SEVEN

'Dr Macek? My name's Edgar Rawls.'

'Pleasure to meet you, Mr Rawls. Please do come in.'

Rawls stepped inside and grinned affably down at his host. Dr Macek was at least nine inches shorter than the American, and over twenty years his senior. His most obvious features were a matted grey beard, pebble glasses, and a potbelly which spilled out of a shiny old suit.

Dr Macek's yellowing office complemented his *fin de siècle* appearance. Most of it was taken up by an ornate walnut desk, ink-stained and scuffed by decades of neglect. Its bookshelves sagged under flaking piles of Serbo-Croat tomes and pamphlets. Long-forgotten generals and politicians gazed down from sepia portraits on the walls, indifferent to the dust and cobwebs surrounding them.

'Do sit down,' Dr Macek said, as he retired behind his desk. 'I am asking myself if you have come all the way over to London just to visit us, which is surprising.'

He picked up an elastic band and wound it slowly around his fingers.

'Yeah,' Rawls said, 'I guess I'd better explain. I'm trying to find a gentleman called Milovan Lalic, who I understand is involved with your organisation. There's some urgent business I need to conclude with Mr Lalic, but nobody seems to know where he is. That's why I'm here; I'm hoping you might be able to put me onto him.'

'I see,' Dr Macek said, looping the elastic around his thumb. 'You are certainly correct in this respect, that Mr Lalic is involved with our movement. As you know, we campaign for a free and democratic Croatia. Mr Lalic is occasionally acting as semi-informal liaison officer for us, from time to time.'

'I understand he also helps with your fund-raising.'

'This is also correct,' said Dr Macek. 'He is periodically instrumental in these matters. But this is not his permanent occupation, and he is often involved with other persons, in other matters.'

'Does this mean he isn't working for you right now?'

'Regretfully, he isn't. We have not been

seeing Mr Lalic for some weeks. Months, even.'

'Is that a fact?'

Dr Macek nodded gravely, as he formed another loop around his fingers.

'Have you any idea who he's working with now?' Rawls asked.

'Regretfully, no.'

'Pretty elusive guy, huh?' Rawls grinned.

Dr Macek waved his free hand in a helpless gesture.

'He is such a person, Mr Rawls.'

'Sure. And I guess there's no way of contacting him? Address, phone number?'

'There is no phone,' Dr Macek said. 'As you know, Mr Lalic is also working in Paris and elsewhere. In London he is normally staying at various hotel accommodations. He leaves us a poste restante address in Paris if we need to be in touch. You are certainly welcome to this.'

'Thanks,' Rawls said. 'But I've already tried that address, and it hasn't worked. You've got no other suggestions?'

'Regretfully, no.'

Dr Macek smiled sympathetically, but he did not look particularly regretful. He gave the elastic band another twist, pinning his thumb to his little finger.

'That's a real shame, Dr Macek,' Rawls sighed. 'One hell of a shame, in fact. You see, I represent Mr Arnold K. Bronstein of New Jersey. Maybe you've heard of Mr Bronstein?'

Dr Macek shook his head.

'I'm not surprised,' Rawls said. 'Mr Bronstein is something of a recluse. He made a sizeable fortune many years ago out of canned vegetables. Since retiring, he's devoted much of his time and wealth to supporting worthy causes.'

'Indeed?' said Dr Macek, with new enthusiasm.

'Yes. Mr Bronstein is particularly concerned with the spread of the Communist threat throughout the world. His favourite motto is "the only good Red's a dead Red", and he's only to happy to put his money where his mouth is.'

'I am pleased to hear this,' Dr Macek smiled, adding another twist to the elastic.

'That's why I'm looking for Mr Lalic. Obviously, Mr Bronstein feels the supreme danger comes from the Soviet Union and China, but he also realises there are other kinds of Communist oppression.'

'Such as Yugoslavia?'

'That's right, Dr Macek. My employer

thinks it's about time the free world put the heat on Yugoslavia, just to remind them they've not been forgotten. Mr Bronstein wants to donate funds to various causes that oppose Yugoslav Communism. These donations would be quite substantial, of course.'

The elastic finally snapped. It must have been quite painful, but Dr Macek managed not to flinch.

'And you were hopeful that Mr Lalic would handle these contributions?'

'Yes,' Rawls said. 'We asked Mr Lalic to draw up a list of organisations which he felt were doing most to oppose the Communist scourge. He did this for us, and we agreed that after we'd checked it out, I'd get back to him to organise the payment. Mr Bronstein OK'd the list last month, but unfortunately we now can't find Mr Lalic. As I say, it's a damned shame.'

'Very regretful,' Dr Macek agreed. 'But why do you need Mr Lalic for paying this money? Can you not merely give it yourselves?'

Dr Macek's expression did not change, but Rawls noticed a little glitter behind the pebble glasses.

'I guess we could with some of the

organisations,' Rawls said. 'But many of the other people operate covertly, and Mr Lalic has their bank account numbers. Obviously, we prefer to leave the whole matter in Mr Lalic's hands, if possible.'

Dr Macek scratched his beard thoughtfully.

'This is understandable,' he said. 'Would you perhaps know which organisations you are proposing to fund?'

'The list is confidential,' Rawls smiled. 'But I think I can tell you that you're on it. However, my instructions are to deal exclusively with Mr Lalic. If I can't find him, I'll have to get fresh instructions from Mr Bronstein. That could take some time.'

'Why is this?'

'For four months of the year, Mr Bronstein takes his holiday on a private island in the Caribbean. During that time he suspends all his financial activities, and remains incommunicado even to his most senior employees. You see, Mr Bronstein has a special project ... it's kind of tricky to explain.'

Rawls gave an uneasy grin, to which Dr Macek replied with an inquiring lift of the eyebrows.

'Well,' Rawls said slowly, 'Mr Bronstein

has a kind of theory about the Russians. He thinks they've put special satellites up in space to attack our food.'

Dr Macek frowned.

'I do not completely understand...' he began.

'High-intensity beams of radiation,' Rawls explained. 'The satellites bombard crop-growing areas of the United States, and irradiate the food. That's what Mr Bronstein believes. He has an observatory in the Caribbean, where he looks out for these satellites.'

'Fascinating,' Dr Macek said diplomatically.

'Yeah,' Rawls said uncomfortably. 'Mr Bronstein's very ... enthusiastic about it all. Now I'm not sure I fully agree with the theory. I have some doubts. But that's not the point, is it? Mr Bronstein's fully entitled to his beliefs. That's the difference between us and the bad guys, isn't it? I mean, that's what the free world's all about.'

'Most true,' Dr Macek said cheerfully.

'Anyway,' Rawls said, 'that's why I can't speak to Mr Bronstein. He began his holiday last week.'

'This is problematic,' said Dr Macek. 'I see why you must be dealing with Mr Lalic.'

He leaned forward and rested his chin on his hands.

'Perhaps,' he mused, 'we might be capable of discovering further details for you. Excuse me, please.'

He left the office, and Rawls was at last able to release the grin he had been smothering. Five minutes later Dr Macek returned, smiling in satisfaction.

'We are most fortunate, Mr Rawls. I have learned something about Mr Lalic's location.'

'No kidding?' Rawls said, trying to look surprised.

'Yes. Mr Lalic is known to be in Yugoslavia at this time. I have learned of his exact address.'

He gave Rawls a sheet of notepaper.

'Why, that's great,' Rawls said appreciatively. 'I'm much obliged, Mr Macek.'

'The pleasure is mine,' Dr Macek said. 'We are most happy to assist friends of the fighting against Communists. Your employer is very right: the only good Reds are the dead Reds.'

EIGHT

Eddie Fulton put down the phone and stared at his note-pad.

'How about that?' he muttered.

He tore out his last page of notes, screwed it up into a ball, and flicked it at the head of his colleague, who was ordering himself a drink.

'Merry Christmas, Bill,' he said cheerfully.

'Same to you, Eddie. What's new?'

Fulton took his pint-glass off the top of the pay-phone and went over to the bar.

'Bill, have you ever dealt with academics? Dons, professors, people like that?'

'Some,' Bill said.

'What did you make of them?'

'Wankers, the lot of them.'

'In what way?'

'Each one I spoke to insisted on lecturing me about the press.'

Bill assumed a whining, pedantic voice: '"Why do you people always sensationalise everything? Why do you write about trivial things? Why do you always ignore our

important findings? My distinguished colleague, Professor Schnitzelgruber, wrote a
sensational treatise on the renal sympathetic
baroreflex in rabbits: why did you not report
this? Why do you print pictures of naked
women?" Et cetera, et cetera. Wankers.'

Fulton laughed and lit a cigarette.

'Have you ever heard of a bloke called
Wyman? Philosophy don.'

Bill shook his head.

'Should I?'

'That's what I've been trying to find out.
He looked me up the other day, and asked
me questions about that piece on Feigl. You
know, the teacher who vanished in Yugoslavia. Apparently Wyman was a friend of
his.'

Bill's face screwed up in sympathy.

'Ouch,' he said.

'It wasn't like that,' Fulton said. 'He just
wanted to know if it was true. By the time
we finished, he'd guessed it was a silly
season special. It didn't seem to bother him,
though.'

'So what's the problem?'

'I don't know,' Fulton said, scratching his
head. 'Something wasn't right about him,
that's all. If he'd given me a bollocking for
maligning his dead chum, I'd have under-

stood. But he couldn't care less.'

'And no sermon on the state of the press?' Bill said. 'No polemics on tabloid titties?'

'Not really. He knew exactly what I'd done and why I'd done it, but it didn't really interest him. He was after something else.'

'What?'

'I don't know. But if Feigl really was a spy, and I had proof, Wyman wouldn't have burst into tears over it. I'm sure of that.'

'What do you mean?' Bill asked.

'It was as if … look at it this way, Bill: somebody says your lifelong buddy's a spy. How would you react? You'd laugh at the idea, or get indignant about it. You wouldn't just sit there, weighing up the evidence for and against, treating it like a crossword puzzle. What kind of a man does that about his closest friends?'

'Someone who's done it for a living?' Bill suggested.

'That's what I thought,' Fulton said. 'So I looked him up in an academic "who's who". He does teach in Rome, as he claimed, but he's only been there for a couple of years. Before that he was a fellow of an Oxbridge college. I phoned them and asked about Wyman's career. They said he'd only taught there occasionally: most of his career was spent at the Foreign Office.'

Bill emitted a low whistle.

'I like it,' he said.

'So did I,' Fulton grinned. 'I looked him up in an old copy of the *Civil Service Year Book*. There he was, listed as the Deputy Head of the Research Co-ordination Department in Whitehall.'

'What's that?'

'Good question. The *Year Book* says its job is to "liaise between the Research, Planning and Records Departments, to ensure a co-ordination of overall planning strategy".'

'That's helpful,' Bill observed.

'It's meaningless,' Fulton said. 'There was a phone number, which I tried. I got a recorded message referring me to the Records Department, so I phoned them. I said I was doing a piece on Civil Service spending – you know, "where's all the public lolly going, the tax-payer has a right to know, and just who are the Research Co-ordination Department when they're at home?" They passed me on to the Press Office, who gave me a load of old cock about ancillary administration.'

'Dick-heads,' Bill said sympathetically.

'Maybe. So I tried a flanker, and phoned the Planning Department. Guess what?

They'd never heard of the Research Co-ordination Department. I said, "Look, according to the *Year Book*, it co-ordinates overall planning strategy, and that means you." They insisted they'd never heard of it, and they'd never heard of Wyman, either.'

'So Wyman's a spook,' Bill said. 'Are you going to chase him up?'

'How?' Fulton said. 'I know bugger all about those people. But I'm wondering if the Feigl piece was right after all. I might just have guessed the truth.'

'Don't get carried away,' Bill cautioned. 'None of this proves anything.'

'It doesn't,' Fulton agreed. 'But wouldn't it be funny if... Bill, who knows about these things?'

'Harold Davis. We buy stories like that from him occasionally.'

'He's difficult, isn't he?'

'He's a shit,' Bill said emphatically. 'He thinks he's several notches above the rest of us. But he is good. He knows the security world inside out.'

'Where does he get his stuff?'

'The horse's mouth. He cultivates Establishment people, goes to their parties, kisses their bums, and picks up their gossip. He's been doing it for so long he thinks he's one of them himself. Like all *nouveaux,* he needs someone to spit on, so he treats other journalists like seedy proles.'

'But we are, aren't we?' Fulton laughed. 'Will he talk to me?'

'He might,' Bill shrugged. 'Try him.'

Fulton nodded and drained his glass.

'Thanks Bill,' he said. 'I think I will.'

NINE

Yugoslavia is a patchwork quilt of races, cultures and landscapes. It comprises eight federal regions, seventeen national groups and three main religions, with little to unite them save for a Communist government and a messy, violent history.

As in Italy, the nation's wealth is spread unevenly: the affluent industrialised north grudgingly shoulders the economic burden of the weaker south. The most prosperous region is Slovenia, in the north-west corner, which shares frontiers with Italy and Austria. Agriculture and industry both flourish here: Slovenia is mountainous, rich in minerals, and enjoys a high standard of living.

Thousands of tourists visit the region, and not just for the favourable exchange rates. Slovenia offers agreeable coasts, tranquil lakes and imposing peaks. Just one example of its scenic attractions is the exquisite valley of Bohinj, sixteen hundred feet up in the Julian Alps, and cradled among forested ridges that reach over seven thousand feet above sea level.

Lake Bohinj, at the western end of the valley, forms a rectangle three miles long and half a mile across. Two small groups of houses are huddled at either end, connected by a road which follows the southern shore. Only the eastern side is populous enough to earn the title of village. A few hotels are tucked away among the woods; the largest of these is the Hotel Zlatorog, at the far west of the lake.

Late on Saturday evening, Wyman checked into the Zlatorog. After dinner, he had a brief conversation with the receptionist, who told him little more about Herbie's disappearance than he already knew.

'Yes,' she said, 'Mr Feigl has come here every summer for many years.'

'Was he always on his own?' Wyman asked.

'His wife came with him once, about twenty years ago, but I don't think she enjoyed her stay. Apart from that, he has always come alone.'

'I suppose he's become quite well known in the area.'

The receptionist frowned.

'Not really,' she said. 'Obviously he was a familiar face, but he never really got to know anyone. I think he enjoyed being left alone.

When other guests tried to make conversation in the restaurant, he always seemed a little embarrassed. He was perhaps a little shy.'

'Perhaps,' Wyman nodded. 'Did he ever talk about the area – why he kept returning, and so on?'

'It's a beautiful place,' she smiled. 'Also, I think there was a sentimental reason. You know that he was here during the war? He was with the Partisans in the mountains.'

'So I heard,' Wyman said. 'He must have made some local friends then.'

'A few, but most of them are dead. I really don't think Mr Feigl came here to see people. He only seemed interested in taking walks in the mountains.'

'Indeed. After all these years he must have got to know the mountains well. Surprising that he should vanish this way, don't you think?'

'I'm not so sure,' the receptionist said thoughtfully. 'These mountains have a deceptive appearance. The lower slopes look gentle enough, and the forest isn't especially dense, but plenty of people have been caught unawares. There are many ways of taking a fall, even on the paths. Also, Mr Feigl was not a young man, and he smoked heavily.

'True. Do you know which route Mr Feigl took when he disappeared?'

She took a map out from under the counter and pointed to the hotel with her pen.

'He left here in the afternoon and walked out along the northern shore of the lake. When he'd gone for about three miles, he turned off the main path and went up a steep track, here.'

She put a cross on the map, and drew a short line upwards, in the direction of the mountain summit.

'About twenty yards up the path is a woodcutter's hut. When he arrived there, Mr Feigl met two other tourists who were going in the opposite direction. They had a brief conversation, and Mr Feigl said he would try for the summit. They warned him that it was a difficult route, but he made a joke about it and went off.'

'A couple of hours later, he came down and returned to the lake path. He admitted the slope had been too tough for him, and he made another joke. Then he walked off, in the direction of the hotel. That was the last anyone saw of him. They've searched the woods thoroughly, as you know. Even the tracker dogs couldn't find him.'

She drew another cross on the map.

'They also thought he might have fallen in the lake here, where the path runs very close to the water. But the divers found nothing, and his body would have surfaced by now. Your embassy people came here a few days ago and took away his passport and belongings. That's all I know.'

Wyman thanked her and returned to his room. It occurred to him that he was not the first tourist to have inquired about Herbie's disappearance: the receptionist had told the story with a fluency born of practice.

He picked up the phone and asked to make an international call. A few moments later he was speaking to his wife.

'You don't really expect to find him, do you?' Margaret said.

'Of course not,' he laughed. 'But they're all baffled by what happened. From what the receptionist tells me, it seems almost impossible that he met with an accident. I got the impression that they're trying to convince themselves that it's true, simply because it's the least implausible explanation. The receptionist says the mountains look deceptively tame, but I don't think she really believes a word of it.'

'And what do you believe?'

78

'I have an open mind,' Wyman said.

'What does that mean?'

'Precisely what it says. If Herbie didn't have an accident, we are left with a whole range of possibilities. Some of them are quite bizarre.'

There was a pause at the other end of the line.

'Can you tell me about them?'

'This phone line goes through the hotel switchboard,' Wyman said slowly.

'I understand,' Margaret replied. 'What did the locals think of Herbie?'

'The receptionist was diplomatic,' Wyman grinned. 'I think they looked upon him in much the same way as his teaching colleagues did: a difficult little man, best left alone. You know, after I escaped from his headmaster's office, I looked around Herbie's flat. There were no letters, no photographs, nothing to suggest any contact with other human beings – even his wife.'

'Do you think he cleared it all out before he left?'

'The thought occurred to me, but I changed my mind. He'd have left gaps: spaces on bookshelves, empty drawers, bright patches on the walls where pictures used to hang. There was nothing like that.

No, I think Herbie was a genuine *tabula rasa:* he'd done his best to strip all moral and social complications off his life, like so many layers of paint.'

'That sounds like the start of a theory,' Margaret sighed.

'And what's wrong with that?' Wyman said warmly.

'Nothing, I suppose. But if the problem becomes theoretical, I can be sure you won't let go until you've solved it.'

'Nonsense,' Wyman snorted.

'And it means you won't be back home for some time.'

'Oh really, Margaret. What on earth makes you–?'

'Bitter experience. You've always enjoyed hopping around Europe on these little jaunts, and–'

'Utter piffle,' Wyman said indignantly. 'This is a perfectly straightforward problem, but I don't think I have the resources to solve it. Tomorrow I shall walk the route Herbie took, and that will be all. The matter will end there. The chances are I shall be back in Rome within three days. And Margaret...'

'Yes, Michael?'

'What on earth are you laughing at?'

TEN

At six o'clock the next morning, Wyman left the hotel and began his stroll around the lake. He was still tired from his travelling the day before, but the dewy freshness of the air soon blew away the cotton wool inside his head. Besides, he consoled himself, this would allow him three hours before the other tourists were up and about. Wyman had little hope of finding anything, but if there were to be any surprises, he would prefer to face them alone.

As the path turned into the woods along the northern shore, Wyman paused to take in his surroundings. They were enough to make a chocolate-box designer squeal in delight. The lake was ringed by dense olive-coloured forest which crept about two hundred feet up the surrounding mountains, and gradually dissolved into bare stone crags stretching thousands of feet beyond. It occurred to Wyman that if Herbie's body was lying undiscovered on a slope, it must be within the area obscured by the woods: any higher, and it would be visible from the ground.

He walked on, and was soon panting from the unaccustomed exertion. Once inside the woods, the path quickly worsened in quality, and took an erratic course between the trees. Occasionally it vanished altogether, and Wyman had to hop across gullies formed by small streams. After ten minutes, he sat down and wiped a cascade of sweat from his brow. He lit a cigarette, and added masochism to the list of Herbie's personality defects.

A little later, Wyman's face no longer felt like a leaky hotwater bottle, and he set off once more. With some relief, he noticed that the path was growing gentler, and it was not long before he arrived at the bypath mentioned by the hotel receptionist.

He scrambled up a grass bank, and made his way to a small clearing about thirty feet ahead. There he found the woodcutter's hut: a sturdy little pine cabin, with one door and two small windows. Wyman peered through the wire mesh on the windowpanes, and could make out a table, a chair and a camping stove.

A narrow track led away from the hut, and snaked up among the trees. Wyman took a long gloomy stare at it, and shook his head. With a sigh of resignation, he tramped up the slope and into the woods. He had only gone a few yards, when something caught his eye. He pulled back a bush and looked down at the ground. Wyman's heartbeat was already pounding through physical toil: what he saw sent it into overdrive.

'Good God!' he exclaimed.

Huddled at his feet was the body of a man, lying face down on a dried pool of blood. Wyman put a hand on its shoulder, and tried to roll it over. This was surprisingly difficult: the corpse was quite rigid, and felt unnaturally heavy. With a desperate heave, Wyman turned the body on its side, and gazed at the face. It had been shot at close range, just below the jaw. Nevertheless, the other features were clearly visible. This was a man in his early sixties, with grey hair and a slender build. It was not Herbert Feigl.

Wyman let go of the body and stepped back a few paces. Instinctively he reached into his pocket for a cigarette. As he lit it, he noticed his hands were trembling violently.

'My kingdom for a hip-flask,' he muttered. 'So who on earth can this be?'

'His name's Milo Lalic,' said a voice

83

behind him.

Wyman spun round, and saw a tall man wearing dark-tinted glasses and a sardonic grin.

'Rawls!' Wyman said hoarsely. 'What the devil are you doing here?'

'Burying a stiff,' Rawls said, holding a shovel aloft. 'What else would I be doing in a Yugoslav resort?'

'Did you kill him?'

'No. I found him here yesterday. It was getting dark, so I couldn't do very much. If some tourist finds the body, the police will check up on everyone in the area. My visa's OK, but it wouldn't take long to find out who I work for. Better just to hide the guy. It could save me a lot of hassle.'

Wyman frowned.

'But if this man has nothing to do with you...'

'I didn't say that,' Rawls said. 'I didn't kill him, that's all.'

'I see,' Wyman said slowly. 'Or rather, I don't see at all. I suppose it's a long story.'

'Score ten for a good guess,' Rawls laughed. 'Give me a hand, will you?'

They lifted the corpse and took it to a spot twenty feet further into the woods, where Rawls had dug a grave.

'Thanks,' Rawls said, as he covered the body with earth. When the grave was nearly full, he threw in the shovel and finished the job with his hands.

'I suppose,' Wyman said thoughtfully, 'this could simply be a coincidence. There's no reason why an American intelligence officer shouldn't just bump into a former English colleague on a mountain in Slovenia. My search for somebody called Herbert Feigl, who is thought to be dead, need have no connection with your discovery of someone called Milo Lalic, who is definitely dead. The two might be entirely separate.'

'And pigs might fly,' Rawls agreed.

'So what brings you here?'

Rawls jabbed his thumb at the grave.

'I was trying to find that mother. I guess I was too late.'

'And what was he up to?'

'He was looking for your man Feigl. That's your connection.'

Wyman gazed upwards and sighed.

'Thank you Rawls,' he said heavily. 'That explains everything.'

'I know the feeling,' Rawls said. 'I don't know about you, but I could use a beer. There's a *restavracija* down on the eastern shore. If you say the word *"pivo"* to the owner, he serves you this fantastic, cold, frothy–'

'Perfect,' Wyman said, and they set off down to the lake.

ELEVEN

Eddie Fulton had no major ambitions. He did not know what he wanted, and had little inclination to find out. Because his aspirations were few, his achievements were even fewer. His life had a scrappy, incomplete quality, punctuated by near misses and wasted opportunities. He might have gone to a university and done well, but instead he took a job on a local paper. He was a good reporter, and with a little effort he would have moved quickly to Fleet Street; with no effort at all, it took him twelve years. With a little care, his marriage might have succeeded; after five years of indifference, Fulton was divorced.

As he drove his rusty Ford along a rainy Oxfordshire lane, Fulton considered the difference between himself and the man he was about to visit. A brief inquiry on the subject of Harold Davis revealed the antithesis of everything Fulton sought, believed in and understood. Davis was driven by categorical ambitions, and every last scrap of his life was dedicated to achieving them. At an early age he had abandoned his bland Essex town, and discarded its clumsy values. He knew where the real power lay and who wielded it. He yearned for a place at the top table, and he soon found a way of getting there.

As a political correspondent, Davis became known as a useful channel for discreet leaks. Politicians and senior establishment figures could rely on him to present their gossip in the manner they wished, and with the desired effect. In return, Davis was admitted to the more exclusive clubs and flattered into believing he was now one of the great and good.

Soon he was admitted to the most secret world of all. The gossip was no longer about MPs and party politics: it was about security, intelligence and spies. As before, he accepted the stories with unquestioning gratitude, and published them with great success. The newspapers paid him well for his articles, and his books made him a fortune. If sales flagged, one of his parliamentary friends would pretend to be concerned, and mutter darkly about possible breaches of the Official Secrets Act. Sales would immediately surge, and the public would read his books in guilty fascination, with no suspicion that they were being duped into believing the official version of events.

It never occurred to Davis that he was being used. He thought of himself as a gifted journalist, with a sensitivity and charm denied to most of his colleagues. He would doubtless find Eddie Fulton gauche and uncouth. As he pulled up outside Davis's home, Fulton grinned in anticipation.

He got out of the car and looked around. The stone-built house looked at least two hundred years old. Like the Volvo estate parked outside, it was too good to be true. Fulton knocked on the door, and was shown inside by his host.

'You understand,' Davis said, 'that I'm only doing this just the once, as a favour. I won't normally have your lot around here.'

'Very good of you,' Fulton said cheerfully.

'It's a matter of principle,' Davis explained, as he led Fulton into the main room. 'This sort of work should be left to those who understand it. I don't deal with other people's stories, so why do they want to poach mine? Each to his own, I say.'

'That's reasonable,' Fulton said. 'But this

is just background.'

Davis was unconvinced.

'They always say that, until I put the meat on the story. Then they run it under their own by-line. It's poaching.'

Fulton pointed to an antique gun above the fireplace.

'Never mind,' he said. 'I'm sure you're used to handling poachers.'

Davis ignored the remark and sat down.

'What exactly do you want?' he asked.

'I'm trying to find out about a guy called Michael Wyman. I have reason to believe he may have been an intelligence officer–'

He was interrupted by a weary groan.

'Forget it, son. Just forget it.'

'What do you mean?'

'You're wasting your time, Fulton. If I'd known you were coming here for that old tale, I'd have told you not to bother. It's a nonstarter. You won't get confirmation from anyone else, and the story is permanently D-noticed. Wyman himself will deny everything, so you might as well–'

'What the hell are you talking about?' Fulton said quietly.

Davis frowned and tilted his head back in mild surprise.

'The Wyman story, of course. I assume

90

that's what you're after.'

'I didn't know there was a Wyman story,' Fulton said. 'I'm looking into something else. Wyman showed up a few days ago and poked his nose in. I want to know who he is.'

'What's your story?'

Fulton recounted the tale of Herbert Feigl's disappearance, and Wyman's peculiar inquiry in the wine bar.

'So I looked into Wyman's background,' he concluded, 'and found that he used to work for a nonexistent department in the Foreign Office.'

'And you decided he was an intelligence officer,' Davis said. 'Well, you were right. He used to work for an MI6 department in Percy Street, specialising in East German affairs. The department was axed a couple of years ago, during the Treasury cuts. Wyman was made redundant, and he's gone back to his old profession. End of story.'

'Is it? Why was he snooping around London, then? Why did my piece bring him running?'

'Isn't it obvious? You've suggested an old friend of his was a spy. Wyman spent most of his life in that business. His first reaction would be to check your story.'

'But he didn't seem upset about it, or–'

'Of course he didn't,' Davis said impatiently. 'He's a professional. He wanted to see if you knew what you were talking about. Once he realised it was rubbish, he'd have forgotten it. That's the problem with you people: not only do you invent these fantasies, but you also believe them.'

Fulton nodded sheepishly, but he was not convinced.

'And that's all there is to it?' he said. 'So what's this other story about Wyman? Maybe there's a connection.'

'Hardly,' Davis laughed. 'This is an old tale. When Wyman was made redundant from MI6, he was left without a pension. Apparently he was very bitter about it, and decided to take revenge. Somehow he managed to swindle his people out of a very large sum.'

'How much?'

'I don't know the exact amount,' Davis said, 'but I think it was in seven figures. In one version it was five million.'

Fulton gave a low whistle.

'I'm impressed. How did he get away with it?'

'I'm not sure. I think he threatened to blow the whistle publicly if anyone took action against him. That would have been enough to keep them off his back. It's a good story, but it's strictly taboo. And it has nothing to do with your missing school-master.'

Fulton lit a cigarette, ignoring Davis's look of disapproval.

'I still think there's more to it than you think. This guy Feigl was an interesting character–'

'No he wasn't,' Davis said dismissively. 'He was a boring little prat who got lost on a mountain. It's not a security story.'

'How can you be so sure?'

Davis smiled smugly.

'Because if it were, I'd have heard about it. Take my advice, Fulton: stick to tits and bums, and leave the serious stuff to people who understand it.'

'Like you?'

'Like me. You can't just barge into the security world, you know. I've spent years getting inside it, and I know how it works. They're not concerned with absentee teachers. They talk about serious issues.'

'Such as?'

'Such as military strategy, electronic surveillance, initiatives like Project Waltz–'

'What's that?'

Davis's smile froze, as he realised he had gone too far. In fact, he knew nothing about Waltz: he had only heard the name mentioned recently by an American guest at his club. But he knew it was not for the ears of people like Fulton.

'Nothing, really,' Davis said quickly. 'It's mostly analytical stuff: the sort of things that interest serious papers.'

'Not the kind I write for?' Fulton grinned.

'No. Oh, there is the occasional story of wider interest. I found one the other day, in fact. There's a Russian emigré in Manchester. He's a Jew called Semyon Gureyvitch. His brother's still in Russia, operating under the name Zhdanov.'

He paused for dramatic effect.

'So what?' Fulton said.

Davis threw up his hands in disgust.

'You really are out of your depth, aren't you laddie? General Zhdanov is the head of the KGB. Public enemy number one. And I've stumbled across a long-lost brother, who's *Jewish.*'

'Who cares?'

'General Zhdanov, for one. They don't like Jews in Russia, you know. So the General must have kept his origins well hidden to get to his present job.'

94

'That's very exciting,' Fulton yawned. 'And what are you going to do with the story?'

'Nothing, probably,' Davis said. 'It's not very serious, is it?'

'Trivial,' Fulton agreed. 'And you're a very serious journalist. I can see that.'

Davis's face tightened with displeasure.

'Don't be cheeky, son,' he said coldly. 'There's more to it than vicars and call girls.'

'My department, you mean?' Fulton chortled, tugging vigorously at his forelock. 'Don't worry master. I know my place.'

TWELVE

'You were right about the beer,' Wyman said appreciatively.

'The food's good too,' Rawls said.

They were sitting at the back of the *restavracija*, watching other tourists come in for their morning coffee. The noisy families and chattering bar staff conveniently smothered Wyman's résumé of his inquiry.

'The fact is,' Wyman concluded, 'none of this hangs together. That path is reasonably tame, especially for somebody who knows it well. I can't believe Herbie had an accident.'

'That makes two of us,' Rawls agreed.

'In that case, he deliberately disappeared. This raises all sorts of strange–'

'Wait a minute,' Rawls said. 'Are you telling me he's still alive?'

'Well, we just agreed that there was no accident.'

'Sure, but I meant that he was rubbed out.'

'Murdered?' Wyman exclaimed. 'By whom?'

'Rawls tilted his head in the direction of the lake.

'By the same firm who took care of Lalic. But I see you're been studying some other angle. Tell me what it is.'

'It's not very satisfactory,' Wyman admitted, 'but it was all I could think of. As I said, I was drawn into all this by the newspaper article suggesting that Herbie was spying for the Yugoslavs. They were just guessing, of course, but I still wonder if it wasn't a good guess.

'You see, it is technically feasible that Herbie *was* an agent. But there are two things which make the idea implausible. Firstly, his personality. He was volatile, and temperamentally unsuited to long-term intelligence work. Secondly, he believed firmly in liberal causes.'

'You've just described a great cover,' Rawls grinned.

'Of course,' Wyman conceded. 'More importantly, there was the obvious question of what a schoolmaster in the middle of nowhere could have done for them. There was only one possibility, although it was very remote.

'Herbie belonged to an international human rights organisation called Freedom of Conscience. They campaign for the release of political prisoners – writers, dissident journalists, and so on. They have a number of local groups in Britain, and Herbie belonged to the Sussex branch. The headquarters in The Hague collect dossiers on the prisoners, and distribute them around the world. Each branch then writes letters to the prison authorities and the head of state, asking nicely for the release of the dissident in question. It frequently bears fruit.

'The dossiers are often very detailed. Apart from information about the prisoner, they contain lots of useful data about the political situation in that country, and precise information about where and how the dissidents are behind held. The methods of collecting all this are kept secret, and there are some governments who would dearly love to know how it's done.'

'Like the Yugoslavs?'

'Exactly,' Wyman nodded.

'And Feigl was their man inside Freedom of Conscience?'

'It was the best I could manage,' Wyman shrugged.

'But you said you weren't satisfied with it.'

'I'm not. It still seems inconsistent with

Herbie's personality, and it still leaves key questions unanswered. Why did he need to defect? Presumably he felt threatened, but by whom? And why did he "arrange" his own disappearance here? You would think that once he'd arrived, there was nothing more to fear. No, there must be some other ingredient.'

'There is,' Rawls said. 'Our buddy on the hill.'

'Lalic? Explain.'

Rawls recounted the puzzle in Bulgakov's debrief, and how he tracked down Lalic to Slovenia.

'Lalic had an arrangement with the KGB,' Rawls said. 'It worked for many years, and he made a few bucks out of it. It seems he got greedy, and they've punished him for it. That was a KGB job up there.'

'How do you know?'

'They were looking for him. Lalic used to get regular money for giving them small items of news about emigré organisations. It wasn't much, and Lalic was getting old. So one day, he had a bright idea: invent something big, and put a heavy price-tag on it. His contact at the embassy, Nadysev, was a jerk: by the time he found out he'd been swindled, Lalic would be somewhere else with a fat wallet. Happy retirement for Lalic.'

'The man was insane,' Wyman said. 'You don't play games like that with the KGB.'

'We know that,' Rawls agreed, 'but Lalic was strictly bottom league, and he didn't realise he was dealing with the bottom league at the embassy. He told Nadysev he'd found a special source, who had a twenty-four carat story to sell. All Nadysev had to do was sign a fat cheque made out to "cash", and Lalic would handle the rest.'

'What was the story?'

'Christ knows,' Rawls said dismissively. 'Lalic was a prick-tease. Sure, he'd found something, but it was probably worthless. He just packaged it beautifully, and gave it a hard sell. Let's face it, he even had us wondering, which is why I'm here. But it was horseshit, and it backfired on him.

'When Lalic made his play, it was so good that the heavies arrived from Dzerzhinsky Square. Nadysev was sent home, and the experts put Lalic's story under the microscope. Instead of paying him the money, they found out who Lalic's mystery source was, and took a look at him. He turned out to be a crummy schoolteacher, who Lalic knew from way back.'

'Herbie? How did they find him?'

'The same way I did,' Rawls said. 'Lalic used to leave phone numbers lying around for his friends to find him, so it was easy to piece together his movements. They found he'd made regular visits to a village in Sussex, near the school. The rest was easy.'

'So what happened to Herbie?'

'When Lalic didn't get his usual cheque, he got worried. His KGB contact had vanished, and everything was going wrong. He guessed the Russians were looking for his source, and he knew what would happen if they found him. So he came out here to kill Feigl before the Russians could ask him any questions. Of course, he was too late: the Russians had already taken care of Feigl. They wanted Lalic, and yesterday they got him.'

Wyman took off his spectacles and squinted at his beer-glass.

'No,' he muttered, 'I'm not persuaded. Lalic had a story. You assume they killed him because it was worthless, but perhaps it was the other way round. Perhaps it was so good they had to silence him. Having extracted the information from Herbie, they lured Lalic out here and killed him.'

'It fits,' Rawls conceded. 'But either way,

Feigl's dead.'

Wyman nodded grimly.

'I suppose so. But why would he have dealt with the KGB in the first place? If he was a Yugoslav agent, he would avoid them like the plague. If he was just an innocent schoolteacher, he'd have even less reason to deal with them. Either way, there's no explanation.'

'Try money,' Rawls chuckled. 'It's the usual incentive for weird behaviour. It wouldn't matter if Feigl was an agent or an honest Joe: he could still use a few extra notes. And remember, it was Lalic who did the haggling: Feigl just had the story.'

'And you believe Lalic took one of these stories and dressed it up beyond recognition?'

'Sure,' Rawls said. 'Maybe it came from a dissident group here. Maybe it's a dirty story about a Party official.'

'Maybe it's a true dirty story.'

'Who cares?' Rawls shrugged. 'I'm not looking for Yugoslav sleaze.'

'So what are you looking for?' Wyman said.

'Nothing. My people were worried by Bulgakov's debrief. They thought Lalic might have been offering something really valuable. He was a mercenary, so if it was good material, we'd have outbid the Soviets for it. Now I know it was all bull, I'm going home. And even if it's true, we're not in the market for low-grade dirt. The case is closed.'

'I see,' Wyman nodded. 'I presume you originally had some theory about what Lalic might have been offering. Perhaps you could tell me...?'

'No theory,' Rawls said. 'I came out here with an open mind.'

'What about the people who sent you?'

'They might have taken a guess, but they didn't tell me about it. What does it matter?'

'Nothing, probably,' Wyman sighed. He lit a cigarette and ordered two more beers.

'You're not satisfied, are you?' Rawls said.

'No,' Wyman said. 'I'm unhappy about the whole thing. You're leaving too many loose ends.'

'You only say that because the guy was your friend,' Rawls observed. 'All that matters is that there was no big story.'

Wyman sighed again and lapsed into silence. When the beer arrived, he made no move to pick up his glass.

'Are you going back to Rome?' Rawls asked.

'Not just yet,' Wyman said. 'Herbie didn't come to Bohinj directly. He told the hotel receptionist that he'd spent a couple of days in Vienna first. He visited Max Gebhard, I understand.'

'Gebhard?' Rawls said in surprise. 'How does a teacher get to know the Austrian president?'

'He wasn't President then,' Wyman corrected him. 'The elections took place after Herbie vanished. Gebhard is a patron of Freedom of Conscience.'

'No kidding?'

'A founder member, apparently.'

'And you think that raises the stakes?'

Wyman shook his head.

'I suspect it lowers them. If Herbie was a Yugoslav agent he'd have come straight here. He wouldn't have wasted time by exchanging pleasantries with a patron of an outfit he was undermining.'

'He wouldn't,' Rawls agreed. 'Unless Gebhard was in on the act.'

'Indeed,' Wyman said drily. 'And Mother Teresa ran their Eastern section.'

'OK, it's unlikely,' Rawls laughed. 'So what did they talk about?'

'Something to do with Freedom of Conscience, I suppose. Perhaps just to wish

Gebhard well in the election. Whatever the reason, Gebhard was one of the last people to have a full conversation with Herbie before he disappeared. He's worth a try.'

'If you say so,' Rawls grunted. 'Sounds like a long shot.'

'It's unpromising, I must admit,' Wyman smiled. 'But it's the last possible clue. Having got this far, I might as well finish the job.'

'I guess so,' Rawls said, 'but I think you're wasting your time.'

He took a long pull from his glass, and slowly wiped a finger across his mouth.

'Damn good beer,' he said approvingly.

THIRTEEN

'Twenty-three miles,' said the President. 'That's incredible! How do I do it, George?'

'Healthy mind in a healthy body,' Bradwell said. 'Your own motto, sir.'

He might have added 'a healthy mechanic'. The tachometer on the President's static bicycle had received further sympathetic adjustment.

'How's the rowing machine coming along?'

'It'll be here in a day or two, sir. The manufacturers wanted a little extra time to produce a ... a suitable model.'

'Suitable? Suitable for what?'

'Why, suitable for the President of course,' Bradwell said hastily. 'Only the very best for the White House, we said.'

'Oh, sure.'

A few feet away, the President's staff pored over Rawls' latest report.

'That seems to be the end of the matter,' said the Secretary of State. 'Rawls thinks it's all over, and I see no reason to disagree with him.'

'Are you kidding?' said the CIA Director. 'This guy Wyman is heading for Vienna. He's going to see Gebhard, for Christ's sake.'

'So what?' said the National Security Adviser. 'He's not going to learn anything.'

'How do you know? Wyman's ex-intelligence, and from what I hear–'

'He's simply being tidy. He knows Feigl saw Gebhard, so he's just checking it out. But he's not expecting to find anything; Rawls is sure about that.'

'You know George,' said the President, 'we ought to let the press in here to see this. They'd love it.'

'Maybe,' Bradwell said uneasily.

'They'd get some great pictures out of it. Good for the image.'

'It could be,' Bradwell said. If a sharp-eyed reporter spotted the tachometer, the consequences could be rather unpleasant.

'I still don't like it,' said the CIA Director. 'Even if he gets nowhere in Vienna, he'll still be wondering about Feigl. There's no body, and no complete explanation. Just because we're satisfied, it doesn't mean that Wyman–'

'Fuck Wyman,' said the Secretary of State elegantly. 'What are you worried about? He only wants to know why they killed his buddy. That's reasonable. We know he's wasting his time. Whatever Wyman finds out, it won't bring him any nearer to Waltz, and that's all that counts.'

'That's right,' the National Security Adviser agreed. 'I say we take Rawls' advice, and just forget the whole thing.'

'A press conference in a gymnasium,' the President said, warming to his theme. 'What an idea!'

'Does Gebhard know about Wyman yet?' asked the CIA Director.

'Sure. Wyman made an appointment yesterday. Gebhard's giving a speech tomorrow night at a party meeting, and he's seeing Wyman afterwards. Shouldn't be any problems.'

'You know the KGB are monitoring Gebhard.'

'Of course they are. They monitor everyone, for Christ's sake.'

'No, this is high intensity. They've got parabolic mikes trained on his office, and they've been trying to bribe his mailman.'

'How do you know?'

'We bribed him first. Everybody takes bribes in Austria.'

'Nice country.'

'"A healthy President and a healthy administration",' said the President. 'How does that sound?'

'Brilliant,' Bradwell lied. 'Very pithy.'

'Yeah, that's how I like it. Full of pith.'

'How about the rest of Rawls' conclusions?' said the National Security Advisor. 'Downgrading Bulgakov's debrief, and so on.'

'I'm not so happy about that,' admitted the Secretary of State. 'Even if Lalic was a dead end, there could be more where he came from. The Soviets may not know the details about Waltz, but they've grasped the general principle. The embassies are all reporting a flurry of activity–'

'Flurry?' exclaimed the CIA Director. 'It's one of the biggest fishing expeditions the Russians have ever mounted. They're squeezing the Yugoslavs, the East Germans, anyone who might know. They think they're onto a winner here, and it can only be a question of time–'

'But that's Rawls' point, isn't it? We can't stop them, so there's no point in trying. But whatever they produce will be contaminated by the fact that *they* produced it. That gives us a hell of an edge.'

'Of course, I can't do it alone,' the

President mused. 'This needs all of us. "Healthy administration" means just that.'

'I'm not sure I follow you,' Bradwell said.

'You've all got to come in on this. We could have Gerry doing press-ups, Ed on weights, and Jim on aerobics. It'd look great. And as for you, George–'

'Me?'

'Yes, you. How about trying your hand on a trampoline?'

Bradwell looked horrified.

'Now, Mr President, maybe you're getting a little carried away here...'

'Nonsense,' said the President cheerfully. 'I can just see it now: the Chief of Staff performing mid-air somersaults for the press corps–'

'Remember,' said the CIA Director, 'this is a two-pronged attack, so to speak. On the one hand they've got the KGB scurrying around Europe, on the other there's quiet but noticeable troop movement on the Czech-Austrian border. And don't tell me that's a coincidence.'

The word 'troop' breathed life into General Cremona.

'If I might offer an opinion here...' he said.

'Sure, Bud. Go ahead.'

'The situation you're referring to has not been fully evaluated by the Pentagon. But the preliminary diagnosis is an upgrading of second-order pre-combat preparedness in the Strakonice-Kraselov sector, with corresponding activity in Vimperk, Slavonice and Hrádek. This suggests a quasi-random routine exercise scenario, but offers the possibility of alternative strategic interpretations.'

'You don't say?'

'In other words,' said the Secretary of State, 'they're telling us to watch our step. It is a little worrying.'

'It's damned unhealthy,' said the CIA Director.

'Unhealthy?' said the President. 'My point exactly, gentlemen. And I've got the answer to your problems.'

The others turned round in surprise.

'What's that, Mr President?'

'This.'

The President stopped pedalling, and affectionately slapped the handlebar of his bicycle.

'You know my motto, gentlemen: a healthy mind in a healthy body. If it's health you're worried about, try this. Good for your body, great for our image.'

111

There was no obvious reply to this, so the staff merely gazed stupidly at the President, while the assistants helped him down. He patted his face with a towel, and, ignoring their goldfish expressions, he pointed encouragingly at the bicycle.

'OK,' he said briskly. 'Who'll go first?'

FOURTEEN

Wyman had never been to a political meeting before. He had always thought of party politics as one of life's necessary evils, like vaccinations and income tax: they were inevitable, but one preferred not to dwell upon them. The same could be said of politicians.

Nevertheless, Wyman could not suppress his interest in the proceedings around him. This particular meeting was being held in a mood of triumph; the party had just fielded the winning candidate in the Austrian presidential election, and was looking forward to further success in the forthcoming parliamentary poll.

The meeting was held in an enormous Hapsburg ballroom, and it reeked of affluence. Between the polished floor and the ornate ceiling sat a large and expensive audience, arranged into long rows of cigars, dinner suits, jewellery and furs. This was not a workers' rally; it was not the workers' party. On the podium before them stood the hero of the moment, Max Gebhard.

From his seat in the second row, Wyman had a splendid view of the new President. He was tall and angular, with snow-white hair and brittle, patrician features. A monocle would not be out of place on him, Wyman thought, but he soon changed his mind: Gebhard had an impish smile, and the twinkle in his eyes suggested softer, humane qualities. His voice was typically Austrian: slow, musical, and almost plaintive. Listening to his speech, Wyman understood why Gebhard was known as a thinking man's politician. He spoke gently and with confidence, without the shrillness of the dogmatist or the hack.

'In a few months,' he began, 'there will be another election, the most important of all. We have been putting a special argument to the electorate, and we have enjoyed some small success.'

There was vigorous applause for this modest reference to his own election.

'You could say,' he went on, 'that we have won half the argument. We now have to win the remainder. In fact, there is not one argument, but many. Perhaps I can remind you of the one that is closest to my heart.'

The audience settled down and allowed

Gebhard to refresh their memories. Their country was neutral, he reminded them, and would remain so for the foreseeable future. But he drew a distinction between political neutrality and what he termed 'cultural neutrality', or 'neutrality of spirit'. In the latter sense, Gebhard said, Austria was not neutral at all.

His tone of voice now shifted, and he spoke more slowly. To Wyman he sounded like a benign schoolmaster explaining something to an unusually stupid pupil, but the audience seemed unperturbed. Gebhard told them that the world was now run by two opposing forces. The opposition was not merely political or economic. It was an opposition of cultures, traditions and values.

The first tradition, he said, put faith in people. It expected individuals to be responsible for their lives. It gave them choice: choice of behaviour, choice of values and choice of governments. And it expected them to take responsibility for the consequences. If they made good choices, they enjoyed the results. If they made bad choices, they could only blame themselves. Gebhard clearly approved of this arrangement.

The other tradition, he said, put absolute faith in the State. Individuals regularly disagreed about important things: this system solved the problem by controlling everything from the centre. Government organised everything: not just factories, farms and schools, but also lives, morals and opinions. This was obviously a Bad Thing.

'The citizens are treated like children,' he said, with a grim smile. 'For most of the time they are controlled and managed. And, not surprisingly, they have come to resemble children: often pleasant, often naïvely charming, but often brutal and violent.

'No doubt someone will say I am being unfair. What about *perestroika?* What about *glasnost?* What indeed?'

He paused to allow some sympathetic laughter.

'Take *perestroika*. This, I understand, means "reconstruction". They want to take their inefficient one-party state, and turn it into an efficient one-party state. An efficient tyranny. Am I really supposed to welcome this?'

There was more laughter, but Gebhard stopped it with a wave of his finger.

'And what of *glasnost?* "Openness".

"Freedom of speech". Yes, freedom to complain about the quality of consumer goods. Freedom to criticise the more overtly corrupt factory managers. This I grant you. But freedom to complain about Lenin? Freedom to demand a nonsocialist state? I rather doubt it.'

There was a loud burst of applause, which Gebhard could not extinguish swiftly. For nearly a minute he smiled politely at his devoted audience. It occurred to Wyman that preaching to the converted could be an exhilarating pastime.

He noticed, however, that Gebhard was glancing at his watch. When the clamour subsided, the President proceeded swiftly towards his conclusion. There could be no doubt, he said, about which of these two traditions Austria belonged to. Theirs was a prosperous, civilised nation, but all could be lost overnight. They should not be complacent. They should be clear about who their friends were, and let them be sure of their amity. This, he assured them, would be the most important message of the election campaign. He thanked them, bowed modestly, and sat down.

Gebhard received a standing ovation, which was sincere, though hardly spontaneous. He stood up, bowed once more, and smiled appreciatively at his audience. After a few minutes the applause began to die down, and Gebhard was led off the stage and out through a side-door. Wyman felt a gentle tug on his sleeve, as an usher asked him to step outside. A few moments later he was outdoors, shaking hands with the Austrian President.

'Pleased to meet you, Dr Gebhard,' Wyman said. 'And thank you for seeing me at such short notice. I hope I haven't–'

'Not at all, Professor,' Gebhard smiled. 'I was most distressed by the news in your letter. I really should have seen you before this meeting. It would have spared you the added torture of my speech.'

'On the contrary, I found it most absorbing.'

'Irritating, as well, I should think,' Gebhard laughed. 'I understand you are a philosopher. Your profession prefers reason to rhetoric, with every justification. Political speeches are so … vulgar, aren't they?'

'I've heard worse,' Wyman said. 'Your speech was a clear summary of your ideas, and you believed what you were saying. That puts you two points ahead of most of your colleagues.'

'I'm flattered,' Gebhard laughed. 'Anyway, Professor, perhaps we can go elsewhere to talk. My audience will be leaving by the front entrance any minute now. If I'm spotted, we'll be here all night. If you'll follow me...'

Gebhard led Wyman to a nearby limousine. They were accompanied by two bodyguards, one of whom held a walkie-talkie. When they were inside, the bodyguard spoke into the radio. Two police cars drove up: one took the lead, the other stayed behind.

As they moved off, the policeman in the front car switched on its siren and lights. Gebhard frowned and tapped a bodyguard on the shoulder.

'No alarms,' he said softly.

The bodyguard relayed the command on his radio, and the front car promptly responded. Gebhard turned to Wyman and grinned.

'We aren't going to the palace,' he explained. 'Nowadays, I find that my home and place of work are permanently besieged by journalists, tourists and paparazzi. All my guests are photographed, investigated and cross-examined. I have learned the need for alternative arrangements.'

'The price of fame,' Wyman sympathised.

'Quite so. But there is no need for my personal guests to suffer. We have an arrangement with a hotel on the Park Ring. It enables me to hold private meetings with a certain amount of discretion.'

'I'm glad to hear it,' Wyman said, as he settled back in his seat. 'I'm all in favour of discretion.'

FIFTEEN

The hotel was obviously well used to Gebhard's custom. Wyman and his host were swiftly escorted to a private lounge on the fourth floor, where more policemen were completing an electronic 'sweep'.

'All clear, sir,' one of them said.

'Thank you,' Gebhard replied. He turned to Wyman and lifted his hands apologetically. 'It has to be done, I'm afraid. Every time I come here, the room must be checked for explosives and microphones. It must cost the taxpayer a small fortune in police time. Please take a seat.'

As the policemen put away their equipment, Gebhard went over to a drinks cabinet and looked inquiringly at his guest.

'Scotch, please,' Wyman said. 'Neat. Is this where you met Herbert Feigl?'

Gebhard poured out a Cognac and a Scotch, and gave the latter to Wyman.

'Yes. Your letter was the first I'd heard of his accident. I was deeply saddened by the news. He seemed a decent man.'

'He was. This was the first time you met him?'

'Yes. As you know, we were both members of Freedom of Conscience. A few years ago Mr Feigl heard that I was visiting London, and he asked if I could visit his local branch in Sussex. I agreed provisionally, but my agenda proved to be unexpectedly heavy, and I had to withdraw. Since then we corresponded once or twice on human rights matters.'

When the policemen had left the room, Gebhard lit a cigarette. He inhaled the smoke appreciatively, and smiled guiltily at Wyman.

'Strictly against the rules,' he said.

'Doctor's orders?'

'Politician's orders. Nowadays it is not acceptable for senior politicians to smoke cigarettes. It upsets the voters.'

'It's the international health craze,' Wyman said, lighting his own cigarette. 'Quite sickening.'

Gebhard shook his head.

'There's a deeper explanation, I think. Tobacco itself is politically neutral: it's the vehicle that counts. Voters don't mind cigars and pipes. These suggest character. But cigarettes seem to indicate weakness. Unfortunately, I like them. So instead of being a pipe-puffing president or a cigar-sucking statesman, I'm a secluded cigarette-smoker. You see, I'm really a very dishonest politician.'

'Your secret's safe with me,' Wyman laughed. 'Herbie was also a persecuted nicotine-addict, you know. It's been suggested that it might have contributed to his death.'

'Indeed?'

'He smoked about fifty a day, which led the Yugoslavs to suppose he had a heart attack somewhere.'

'You sound as if you don't agree.'

Wyman shrugged.

'It's possible,' he said. 'May I ask why he came to see you?'

'Of course. He wanted to wish me luck in the elections. He also wanted to talk about a certain Czech dissident whom we've been trying to get released from prison.'

'I see,' Wyman muttered. 'Did you also perhaps discuss the case of any Yugoslav dissident?'

'No, just the Czech.'

Wyman shifted uneasily.

'Was that discussion confidential, or can I...?'

'Not in the least,' Gebhard laughed. 'Quite simply, Feigl's branch has been campaigning for the release of a Czech poet, and Feigl wished to know if I might add my voice to the chorus. Normally, this would have been quite straightforward. But now I was standing for the Presidency, and things were a little more complicated.'

'I understand,' Wyman said.

'I told Feigl I could no longer write any letters of this sort as a private citizen. But I promised I would mention it to the Czech embassy at the first opportunity.'

'And that was all he was here for?'

'Yes. Oh, there was some small talk, of course. He also asked me to sign half a dozen copies of one of my books.'

'Then he left?'

Gebhard nodded, and smiled curiously at his guest.

'Now,' he said, 'can I ask you a question? You said in your letter that the Yugoslav police were satisfied that he had had a fatal accident, and it was purely a matter of time before his body turned up. You obviously don't share their confidence. May I ask why?'

'I'm not saying they're wrong,' Wyman said carefully. 'In fact, I expect they're right.

I'm simply perplexed by the absence of his body. If Herbie did have a coronary, he might have shown symptoms of illness shortly beforehand. After he left Vienna, he went directly to Bohinj. It's quite likely that you were the last person to have a full conversation with him before he died. That's why I asked to see you.'

'I understand,' Gebhard nodded. 'You're wondering if I might have noticed signs of stress, or something like that.'

'Exactly,' Wyman said.

Gebhard took another long puff of his cigarette and gazed pensively at his brandy glass for a few moments. Finally, he exhaled a long stream of smoke and shook his head.

'I'm sorry,' he said. 'He seemed perfectly well to me. I don't recall any symptoms of that kind. He struck me as a calm, reflective person. Reasonably content with the world.'

'Did he talk much about himself?'

'Not really. He mentioned his school. He seemed very fond of the place. But we spent more time chatting about my book.'

'The one you signed for him?'

'That's right. *Austria: East or West.* Perhaps you have heard of it.'

'Yes,' Wyman said. 'I haven't read it, but I understand it's a full statement of the views you made in your speech tonight.'

'That's right. I wrote it about two years ago, when I decided to run for the Presidency. I hoped it would be something of a manifesto. Sadly, I was right.'

'Why was that sad?'

'Because,' Gebhard laughed, 'as with all manifestos, nobody read it. Even the press ignored it. Oh, it was reviewed here and there, but only by academics. It was treated as a learned discourse, written for the benefit of political theorists. That wasn't what I had in mind.'

'I wouldn't worry about it,' Wyman said. 'As an academic, I've often wondered what would be needed to bring my work to wider attention. I once considered scattering liberal doses of violence and pornography throughout my essays, but I soon abandoned the idea. It would only provide salacious amusement for my colleagues.'

'Quite so,' Gebhard chuckled. 'I fear the academic is doomed to speak solely to his colleagues. When I began writing, I entertained fine ideals about raising the communal standard of political discourse. I now know better.'

'I read some of those books,' Wyman said. 'I thought they were very interesting. *A*

126

Defence of the Open Society, and your second one...'

'*Bureaucracy: the Twentieth Century Plague.*'

'Yes. I'm afraid I've forgotten most of the arguments, but I recall being intrigued by them. I must read them again.'

'In that case,' Gebhard said, 'you shall have signed copies. No, Professor, I insist. I'll send them to your hotel tomorrow. I'm only sorry that I can't give you more help with your inquiries.'

'It doesn't matter,' Wyman shrugged. 'I didn't really expect you to produce any vital clues. But this was the last unexplored part of Herbie's itinerary. I had to make sure. It may sound odd, but I suppose I felt I owed it to him.'

'I understand,' Gebhard said.

'There's just one more thing,' Wyman said. 'This may appear highly impertinent, but...'

'Go ahead.'

'When Herbie visited you, you were extremely busy. Your campaign was in its final stages, and there must have been a great deal on your mind. I'm surprised you could find the time to see him.'

Gebhard smiled and took another sip of his brandy.

127

'Professor,' he said, 'right now there are several million people who think very highly of me. I could knock on any of their doors, and they would all give me a hearty welcome.

'That can change very quickly. I don't think of myself as a radical politician, but by Austrian standards I am held to be unusually progressive. Such people can fall from grace with extraordinary speed. One should never forget that, I think. One should always keep a decent supply of personal friends, just in case.

'Your friend respected me before I ever thought of standing for office. I appreciated that, and I found time for him. I didn't know him very well, but I had the impression that he was not a particularly happy person. I suspect he had few close friends.'

'You were most observant,' Wyman said.

'But the point is,' Gebhard went on, 'he did have *some* friends. You, for example.'

He stubbed out his cigarette and immediately took another one. Before lighting it, he paused and looked intently at Wyman.

'If I should ever disappear,' he said quietly, 'I should like to think there is someone who'd come looking for me. I should like that very much.'

SIXTEEN

Vienna is a whipped-cream city. Its inhabitants seem to believe that nothing looks right unless it is adorned by elaborate milky swirls. This not only applies to their famous pastries: it is true of their soup, their coffee and even their buildings. Viennese architecture reflects the Viennese taste in food. It is elegant, rich and florid, and it leaves nothing to the imagination. Taken in excess, it can produce unfortunate after-effects.

These thoughts occurred to Wyman as he sat in a *Konditorei* on the Kärtner Strasse. The item of food on his plate had begun life as a gateau. Several layers of jam, icing, chocolate and cream later, it bore an alarming resemblance to an Alpine peak. The coffee beside it had been subjected to a similar process. It lay hidden beneath an explosion of frothy milk, topped by the ubiquitous dollop of piped cream, and finished with a sprinkling of powdered chocolate. Through the window, Wyman could see the sumptuous buildings of the Stephans Platz, and the magnificent spire of the cathedral. The similarity was disturbing.

Wyman knew his indigestion was largely psychosomatic. He understood that it resulted from lingering traces of Puritan guilt, and the Anglo-Saxon dread of excess. He appreciated that the problem was aesthetic, and not dietary. Unfortunately, his stomach understood none of this. It felt definitely queasy. Wyman abandoned the gateau as a lost cause, and concentrated on the coffee. With a decisive scoop of his spoon, he lopped off the whipped-cream head-dress and put it down beside the gateau. At once, the coffee ceased to intimidate him, and he took a long, happy slurp.

He looked at his watch, and saw he had four more hours to kill before his plane left for Rome. With the deepest reluctance, he had decided to abandon his inquiries. Despite all the unanswered questions, Wyman realised that there was nothing more he could do. He must assume that Herbie, like Milo Lalic, was buried somewhere in the mountains above Lake Bohinj. Who had killed him, and precisely why, would probably never be known.

His only souvenir of the affair would be the four books which Gebhard had signed and dispatched to Wyman's hotel that morning. Despite his instinctive distrust of politicians, Wyman rather liked the Austrian President. Apart from his quiet charm, he possessed a humane, civilised quality which lifted him clear of the shark-pool of contemporary politics. Of course nowadays such qualities counted for nothing, and Gebhard must also be capable of polished ruthlessness. But, Wyman suspected, if a few more Gebhards led a few more countries, the West might perhaps emerge from its slough.

At least the fellow has *ideas*, Wyman reflected, as he picked up one of the books. At least he *thinks*. At least he has the decency to put his own thoughts on paper and defend them, rather than leave the job to his ghostwriter and his advertising agency. An honest politician is always too much to expect, but is it really so outrageous to ask for one who can read and write?

Wyman stopped and looked up from the book. Something was wrong. He fumbled in his jacket, and drew out his note-pad. The Hotel Zlatorog had kept an inventory of the items left behind by Herbie Feigl. Wyman had copied the inventory, though it showed nothing of interest. Apart from his passport and spare cash, there were his clothes, toiletries, travellers' cheques, alarm clock and some magazines. That was all.

'How very curious,' Wyman muttered.

Gebhard had signed six copies of his own books for Feigl. These were not listed on the inventory, so presumably they were not in Feigl's room. What had become of them? Wyman quickly ran through the possibilities. Had Feigl mailed them home? It seemed unlikely: the books were almost certainly for Feigl himself. Either Herbie had left them in the hotel, or they had gone with him on his last walk. The latter option was absurd: he might have taken out one volume, but not all six. Had they been stolen? And if so, why? It made no sense.

The only remaining possibility was that there were no books, and Gebhard was lying. That seemed equally fantastic. Why should Gebhard invent such a story? It was too easy to check, and it would gain him nothing.

Wyman frowned and put away his note-pad. This was the last straw. His knowledge of the Feigl affair was incomplete, and he had finally accepted that it must remain so. The facts were sketchy and limited. But he now realised they were also contradictory, and he would not tolerate this. By profession, Wyman was a logician. He loathed inconsistency.

There was only one avenue left to explore. Herbie had got into trouble because of his contacts in Yugoslavia. These went back over forty years: Herbie had served in Yugoslavia during the war, and visited it regularly afterwards. Rawls regarded this line of inquiry as sterile. He was probably right, but Wyman had nothing else left to investigate. Even if it were fruitless, a quick search through Herbie's past would at least convince him that the case must be laid to rest.

Wyman made up his mind. He would not go home on the afternoon flight, but would return to London. The matter should be settled within two days. A quick phone call would placate his wife.

He turned round and caught the eye of the waitress.

'Another coffee please,' he said.

He noticed the redundant dollop of cream from his last cup, and added hurriedly: 'Black, please.'

SEVENTEEN

General Zhdanov was not in a good mood. His desk creaked beneath the weight of a thousand files, dossiers and reports. There were pink forms and blue forms, intercept summaries, intelligence digests, photograph analyses and a small mountain of internal memoranda. Some people in the KGB were fascinated by this sort of thing. Others found it depressing. But General Zhdanov belonged to a third category: he found it highly infuriating.

He threw down his pen and snorted.

'Bollocks,' he muttered, and in a voice that could be heard throughout most of Dzerzhinsky Square, he yelled out: 'Kuleshov! Get in here.'

There was a patter of anxious footsteps, followed by a tap on the door.

'Come in, you rodent,' Zhdanov bellowed.

Kuleshov crept into the office, and gazed timidly at his chief.

'Is something wrong, General?'

Zhdanov waved at the papers on his desk.

'This,' he said indignantly. 'It's a fucking disgrace. When are you going to get it into that bidet you call a head that I am not one of your piss-arsed paper-pushers? I asked for a report, not for the Belorussian annual paper quota.'

'But, General,' Kuleshov spluttered, 'I've included my own synopsis of all this material. It contains all the salient points.'

'You mean this compost?'

Zhdanov picked up a hefty slab of a document and brandished it at his assistant.

'Who do you think you are, Tolstoy or something? "Salient points", my arse. This has more salient points than the Himalayas. Sit down, maggot.'

Kuleshov did as he was told.

'I have a theory,' Zhdanov growled. 'When a job is simple, and it's carried out cleanly, the reports are clean and simple. Conversely, when the job is messy and sloppily handled, the reports are messy, opaque and very, very long.'

With one sweep of his beefy arm, the General wiped his desk clear of all its clutter.

'Now,' he said, 'I know the facts. I want your conclusions. A verbal synopsis, Kuleshov. And if I hear one piece of evasiveness, just one, you'll be using one of those reports as a suppository. Get on with it.'

Kuleshov took a deep breath and got on with it.

'We are … satisfied by recent events. The *shavki* Lalic is dead, and the Americans appear to have abandoned their inquiries in that sphere. Wyman also appears to have lost heart, and we believe he will soon return home. This will therefore allow us to resume our search for Feigl without further interference. It is very … satisfactory, General.'

Zhdanov stared at him in disbelief.

'And that's it?' he gasped.

'Why, yes.'

'Very satisfactory?'

'Yes, General.'

'You amaze me, Kuleshov, you really do. Firstly: Rawls has gone home. This is because Lalic is dead, and he was their only line of inquiry. But it doesn't mean they've lost interest.

'Secondly: Wyman has not gone home. After he visited Gebhard, he was supposed to return to Rome. He didn't. He went to London. Why? He's not happy. Maybe Rawls bothered him. Maybe Gebhard bothered him. But there's no indication that

136

he's "lost heart".

'Thirdly, our "search for Feigl" is proving to be an unmitigated disaster. That's what you've been trying to hide from me with all this paperwork, isn't it? No, don't deny it. I smell a fuck-up here.'

Zhdanov put his feet up on his desk and emitted another groan of frustration.

'Useless,' he lamented. 'Absolutely useless. We're inches away from sealing the fate of that bastard, and you can't see it. We can do it, Kuleshov, we really can. We could screw him, if only–'

'Who do you mean, General?'

'That turd Gebhard, of course. Don't you see? I know what he's doing, and the Americans know that we know. But we're helpless without that extra little particle of proof...'

Zhdanov's voice trailed away, as he sank into deep thought. Kuleshov watched him nervously. The contemplative Zhdanov could be even more unsettling than the rabid version.

'Very well,' Zhdanov said eventually. 'These are my orders. The search for Feigl will be intensified and extended to all parts of Europe. Wyman will be monitored. So will Rawls. You will also keep an eye on this

English journalist, Fulton.'

'With respect, General, Fulton is of no significance whatsoever. His article was entirely speculative–'

'Of course it was,' Zhdanov snapped. 'But he's curious, and he's asking questions in Yugoslav emigré circles. It's just possible he might discover something, and I'm leaving nothing to chance.'

'I understand, General.'

'I hope you do,' Zhdanov said meaningfully. 'You'll keep me fully informed, of course. And I don't mean this crap.'

He jabbed his thumb at the paper strewn about the floor.

'I mean verbal reports,' he said. 'At least four a day, in this office.'

'Not by telephone?'

'No. I hear they've been asking questions over in the Kremlin. They want to know what's happening. Some prick in the GRU was sent here to grill me. I told him to fuck off, but I don't suppose we've heard the last of it.'

Kuleshov was appalled.

'Do you mean they might be listening in on our calls?'

'Don't be so shocked,' Zhdanov grinned. 'We don't hold a monopoly on these things, you know. Our beloved Party Secretary thinks I'm developing something of an obsession about this business.'

'But surely he's as worried as we are–'

'Yes, yes, but he's asked for a more delicate approach. Delicate! If only he knew. If I had my way, I'd fly to Vienna tonight and dis-embowel that bandit with my bare hands.'

'You ... feel that strongly about him, General?'

Zhdanov closed his eyes and summoned his last shred of patience.

'Very astute of you, Kuleshov. Yes, I hate him very, very much. Now get out.'

EIGHTEEN

The Public Records Office has two main buildings in London. There is a big, ugly Victorian building on Chancery Lane, and a big, ugly modern building at Kew. One could spend many hours debating which of the two is the most unpleasant: in this case, nineteenth-century pomposity would probably be beaten by twentieth-century brutality, if only by a short head.

The Kew building is a vast, crude slab of concrete and glass covering an area of waste-ground beside the River Thames. Its Orwellian appearance is matched by its interior: in the air-conditioned reading-room, visiting researchers request documents using computer terminals, and they are paged by electronic bleepers when the material is available.

Wyman had always felt somewhat intimidated by anything involving silicon chips, and the surgical efficiency of the Kew office brought out his worst fears. But, to his surprise and relief, he had no trouble in finding what he wanted. The WO/202 series of records contained documents to and from British military missions to occupied territories during the Second World War. Wyman spent much of one day reading through everything he could find on missions to Yugoslavia.

Most of the files consisted of bundles of typewritten signals, which were stuffed into battered cardboard folders and tied up with string. The signals were in vaguely chronological order, without any explanatory material. Many of them were missing, either because they had been lost, or because they were still deemed to be too politically sensitive for public exposure.

The documents ranged from brief operational dispatches to detailed reconnaissance. There were long intelligence reports on enemy activity, as well as confidential memos concerning Allied groups and individuals. From all this material, Wyman built a vivid, if fractured, picture of events in the years 1942 to 1945, when small groups of Allied servicemen were parachuted behind enemy lines to make contact with resistance groups and to offer them help in their struggle against the occupying forces.

Finally, Wyman tracked down the dispatches to and from Lieutenant Herbert Feigl. Herbie had been in charge of a four-man unit sent to liaise with a detachment of Tito's Partisans in the Julian Alps, late in 1944. The area acquired a special importance after October 20, when Belgrade fell to the Allies. In Croatia and Slovenia, the Germans built up their last line of defence, and Herbie's unit lay behind that line. The Allies' final push did not take place until the last two months of the war, when nearly 100,000 Germans were killed, and over 200,000 were captured. In Slovenia, the intervening period was confused and bloody. Some areas, such as Bohinj, were liberated quickly. Others remained occupied until the very end. The rest was no man's land, exposed to retreating German units and assorted hangers-on. The latter included remnants of the Ustase, the notorious Croatian Fascists, whose atrocities rivalled those of the German SS.

Herbie's dispatches reflected the chaos of this time. Many of his signals were simply requests for further rations and arms. There were regular intelligence reports, chiefly detailing the movements of German troops. Occasionally, Herbie would send careful assessments of his hosts, the Partisans.

Although relations between the Slovenes and the British were usually cordial, they were not without problems. The Partisan leader, whose code-name was 'Coleridge', was clearly suspicious of all outsiders. Before giving any information, however routine, to Herbie's unit, Coleridge would insist on getting clearance from his own headquarters in Ljubliana. This led to delays, and much irritation on the British side.

Herbie's dispatches for February and March of 1945 highlighted these difficulties. The Bohinj area, though nominally free, still suffered frequent incursions by stray German troops. The Partisans organised a small prison camp at Stara Fuzina, to the east of Bohinj, to house those who were captured alive. These prisoners were of great interest to the British, since they were a potential source of useful intelligence. Herbie was ordered to seek access to the camp and question its inmates. Unfortunately, Coleridge was possessive about his new charges, and would not meet Herbie's request. Using his code-name 'Rainbow', Herbie explained the problems in a bitter signal to his commanding officer.

From: Rainbow
To: Glamis

Coleridge still denies us access to Stara Fuzina stop He assures me that we may interrogate his prisoners in due course but will not say when stop He refuses to answer specific questions on this subject so the following information is based entirely on gossip from his men who are not wholly reliable stop

I understand the compound contains about sixty repeat sixty men stop Of these thirty repeat thirty are Germans including eight repeat eight officers and three repeat three SS men plus two repeat two Italians as well as five repeat five Ustase and five repeat five Slovenian collaborators stop

Some of Coleridge's inner caucus are demanding that the SS and Ustase and collaborators be shot now stop Coleridge urges caution and says they should await further orders which is entirely typical stop I have told him we would be most displeased if executions were carried out particularly if we were not allowed prior interrogation stop

It is also rumoured that the compound contains a Wehrmacht intelligence officer stop I have not been told of his name or rank and I do not know if he is a Nachrichten-offizier or an Abwehroffizier stop Apparently he was once stationed near Kragujevac in Serbia stop Do you have information about such a man query I can also confirm that the Ustase officer Capone is captive here and I have sought permission to interrogate him stop Coleridge is typically unhelpful about this stop He is the perfect Commissar ie a pompous officious bureaucrat stop I would be most grateful if you could speak to his superiors message ends

The reply from Glamis was missing from the file, as were several exchanges which followed it. The next message suggested further problems with the obstreperous Coleridge.

From: Rainbow
To: Glamis

Coleridge now claims his radio link with Ljubliana is being jammed stop I believe this is merely another excuse for further delays and indecision but I have no means of proving this stop Is there any way you can check this with Ljubliana query message ends

After this there were further gaps, and then a message from Glamis which indicated a disaster at Stara Fuzina.

From: Glamis
To: Rainbow
Dismayed by your last message stop Please send list of all who escaped stop Coleridge has sent his own explanation to Ljubliana stop Would appreciate your version message cnds

Herbie's reply was predictably caustic.

From: Rainbow
To: Glamis
The explanation is simple stop The inmates heard that some were to be executed and demanded confirmation or denial from Coleridge stop Coleridge refused to comment except to say he was awaiting orders from his superiors stop They therefore decided to risk a mass escape stop Twenty three repeat twenty three prisoners were killed in the escape attempt stop The rest escaped stop
Coleridge blames his men for not implementing the rules correctly which is

146

rubbish stop Since Coleridge never gave us access to these prisoners we have lost a golden opportunity to interview the Abwehroffizier and Capone stop I have made my feelings plain to Coleridge and would be obliged if you did the same with his superiors stop The list of escaped prisoners is as follows

The rest of the message was lost, and the next entry was a note of commiseration from Glamis.

From: Glamis
To: Rainbow
You have our sympathies stop We regret you could not interrogate the Abwehroffizier but feel this is a minor point stop Had he been a Nachrichtenoffizier the loss would have been far greater stop More unfortunate is loss of Capone stop Nevertheless we have passed on your remarks about Coleridge to Ljubliana and heartily endorse them message ends

Wyman closed the file and grinned at the thought of Herbie wrangling with a 'pompous officious bureaucrat'. Herbie did not suffer fools gladly, and Coleridge must have been a constant source of irritation. He also wondered what the difference was between an *Abwehroffizier* and a *Nachrichtenoffizier*. Presumably the distinction was significant. And who was the Ustase officer code-named Capone? He was awoken from these thoughts by a light tap on his shoulder. He turned round and beheld a familiar, shabby face.

'Hello, Professor. Having fun?'

'Eddie!' Wyman exclaimed. 'What brings you here?'

Fulton pointed at the file.

'The same as you,' he said. 'Interesting subject, isn't it?'

'Indeed,' Wyman said heavily.

'Maybe we could chat about it,' Fulton suggested. 'In the cafeteria downstairs.'

'Very well,' Wyman sighed. 'If you insist.'

'Oh, I insist,' Eddie smiled.

NINETEEN

'I don't know what you're up to,' Wyman said, 'but you should abandon it. You're wasting your time.'

'And you're not?' Fulton said.

'I doubt if we're after the same thing,' Wyman said. 'But if it's any comfort to you, I'm probably wasting my time as well. The difference is that I'm on holiday, and you aren't.'

'Oh, that doesn't matter. And I suspect we are after the same thing. You want to know about Feigl. So do I. Perhaps we can pool our information.'

Wyman found this suggestion highly amusing.

'I really don't think–'

'Wait a minute,' Fulton broke in. 'You caught me out the other day, I'll admit that. But I've done some homework since then.'

'It must have made a pleasant change for you,' Wyman grinned.

Fulton took a deep breath, and his voice dropped to a whisper.

'OK. I suppose I deserved that. But then, I wasn't to know I was dealing with the man who screwed MI6 for a few million and did a runner, was I?'

Wyman's smile dissolved.

'Be careful,' he said slowly. 'I don't know what you have in mind, and I couldn't care less. But you'd be wise to forget that story. It could get you into a lot of trouble.'

'Me or you?' Fulton said smugly.

'You, Eddie. I am perfectly secure: you aren't.'

'No joke? So who's going to sit on me, then?'

'The people I embarrassed. I wounded their pride, you see. They're very big on pride, because nowadays it's all they have left. They'll do anything to protect their dignity. They won't let you use that story, and they'll punish you for trying.'

'I'm terrified,' Fulton said. 'Really, I am. Don't worry, Professor, I'm not interested in your funny story. I only mentioned it to prove a point. Like I said, I've been doing some homework.'

'On Herbie Feigl?'

'Right.'

'I presume you've now abandoned your original theory – that spying nonsense.'

'Abandoned it? You're joking, of course. I've refined it.'

'Oh dear.'

'Just listen, will you? In 1944 Feigl was sent to Slovenia, to liaise with the Communist Partisans. The Germans were fighting a nasty war in Yugoslavia. Feigl was young, impressionable and Jewish. The conditions were perfect for a conversion.'

'To Communism?'

'Sure.'

'Whose brand?' Wyman said. 'Lenin's or Tito's?'

'At that stage there was no difference,' Fulton said. 'He became a long-term agent for them, and—'

'Which "them" do you mean? The Soviets or the Yugoslavs?'

'I'm not entirely sure,' Fulton admitted. 'The Soviets, I think. There were a lot of Russians around in '45, and Feigl must have known some.'

'It's getting a little thin, isn't it?' Wyman grinned. 'Some more homework is needed, I think.'

'Maybe,' Fulton said obstinately. 'But I'm sure I'm on the right track.'

'And I'm sure you aren't. Herbie did not enjoy perfect relations with the Partisans. If you read those files, you'll see that–'

'You mean Coleridge?' Fulton broke in. 'That was just a personality clash. Even the most committed Marxists have those, you know. In fact, they're especially prone to them. It doesn't prove that Feigl wasn't converted.'

Wyman shook his head.

'Let me tell you something from my own experience, Eddie. If you convert someone in an army, you tell him to stay there. Military secrets are useful. If he has to leave, you tell him to go into another useful occupation, like the civil service. You don't tell him to become a teacher. Teachers aren't very useful, you see. So why was Herbie a schoolmaster for over thirty years? What was he doing for them? Indoctrinating nine-year-old boys with dialectical materialism? I rather doubt it.'

Fulton refused to be beaten.

'He was up to something, Professor. There's a lot going on right now, and I think he was part of it.'

'Oh rot,' Wyman snorted. 'There's nothing of any interest–'

'That's all you know,' Fulton said desperately. 'You've been out of it too long, Professor. I've come across one or two things that would amaze you.'

'I'm sure you have,' Wyman said drily.

'Have you heard of something called Project Waltz?'

'Funnily enough, I haven't. Tell me about it.'

'That's my point,' Eddie said. 'The security world's humming with the story, and you know nothing about it. Another thing; I bet you didn't know that General Zhdanov, the head of the KGB, is Jewish.'

'I have to confess I didn't,' Wyman said mildly. 'Does he know?'

'Oh, very droll, Professor. But it's true. His real name's Gureyvitch, and he's got a long-lost brother living in Manchester. Even MI6 haven't heard about that one.'

'That wouldn't surprise me,' Wyman laughed. 'But you still haven't told me about this Project Waltz. No, don't bother. I know what you're trying to do, and it won't work. You won't seduce me with a few shreds of security gossip.'

'What do you mean?'

'You don't know what Project Waltz is, any more than I do. You've just heard the name somewhere, and you're trying to impress me. You think I'm a possible source for your story. Unfortunately, I won't be a source and there is no story. Go home, Eddie.'

'That's your last word?'

Wyman nodded gravely.

'Pity,' Fulton said casually. 'I think we could have done business. We both want to find out about Feigl, and we've both got relevant information. You know the KGB are involved in this, and I've–'

'What makes you say that?'

'Feigl knew a man called Milo Lalic, who I'm trying to trace. They say Lalic was a KGB informant. Now if I can find Lalic, we're home and dry. Once we establish contact with the Soviets ... what are you laughing at?'

'You're quite mad,' Wyman said. 'Absolutely potty. Are you seriously considering dealing with the Russians?'

'Why not? I bet they know what's going on.'

'My God,' Wyman said hoarsely. 'You really mean it.'

'Of course I do. We've got leverage, haven't we?'

'You mean this Zhdanov tale?'

'Exactly. I bet he's been sitting on that story all his life. I envisage a little deal–'

'Eddie–'

'A simple exchange–'

'Eddie–'

'Easy enough–'

'Stop it,' Wyman protested. 'For God's sake man, you're so bad, you're embarrassing. Do you seriously think you can just sit down and haggle with those characters?'

'No, I don't. But you could.'

'What?'

'You heard me. You know those people. With my information and your talents. I think we could get the truth out of them.'

Wyman got to his feet and picked up his cigarettes.

'Enough,' he said firmly. 'I'm going home. And you can go back to the *Boy's Own* comic you came from. Goodbye, Eddie.'

Fulton watched in silence as Wyman stepped out of the cafeteria. He leaned forward and stubbed out his cigarette with superfluous force.

'Fuck it,' he said.

TWENTY

'Good morning, Karl,' said Max Gebhard, as his secretary walked into his office.

Karl Weber put down the morning's mail on the President's desk and scowled at the cigarette in Gebhard's hand.

'Good morning,' he grunted. 'Have you thought about cutting down on those things?'

Gebhard nodded cheerfully.

'Oh, yes,' he said. 'I've thought about it.'

'At least you could change to a milder brand. You could resurface a road with the tar in one of those.'

'Probably,' Gebhard admitted. 'But it's taken me the last fifteen years to grow used to filters, never mind low tar content. You'll just have to bear with me, Karl.'

Weber sighed disconsolately, and sat down in front of Gebhard's desk.

'You're incorrigible,' he said.

'True,' Gebhard agreed. 'Now, stop lecturing me and go through the agenda.'

Weber referred to his notes.

'This morning's free,' he said, 'which is very useful. You can clear some of the correspondence you've been neglecting. You still haven't written to eight of the parliamentary candidates–'

'You write the letters, I'll sign them.'

'No,' Weber said emphatically. 'Some of them are old hands, and can spot the difference. You have to write at least one letter.'

'And you'll send copies to the others?'

'Exactly.'

Gebhard nodded.

'Very well. What else?'

'You're having lunch with the French ambassador today. That clears the decks from half-past twelve to three o'clock. Then you're seeing the Americans.'

'Ah, yes,' Gebhard smiled. 'Where are we meeting them this time? On a park bench somewhere? Out in a field? Well away from prying eyes and wagging tongues...'

'Quite right too,' Weber said. 'Vienna is such a rumour-factory, they're perfectly entitled to worry about security.'

'I suppose so,' Gebhard sighed. 'I understand the need for security, but do they have to be so *melodramatic?*'

Weber shrugged and returned to the agenda.

'Next, you're seeing the Chancellor for a couple of hours, and after that you've got a radio interview here–'

'I thought it was television.'

'That's tomorrow. You should read your diary.'

'I beg your pardon,' Gebhard grinned. 'I was distracted by the thought of all my correspondence.'

'It's no joke,' Weber said sternly. 'You've built up quite a backlog there, you know. And it's getting worse every day. Just look at this.'

He pointed to the pile of letters and parcels he had just brought in.

'That reminds me,' Weber said. 'Who do you know in Budapest?'

Gebhard shrugged.

'Budapest? One or two people, I suppose. Why do you ask?'

Weber pulled out a brown parcel from the heap of correspondence. Like the rest of the mail, it had already been opened and given the routine check for explosives. Gebhard took the parcel and examined it.

'The address is written in block capitals,' he said. 'It could be from anyone.'

He opened it and drew out the contents: a copy of one of his own books.

'Oh, this isn't unusual,' he said. 'People often send me my books to be signed. They usually do it through the publisher, but I suppose we must expect them to come here now.'

'I think you're wrong,' Weber said. 'Look inside.'

Gebhard opened the book and saw his own signature on the flyleaf.

'Curious,' he said. 'Isn't there a letter with this?'

'Apparently not,' Weber said. 'I phoned the Post Office to make sure it hadn't fallen out while they were checking it. They insist it's all here.'

Gebhard frowned and stubbed out his cigarette.

'I don't understand. Perhaps this is some sort of joke.'

'Perhaps,' Weber said. 'But if so, it's wasted on me.'

'It is a little opaque,' Gebhard agreed. 'Maybe they've written something inside the book.'

He quickly went through all the pages, but found nothing.

'It's untouched,' he said. 'This book hasn't even been read. I don't understand it, Karl. The book was bought in this country: the price tag is still on the back. Whoever sent it was either a Hungarian visitor to Vienna, or an Austrian visitor to Budapest. What does it mean?'

'You signed it,' Weber observed. 'Do you recall meeting any Hungarians with an odd sense of humour?'

'No,' Gebhard laughed. 'And I probably never met this person, anyway. The publishers asked me to sign about two hundred copies for the bookshops just before the election. They knew it would sell well. And I've no idea how many more I signed at rallies and meetings.'

'Do you normally just sign your name?'

'What do you mean?'

'Don't they ask you to put something first? "To Johannes, with fond regards", or something like that?'

'I suppose so,' Gebhard said slowly. 'Some just ask for the signature, when they want to give the book as a present to someone, but haven't decided whom.'

'But there are fewer of those?'

'Yes,' Gebhard said. 'But I couldn't recall…'

He lapsed into thoughtful silence.

'Don't worry about it,' Weber said. 'There are odd people everywhere.'

160

'That isn't an explanation,' Gebhard said pensively. 'It's an excuse for not having one.'

'Are you bothered about it?'

Gebhard looked up and laughed.

'Good heavens, no. But it's an interesting puzzle, isn't it?'

'Yes,' Weber said. 'And I'm glad to see it's stung you out of your lethargy.'

He took Gebhard's backlog of correspondence out of a tray, and put it on top of the President's desk.

'To battle,' he said.

TWENTY-ONE

St John Travis de Beaumont Ashbroke-Sands inhabited an office somewhere in London's Whitehall. Few people knew precisely what he did there, but it was assumed to be something important and discreet. In fact, he did very little. Most of his time was spent reading reports from his juniors. He would correct their spelling, improve their punctuation, add his signature to the document, and pass it on to his minister. He had done little else for the last twenty years, and the next twenty would run along similar lines. This should be enough to secure him a knighthood and an index-linked pension, though neither of these things particularly interested him.

He was something of a dinosaur. Over nine centuries of recorded existence, his family had undergone many shocks. It had faced the usual hiccups arising from assassinations, feuds, inbreeding, civil wars and pox, and had coped admirably. But it was completely unprepared for the worst trauma of all: the twentieth century. For the first time in history, members of the family actually had to *work*. The blow was too great for such an old and noble clan. They began to die in large numbers.

St John Ashbroke-Sands was the last of his line. His older brother had died in a hunting accident, and his younger brother had shot himself after being caught coupling with a Jesuit priest. (The coitus was excusable, the Catholicism was not.) And one whiff of St John's cologne made it clear to the most casual observer that he would not be adding to his tribe.

Like most dinosaurs, he was a good-humoured sort. He tolerated his juniors' impudence, and they in turn put up with his frequent bouts of petulance. He was slow and fat, and perspired copiously. The juniors used him as a seasonal guide. In winter, two small patches of sweat would form beneath the armpits of his lilac-striped Jermyn Street shirts. As the year went on, these patches would darken and spread. By early August, they would coalesce in the centre of his chest, gluing down his lurid silk ties.

It was now late August, and the sweat patches had begun to recede. By some miracle, his desk was free of letters, memos and circulars. With some satisfaction, he sat back in his chair, put his feet on the desk, and wondered idly how long this blissful quiet would last. It lasted precisely twenty-eight minutes, until Cummings, one of his juniors, burst into the office.

'Good morning Singe,' Cummings said loudly.

Ashbroke-Sands frowned.

'Can't you knock, reptile?'

Cummings ignored the remark, and threw a memo down onto the desk.

'In case you were getting bored, Singe,' he explained.

'Don't call me Singe, you earthworm.'

'Sorry, Singe.'

Ashbroke-Sands picked up the memo by its corner, as if it were a piece of used toilet-paper.

'What's this?' he said disdainfully.

'Try reading it,' Cummings suggested. 'You can read, can't you? I once heard a rumour to that effect.'

'Well you heard wrong, microbe. Tell me what it says.'

'Once upon a time there was a computer at the Public Records Office...'

'Oh, piss off Cummings.'

'...and each request on it was logged, as was the number of the reader who requested it...'

'You're being very boring, you know.'

'...and because some files are more sensitive than others, the computer keeps an eye on who takes these out. For example, there's the WO/202 series, "British Military Missions During World War Two"...'

'Balls,' Ashbroke-Sands said impatiently. 'I don't want to know.'

'Oh yes you do, Singe,' Cummings said.

'Why?'

'Because the whole series on Yugoslavia – all of it – was pulled out by one man on one day last week.'

'A bloody historian,' Ashbroke-Sands said. 'Who cares?'

'You care,' Cummings said. 'You see, the PRO computer cross-referred with our system, and guess who popped out?'

'The Dalai Lama? Vlad the Impaler?'

'A certain Michael Wyman, MA, PhD.'

'Really?'

Ashbroke-Sands was impressed. He put his feet down and studied the memo.

'So you know who he is?' Cummings said. 'I didn't. I asked our computer for his file, and it told me to sod off.'

'Quite right too,' Ashbroke-Sands grinned. 'That file's only available to masters and prefects.'

'That's what it said on the screen. It told me to refer the matter to my superior on your grade, ie you. So who's Wyman?'

'Nobody,' Ashbroke-Sands said. 'He's absolutely nobody. But he was somebody once. One of the great and good, in fact.'

'What happened?'

'He fell from grace.'

'How?'

Ashbroke-Sands shook his head.

'Sorry,' he smiled. 'End of story.'

'Oh come on Singe,' Cummings laughed. 'Play the white man.'

'No, I bloody well won't. This is all mine. Go away, maggot.'

Cummings got to his feet and frowned.

'You're not serious are you?' he said.

'I'm entirely serious,' Ashbroke-Sands said.

He jabbed a fat finger at the print-out attached to the memo, indicating a series of codes at the top of the page.

'Do you know what this means, lizard? It means our computer requests the pleasure of my company at once, alone. It means something has just erupted.'

'It means you're going to have to do some work for a change,' Cummings laughed. 'Poor old Singe.'

Ashbroke-Sands pointed at the door.

'Out, vermin.'

Cummings shrugged and opened the door.

'If you change your mind—'

'*Ave atque vale.*'

'Cheerio.'

When Cummings' footsteps had receded down the corridor, Ashbroke-Sands went over to his computer. He keyed in his password, and entered the codes on his memo. The computer acknowledged his entry, and presented him with the following:

PRO SERIES WO/202 WITHDRAWN 22/8 BY
READER NO. S'111842 M. G. F. WYMAN
WYMAN, Michael (1926–):
see MoDX CI 358.992(V)
SIS200048 (1953–1983)
Sec5ROMSta60–65
ConBlack★★(Grünbaum)83
★★SECURITY CLEARANCE WITHDRAWN
6/83 see also WYMAN,Margaret (neé RAMSAY)
MoDX CI 879.417 (S)
PRESS 'F' FOR MORE

'I know his story, you beastly machine,' Ashbroke-Sands muttered impatiently. 'Get to the point, will you?'

He pressed the 'F' key, and the beastly machine promptly got to the point.

CIA/NSA REQUEST FOR BLANKET SURVEILLANCE OF PRO SERIES WO/202 SUBMITTED 6/3 (DJF39Looq PRIORITY)
REQUEST CLEARED BY JIC ON 8/3, ENTERED 9/3 (JIC387/13/9.3)
PLEASE SUBMIT ALL ABOVE FILES (HARD COPY) PERSONALLY TO H. A. BERMAN (SecLia 377) GROSVENOR SQUARE
ENDS

In other words, the Americans had expected someone with an unusual background to sift through the WO/202 file at the Public Records Office. Why anyone should be interested in these old files, and why anyone else should wish to be informed of this interest, was a mystery to Ashbroke-Sands. But, according to the computer, the request had been sent to the Olympian heights of the Joint Intelligence Committee, and who was Ashbroke-Sands to argue with such an exalted body? His order was clear enough: he was to take all this information to a gentleman called Berman at the US embassy in Grosvenor Square, who would doubtless know what to do with it.

Ashbroke-Sands disliked being an errand-boy, especially at the behest of a computer. But he recognised that some duties could not be entrusted to lower forms of life, such as Cummings, even if this meant the end of a peaceful day.

He stood up, straightened his tie, and ran a comb through his brilliantined hair. As he left the office, he cast one last rueful look at the memo on his desk and shrugged philosophically.

'Ours not to reason why,' he sighed.

TWENTY-TWO

Dr Macek was emphatic.

'He is departed to Yugoslavia. This is all I know.'

'Perhaps he left an address, or a date of return. Something like that.'

'No, Mr Fulton. We have nothing like this.'

Eddie Fulton nodded slowly, as it dawned upon him that he was getting nowhere. If the bearded, corpulent gentleman sitting before him knew the whereabouts of Milo Lalic, he kept the fact well hidden.

'I do not understand,' said Dr Macek. 'For several months at one time, Mr Lalic is not here and is somewhere else instead. Nobody is distressed by this. Then, at once, two people request me for his location. Why?'

'Two?' Fulton exclaimed. 'Who was the other one?'

'A different person,' Dr Macek said helpfully.

'An Englishman, perhaps?' Fulton suggested. 'A man called Professor Wyman? He's got white hair, glasses; about your age.'

Dr Macek laughed.

'No. It was not such a man. And, Mr Fulton, I repeat that I cannot help you with the location of Mr Lalic, which is most regretful to me.'

'That's a pity,' Eddie said. 'I was led to believe you were a close associate of his.'

Dr Macek frowned in suspicion.

'May I inquire who told you this?'

'Oh, just one of our sources.'

'An informer to your newspaper?'

'Something like that.'

Dr Macek scratched his beard thoughtfully.

'This is very strange to me,' he mused. 'At once you are interested in us. Why now? For many years the newspapers have not responded to our overtures.'

Fulton gazed at him blankly.

'Overtures?'

'Yes. We send out missives to all the newspapers with much regularity.'

'Oh, you mean press releases?'

'Yes. For example, this.'

From his desk drawer, he drew out a photocopied document and flicked it indignantly across the desk. It was entitled 'Bulletin of the Campaign for a Free Croatia', and consisted of twenty pages of closely-spaced type. Fulton did not know its contents, but he could guess.

'This information is never employed by the newspapers. Why?'

Eddie coughed uneasily.

'I ... I can't really say. You see, these releases are normally sent to the Foreign Desks, and I usually handle Home News. I can't think why they don't use them, Dr Macek, I really can't.'

But it was too late. This was clearly one of Dr Macek's favourite subjects, and Fulton would not be allowed to escape.

'Our staff,' Dr Macek said sternly, 'are examining the newspapers each day. Our information is not employed. Instead, we see pictures of unclothed prostitutes. We read only about television actors and musicians who ingest narcotics, which is disgusting. Why are these more important than our struggle?'

'Well of course they aren't,' Eddie said. 'Unfortunately, the readers–'

'Readers!' Dr Macek hissed in distaste. 'Pah! Is your newspaper a state collective? Who is editing in charge? The readers?'

He picked up the press release and waved it under Eddie's nose.

'Newspapers are for important information,' he said. 'This is the most important of information. If you tell your readers about us, they will no longer want unclothed prostitutes. They will want to know of our struggle.'

'That's – that's an interesting theory,' Eddie gasped. 'I'll pass it on.'

'Of course,' said Dr Macek. 'Take this personally.'

He gave Fulton the press release, and took out a dozen more from the drawer.

'Take these also. They are most important. Once the editors in charge have absorbed all of them, they will understand our situation better. Tell them I am permanently available for comments.'

Eddie stood up and collected the documents.

'Thank you very much, Dr Macek,' he said, trying hard to look grateful. 'And if you hear anything from Milo Lalic–'

'I will give you immediate contact,' Dr Macek assured him. 'Good-day, Mr Fulton.'

Eddie waited until he was half a block away from Dr Macek's office before he allowed himself to erupt into laughter. He saw a litter-bin, and was just about to put Dr Macek's press releases into it, when he noticed that Boris was loitering on the other side of the street.

'Boris' was the name he had given to the man who had been following him for the last couple of days. He assumed that Boris belonged to the KGB, and that his presence indicated Eddie was onto something. Eddie had been in low spirits until Boris appeared. Now he was in an excellent mood.

He crossed the street and tapped Boris on the shoulder, as the latter was pretending to adjust his wrist-watch.

'Hello, Chief,' Eddie said brightly. 'Fancy a chat?'

Boris appeared to be surprised.

'Who are you?' he said.

'Oh, do me a favour,' Eddie chuckled. 'We don't have to go through all that, do we? Just tell me what it's all about.'

Boris was unimpressed.

'You are making a mistake,' he said flatly.

'No I'm not,' Eddie persisted. 'It's something to do with the Herbert Feigl business, isn't it?'

'Who?'

'You know he's out of the country, so what's all the fuss about?'

Boris shook his head.

'I do not understand you.'

'Or are you after those characters?'

Eddie waved in the direction of Dr Macek's office.

'If you want to know about that outfit, I can ease your workload.'

He gave Dr Macek's press releases to Boris, who accepted them in astonishment.

'It's all good stuff,' Eddie assured him. 'First-rate material. From the horse's mouth. Cheerio.'

Eddie walked briskly away, but Boris did not follow him. As Eddie later described it to his colleagues, Boris stood perfectly still, gazing at Eddie as if the latter were a turd in a swimming pool.

TWENTY-THREE

The high-speed train clattered steadily towards northern England. Wyman sat alone in a first-class compartment, with mile after mile of pasture and moorland gliding past him under a hazy August sun. He resisted the temptation to allow the rolling scenery to lull him to sleep, and fixed his attention upon one of the books Max Gebhard had given him.

Gebhard wrote the book in 1951, when working for an international law firm in Paris. It was the first of several works which would establish his reputation first as a principled lawyer, and later as a scrupulous politician. The former was a rare creature, but the latter was thought to be extinct, if it had ever existed at all.

The standard explanation for Gebhard's probity was that he had no experience of the ugly realities of high office. He had briefly served as a member of parliament in the early 1960s, and had acted as a semi-official legal adviser to two governments. He had also worked on several United Nations consultative bodies, and had lectured in Law at a number of European universities. He was perhaps best known for his involvement with Freedom of Conscience, the international human rights organisation.

The most extraordinary thing about Gebhard was that such idealistic, academic qualities should have any appeal for the Austrian electorate, who by tradition have little use for such things. Indeed, five years earlier, few Austrians would have dreamed of voting for him. So what had changed?

From 1945 to 1966, Austria was ruled by a 'grand coalition' of the two main parties, the Socialists, or SPO, and the conservative People's Party, or OVP. This coalition reflected a strong national consensus that continued long after the coalition was broken, when the SPO ruled on its own, or with the help of smaller parties. All politically appointed organisations, including those which run the nationalised industries, were legally obliged to contain equal numbers of SPO and OVP members.

This made for a stable, if highly tedious, system, but the Austrians value stability far higher than electoral variety. They are a prosperous, complacent people, with few scruples in moral, political or financial matters: day-to-day corruption is commonplace, and politicians are regularly accused of taking bribes.

In foreign affairs, there was also little incentive for taking positive stands. Austria regained full political independence, and neutrality, with the *Staatsvertrag* of 1955. The Soviet Union withdrew the last of its troops, on the understanding that Austria would not allow military bases on its territory and would not join political or military alliances.

All this changed when the United States and the Soviet Union agreed to abolish all European medium- and shorter-range nuclear weapons. Suddenly, the great powers were forced to think exclusively in terms of conventional defence. Austria, hitherto a political no man's land, re-acquired its historical strategic importance. The Austrians gradually remembered something they had virtually forgotten, that their country lay next to Hungary and Czechoslovakia. There was no immediate threat: on the contrary, Europe was as stable as ever. But Austria's supine approach to the rest of the world had to be reconsidered.

Two broad options were open to the

Austrians. They could either carry on as before, and pretend that no new problems existed, or they could adopt a new, more assertive stand. The first approach seemed increasingly impractical. Stories were already circulating of a sharp increase in the number of Warsaw Pact exercises on the Czech border, with corresponding activity in Hungary. Perhaps these were merely rehearsals for defensive manoeuvres, perhaps not. In either case, they suggested that Austria could someday be a battleground, whatever its inhabitants might wish.

Unfortunately, the second option was also fraught with problems. Austria was a neutral state, and obliged to remain so. It could not join Nato, even if it wanted to, and it could not harbour protective foreign troops. Given these limitations, how could Austria assert itself?

It was at this stage that people remembered Max Gebhard. For years he had argued for closer ties with the other Western countries, including the United States. Such ties had to be carefully devised: some could be made formally, such as trade agreements; other, more contentious links could take the form of 'understandings' and quasi-official agreements.

The OVP took up Gebhard's ideas with relish. Foreign policy, which had formerly played little or no part in Austrian politics, became an important issue. Coupled with the general swing to the right throughout the West, the new approach seemed sure to give the OVP an unprecedented overall majority in the general election next December. In the meantime, Gebhard was elected President. This was technically a symbolic position: the policies had to be implemented by the government. But Gebhard was the architect of those policies, and he would present them to the outside world.

A Defence of the Open Society was Gebhard's first step on the road to these policies, and the Presidency. It was well written, and it dealt with a general political theme. The term 'open society' was normally used to describe societies with 'freedom of speech', or, more precisely, societies where all citizens may effectively criticise those in authority. Obviously, 'closed societies' were those in which this could not happen.

In this book, Gebhard widened the application of the term 'open society'. He took it to mean societies which maximised the freedom and responsibility of the individual, and kept the authority of laws, governments and official bodies to a minimum.

As its title suggested, Gebhard's book promoted the idea of the open society, but it considered the other argument in detail. Closed societies were, after all, not without their advocates. For most of its history, Russia had been run along such lines, and in the 1920s and 1930s the closed society was a popular notion in Europe, in the form of either Fascism or Communism. The general idea was that societies suffered from giving too many moral choices to individual citizens. There would invariably be crime, conflict and instability. Far better, it was thought, to let governments decide as much as possible. Individuals could then relax, untroubled by difficult decisions and moral dilemmas.

Why Gebhard had chosen to write about this theme was made clear in the preface to the book:

'In 1940 I began my training as a lawyer, confident that laws and those who form them are sufficient to ensure the well-being of a nation. My later experiences as an officer in the German army taught me otherwise.

'I saw what happened when personal responsibility was completely abandoned in favour of rules and impersonal directives. Since then I have considered this subject in detail, and although I recognise the cogency of many arguments for the closed society, and the confusion and risks attached to the alternative, I feel we must take those risks, and govern our nations accordingly.'

Wyman grinned as he read this paragraph. He could not help reflecting that Gebhard was being wise after the event, but he dismissed this as an uncharitable thought. After all, Gebhard had remained true to his beliefs. He was a stern critic of the Soviet system, and other oppressive societies. Perhaps he was too polished – facile, even – but his heart was in the right place. Not a bad chap to have as your president, Wyman thought.

TWENTY-FOUR

Major Hampton was a gnarled, sunburnt gentleman who acquired anecdotes the way other people collect fine wines. They were all carefully stored and labelled, and he had one for every occasion. Most of them were about himself, of course, because the Major's career had been long and varied.

He had enjoyed a 'good war', and followed it with service in Palestine, Berlin and Korea. After leaving the army, he found work with a company in Rhodesia, and fifteen years later, he bought a farm there. His luck ran out in the late seventies: in the space of eighteen months, his family was killed in a guerilla raid, Rhodesia became Zimbabwe, and his farm was turned into a state co-operative. He returned to England virtually penniless, and retired to a council house in a suburb of Leeds.

The Major's anecdotes were two-edged weapons. His stirring war stories would buy him drinks in the local pub, and win over young admirers. His more bloodthirsty tales served another purpose: well-meaning social workers and prying neighbours were easily repulsed with gruesome stories from the Rhodesian bush, in which recalcitrant black farmhands were flogged within inches of their lives.

But his guest today was not interested in military heroism or colonial savagery. Wyman wanted to know about one of the Major's old army colleagues, a Lieutenant Herbert Feigl.

'Never saw him again, after the war,' Hampton said. 'We corresponded once or twice, and there was talk of a reunion, but nothing came of it. What's your interest?'

Wyman explained about Herbie's disappearance, and the speculation in Eddie Fulton's newspaper.

'It's been suggested that Herbie might have been a Communist spy,' Wyman concluded. 'The idea is that he was converted during the war, in Yugoslavia. Now, I understand you were with him in Bohinj–'

He was interrupted by Major Hampton's roar of laughter.

'Converted?' Hampton chortled. 'That's a good one. And who was supposed to have converted him? Nincik, perhaps?'

'Nincik?'

'The Partisan area leader: we code-named him Coleridge. Herbie couldn't stick him. Nor could I, come to that. But Herbie was in charge, and he had to deal with the bugger.'

'What was wrong with him?'

'Nincik was a pompous prig. Typical bloody Slovene: he had no sense of humour, and everything had to be done by the book. Trouble was, the book in question was written by Marx, and it said nothing about British liaison officers. So Nincik tried to pretend we didn't exist. Drove Herbie mad. I had a CO like that once in Korea–'

'I see,' Wyman said quickly. 'Could you tell me about the prison compound at Stara Fuzina? I believe there was a mass escape early in 1945.'

'Yes,' Hampton nodded. 'Herbie burst a blood-vessel over it, and he had every right to. Nincik's security was nonexistent, and if he'd let us inside the place we'd have given him some useful advice on the subject. But Nincik knew better.'

The Major sat back in his chair, and his voice acquired the low, relaxed cadences of the inveterate raconteur.

'You see, things had reached a tricky stage by this point. Most of the country had been liberated, but the rest was sheer bloody chaos. The Germans were in retreat. They'd formed what we thought was their last line of defence, and that was crumbling. As they fell back, we were wondering if they would regroup and form yet another defensive barrier, or simply scuttle over the border.

'That was the big question, and any one of those POWs might have known the answer. HQ Slovenia was screaming at us to interrogate the buggers, but Nincik used any excuse to stop us. I even tried to sneak into the compound one night, but I was caught. By the time HQ Slovenia got through to the Partisan HQ at Ljubliana, it was too late: they'd escaped. All because of that little pillock Nincik.'

'Why was Nincik so difficult?' Wyman asked. 'Was it simply the bureaucratic mind, or was there more to it?'

'Nincik was known as "the Commissar" even among the Partisans,' Hampton said. 'Loved committees, loved wrangling over sub-section 5, paragraph B. Meat and drink to him. They said he made up for it by being a good fighter, but I never saw the evidence. It wouldn't be too surprising, though; if the rule book said "kill", he'd have killed all right. He'd have murdered his mother if the

186

book told him to.

'But you're right, there was more to it. Herbie was German, and that upset Nincik no end. We tried to explain, but it made no difference. The book told him to hate Germans, you see. Once I took him aside and said, "Listen, Nincik, Lieutenant Feigl has just as much cause to hate them as you have. He's Jewish." It was a bad move, and just made things worse.'

'Nincik disliked Jews as well?'

'The trouble,' Hampton said, 'lay in finding someone Nincik *did* like. Miserable bastard. I pointed out that Marx was a bloody German Jew, and I hadn't heard Nincik complain, but he just stared at me as if I'd blasphemed or something. I suppose I had.'

'Marxists can be a little touchy,' Wyman sympathised. 'I had a look in the Public Records Office at Herbie's dispatches on the subject. There was a German officer in the Stara Fuzina compound, and Herbie had heard a rumour to the effect that he was some sort of intelligence officer. Your HQ was anxious that Herbie should interview him, but of course it never happened. There was some question as to whether the man was a *Nachrichtenoffizier* or an *Abwehr-*

offizier. I don't know the distinction, but apparently it was significant.'

Hampton nodded.

'Can't remember the fellow's name, but I know who you mean. Nincik's boys used to talk about him: a stiff-necked young sod, who obviously had some clout among his own people. Even the SS boys treated him with some respect, and they normally wiped their boots on *Wehrmacht* people.

'The important thing for us was to establish exactly what this chap did for his living. We guessed he was an intelligence officer, but that could mean anything. To be really useful to us, he had to be a *Nachrichtenoffizier*, a field-intelligence officer. Such a man would have been responsible for daily reports on the state of the enemy forces. He'd have advised the generals about where their own troops should be sent, and he'd probably have a good idea of what the top brass were planning in the way of a retreat. This of course was what we were all after.

'Unfortunately, this chap wasn't a *Nachrichtenoffizier*. After he escaped from the compound with the others, our people found out he was only an *Abwehroffizier*, which would have been next to useless. So he wasn't such a big loss after all. Herbie was still incensed by the whole thing, though.'

'I'm not surprised,' Wyman grinned. 'Herbie's tantrums were quite entertaining, as I recall.'

'Volcanic,' Hampton laughed. 'Quite a good soldier, but he had a very short fuse. You know, he'd probably have made Captain if it weren't for his temper. He even blew up on Maclean once.'

'Fitzroy Maclean?'

'Our beloved leader, yes. There'd been problems with the supply drops. The bomber squadrons who delivered our gear had been diverted to other duties for a while, such as dropping bombs on the enemy, or something equally trivial. It was a problem throughout the war, and Maclean did his best to brown-tongue the top brass into keeping up a decent supply. But it wasn't constant, and during big offensives we'd get nothing for weeks at a time. *C'est la guerre*.

'But Herbie didn't see it that way, of course. Oh, no. Herbie had to have his supplies dropped with clockwork regularity, or there'd be hell to pay. So when Herbie was finally introduced to Brigadier Maclean, the big man had quite a shock. Maclean was a splendid fellow, you see, and everyone admired him. Even the Partisans. He was used to getting respect. He shook Herbie's hand, and asked him how things were getting along. Herbie went puce and did his Vesuvius impersonation.'

Hampton assumed a ridiculous mock-German accent.

'"Ve haff no supplies. Ve haff no ammunition. Ve haff no boots. Ve haff no razors. It is ein disgrace. It is inefficient und intolerable. Vot are you going to do about zis?" He practically called the old man a pig-dog.

'Maclean took it splendidly, of course. For a split second, there was a look of sheer horror on his face, but it vanished at once. Then he nodded solemnly, took out his note-pad and pencil, and said, "Thank you, Lieutenant. I'll see to it at once. Let me see: ammunition, boots, razors ... and sedatives."'

Hampton slapped his thigh and roared with laughter.

'Poor old Herbie,' he boomed. 'Never knew what hit him.'

'Wyman allowed himself a quiet chuckle.

'Very good,' he smiled. 'But I'm still unclear about the Stara Fuzina story. You say the inmate was the wrong sort of intelligence officer. What did an *Abwehroffizier* do?'

'Technically, he too was a field-intelligence man. In practice, he was less concerned about enemy troops, and more involved in tackling resistance. In Yugoslavia, *Abwehroffiziers* were responsible for rooting out Partisans and their supporters. Of course, that included people like Herbie and myself. If we'd been caught, we'd have been interrogated by an *Abwehroffizier* before being shot, and bugger the Geneva Convention. As you can imagine, they weren't exactly popular. If Nincik and his boys had known one of them was in their hands, they'd have shot him immediately. Fortunately for him, they never guessed.

'Come to think of it, the *Abwehroffiziers* were a pretty nasty bunch. They tortured all their suspects, and they organised the reprisal squads which wiped out entire villages. They sent quite a few people off to concentration camps, as well. They often worked hand in glove with the Ustase, who also did a nice line in barbarity. In fact, we reckoned it was one of the Ustase who sprang the *Abwehroffizier* and the others from Stara Fuzina.'

'How was that achieved?'

'Good question,' Hampton said thoughtfully. 'Nincik's men claimed that the prisoners had overpowered a couple of them, held them hostage, and forced the other guards to open the entrance to the compound. By the time the alarm was sounded, half the POWs had bolted. There was a shoot-out, and a few stragglers were killed, but most got away.

'It all seemed suspiciously easy. We thought at least one of the guards had been bribed, but we couldn't say anything, of course. The average Partisan would never had done a thing like that, but by 1945 things weren't so straightforward. Tito had offered an amnesty to many collaborators in return for their support, and the Partisan ranks were swelled by all sorts of characters, some of whom were downright criminals.

'Furthermore, one of the Ustase was known as a bit of a wheeler-dealer. He was a corrupt little Croat who bribed his way in and out of everything. It's my guess he bought their way out of the compound.'

'Was this the man you code-named Capone?'

'That's right,' Hampton grinned. 'Quite

apt, don't you think? Herbie and I had run across him once before, elsewhere. From our point of view, he was the real loss. The *Abwehroffizier* would probably have told us nothing, but Capone would have sung like Caruso if we'd offered him money and a safe passage.

'You see, he hadn't joined the Ustase for ideological reasons, or anything like that: he was simply in it for the loot. The Fascists appeared to be the winning team, and he thought he could profit by signing on with them – bribes, confiscated property, and so on. He dealt in just about everything, including information. We kicked ourselves when he got away.'

'That's very interesting,' Wyman said quietly. 'Very interesting indeed. Do you remember what Capone's real name was?'

Hampton shook his head.

'I'm sorry, I don't. *Anno Domini*, I'm afraid. But I never was good on names.'

'Was it Milovan Lalic, by any chance?'

Hampton emitted a surprised whistle.

'Gosh,' he exclaimed, 'it bloody well was! How did you know?'

Wyman sat back in his chair and grinned in satisfaction.

'An intelligent guess,' he said smugly.

TWENTY-FIVE

At last the President had his rowing machine. Like the exercise bicycle, it had been carefully doctored to give its user the delusion of superhuman strength. A more cynical soul might have been a trifle suspicious of the childish ease with which one could flick the oars back and forth, but the President's professional scepticism evaporated in the gymnasium. He wobbled merrily away on the machine, like a faulty pendulum, spurred on by George Bradwell's enthusiastic white lies.

'Very impressive, Mr President,' he beamed. 'I'm amazed at how quickly you've got the hang of it.'

'It's no big deal,' the President panted modestly. 'One of these items is much the same as any other. This baby needs no more effort than the bike.'

'I'm delighted to hear it,' Bradwell said, with feeling.

The President's doctor was horrified by his charge's latest toy: he referred to the rowing machine as a 'mechanical Lee Harvey Oswald', and it had taken Bradwell several weeks to persuade him that the new machine was as harmless as its predecessor.

Meanwhile, the security advisers were assessing the latest report from the US embassy in London.

'I knew it,' said the CIA Director bitterly. 'I knew we shouldn't have been so complacent about Wyman, and I was right.'

The National Security Adviser was unmoved.

'You want a medal?' he suggested.

The CIA Director threw up his hands in fury.

'Kiss my ass,' he shouted. 'First you say Wyman's given up and gone home. Nothing to worry about, you say. Now he's gone back to England, pumping everyone in sight, and all you can do is sit there and jerk off. Just kiss my ass, will you?'

'Relax, relax,' soothed the Secretary of State. 'Wyman won't get anywhere. England's been disinfected, just like everywhere else. He's wasting his time.'

'How do you know? There are dozens of people there who could talk to him. It just needs one slip, and then what?'

'It won't happen, I promise. And all

relevant documents have been taken out of the files and locked away.'

'Wyman has plenty of contacts in the civil service. What if he persuades one of them to open the door?'

'Impossible,' said the National Security Adviser. 'Everything on paper is in the hands of the Director-General of MI5, who keeps them in his safe. If Wyman has any buddies, they're in MI6. 5 and 6 hate each other. There's no risk.'

'Know anything about steroids, George?' the President said thoughtfully.

'I – I beg your pardon?'

'You know, anabolic steroids. The things athletes take.'

Bradwell was aghast.

'You can only get them on prescription, Mr President. Otherwise they're illegal.'

'Oh, sure,' the President said impatiently. 'I know *that*. But, uh, what exactly do they *do* for you? Any idea?'

'Oh, God...'

'I was just asking, George.'

'Furthermore,' said the CIA Director, 'there's the journalist, wassisname, Fulton. He's been asking questions as well.'

'He's nobody,' said the Secretary of State dismissively. 'Screw him.'

'Not so fast. It was his article on Feigl that dragged Wyman into all this in the first place.'

'And did you read that story?' said the National Security Adviser. 'The man isn't even a good guesser. If that's the best he can do, we can leave him to it. I don't intend to lose any sleep over some shit-for-brains reporter.'

The CIA Director had an ace up his sleeve.

'In that case,' he said deliberately, 'why have the Russians put a tail on him?'

The others were impressed.

'Jesus. Are you sure?'

'If course I'm sure. Now maybe you people can start to take this seriously. As a matter of fact, I've looked into this guy Fulton, and I don't think we'll get all that much trouble from him. He isn't a professional like Wyman, thank Christ.'

'I hear they build up your muscles,' said the President. 'That might solve a few problems, George. All this exercise is great, but it hasn't had much visible effect. Steroids could be the answer.'

'It does take a while for the physique to get moving, Mr President. If you let it happen naturally, I'm sure it's just a matter of time before–'

'Yeah, but maybe we could speed things up a little. A few pills wouldn't hurt, would they?'

'Of course, Wyman is still our biggest problem,' said the CIA Director. 'We simply don't know what he's capable of finding out. That makes me very nervous, because I know the damage one smart-ass can do if he's determined enough to do it. Now are you prepared to sit and watch him do the KGB's work for them?'

'I take your point,' said the Secretary of State reluctantly. 'If anyone can find out, Wyman can.'

'So what are you suggesting?' said the National Security Adviser. 'We scare him off? That's asking for trouble, and you know it. Take him out? Even more risky, if we don't know what he's doing.'

'Why not use him?' suggested the CIA Director.

'How?'

'Wyman isn't going to give up. OK, let's leave him to it.'

'But a minute ago, you–'

'Let me finish. We leave him to it, but we watch him every step of the way. If Wyman gets nowhere, everything's sweet. If he finds something, we grab him, and we grab whatever he's found. We'll be testing our own security, and we'll have complete control over what happens.'

'Sounds interesting,' said the Secretary of State.

'Sounds like a waste of time,' muttered the National Security Adviser.

'What do you think, Bud?'

General Cremona shook his head reluctantly.

'This is not a military concern,' he began. 'It has no immediate ramifications–'

'Hold it, boys,' said the President. 'Any of you guys know anything about anabolic steroids? What they are, how they work, and so on? I just asked George here, and he's no use at all. How about you?'

'Anabolic steroids?'

'That's right.'

The Secretary of State shook his head.

'Sorry, Mr President. Analgesics are my limit.'

'Can't help you, Mr President,' said the CIA Director. 'I'm into multivitamin tablets.'

'Are they legal?' asked the National Security Adviser.

'Multivitamins? Of course they're legal.'

'No, *steroids*, you schmock. I thought steroids were controlled.'

'Don't worry about that,' said the President hastily. 'How about you, Bud? No good asking you either, I guess.'

'I know a little,' General Cremona admitted modestly.

'Why, that's great!' the President exclaimed. 'OK, let's have it.'

'A steroid is any of a class of natural or synthetic organic compounds which have a molecular structure of seventeen carbon atoms arranged in four rings. In the elementary steroid nucleus, the carbon atoms are bonded to twenty-eight hydrogen atoms. Small modifications in the structure can result in–'

'Hold it! What about anabolic steroids?'

'They're a particular kind of steroid, occasionally prescribed to post-operative patients to enhance tissue regeneration and muscle growth.'

'Muscle growth! Great! How about side-effects?'

'The medical authorities assert that prolonged employment of steroids can result in cancer of the liver, abnormalities of the sex organs and heart disease.'

The President nodded glumly.

'Is that a fact?' he sighed. 'Well, thanks anyway.'

The others gazed at General Cremona with new respect.

'Damned impressive, Bud,' said the Secretary of State.

'Where'd you get all that stuff?' asked the CIA Director.

General Cremona shrugged bashfully.

'Oh, just picked it up in *Reader's Digest*,' he said.

TWENTY-SIX

'Remember your Hungarian admirer? He's moved.'

Karl Weber put another parcel on Max Gebhard's desk. The Austrian President looked at the label and frowned.

'Same writing, same block capitals,' Gebhard observed. 'But now he's in Kistelek, wherever that might be.'

'South-east of Budapest, not far from Szeged.'

Gebhard opened the parcel, and pulled out another copy of his own book. As before, Gebhard's signature was on the flyleaf.

'No letter and no explanation. What do you make of it, Karl?'

'A madman, perhaps?'

'That explains nothing,' Gebhard said, shaking his head. 'Whoever he is, he's trying to tell me something. I just don't understand.'

'Perhaps we should have a word with Security,' Weber suggested.

'We could, I suppose, but what can they do? It seems fairly harmless to me.'

'There's no rational explanation, which means the sender is mad. If so, he could be dangerous.'

'Really, Karl,' Gebhard laughed. 'I think you're being a little melodramatic.'

'I'm being logical.'

'Nonsense. You can't say an action is irrational merely because you can't see a reason for it. And even if it were pointless, it doesn't follow that the man's mad. He could just be a harmless eccentric.'

'But what if he isn't?' Weber persisted.

'He's in Hungary, I'm in Austria. He's going to have trouble getting to me.'

'It can be done. I think we should mention it to the Hungarian embassy. They might know of some–'

'Don't be silly, Karl. At best they would just laugh at us. At worst, they would remind us that there's no law against sending people copies of their own books. I'm not in good odour with our eastern neighbours, remember. For some time now they've been trying to make out that I'm a dangerous paranoiac. This would be exactly...'

His voice trailed off, and he gazed

thoughtfully at the parcel.

'I wonder...'

'A trick?'

'Why not?' Gebhard said quietly. 'There *is* no law against it, is there? And if the story were presented in the right way, it would make me appear quite paranoid. "Gebhard receives copy of his own book – suspects Communist plot." That's the last thing we need.'

'If you're right, we must expect more of the same. Not necessarily more books, but other devices of this kind.'

Gebhard nodded.

'Yes,' he said. 'And we shall ignore them. Don't tell anyone about this, Karl, not even Security. If this is a dirty trick, the best thing is to forget about it. If it isn't, we have nothing to fear.'

He picked up the book and grinned.

'Anyway, Karl, look on the bright side. This book attacks their political system. If they've been spending government money on it, it will be pleasantly ironical, don't you think?'

TWENTY-SEVEN

Wyman picked up his briefcase, and squinted upwards at a video display. Departures are not announced verbally at Gatwick Airport, and travellers have to make sense of the information shown on screens throughout the buildings. According to the display, Wyman's flight for Rome would leave in just over an hour. He decided to go through to the departure lounge and spend the remaining time in the duty-free shop.

As his passport was being examined, an airport official strolled up and tapped Wyman on the shoulder.

'Professor Wyman? Would you step this way, please?'

'Certainly,' he said. 'May I ask why?'

'Someone would like to speak to you.'

'What about?'

'Just follow me, please.'

The official escorted Wyman through passport control, and led him into a small room off the departure lounge.

'Here you are, sir. This gentleman would like a word.'

The official went out, leaving Wyman in the company of an oily, corpulent creature in a crumpled Savile Row suit.

'Hello, Professor,' said the man. 'My name's Ashbroke-Sands.'

Reluctantly, Wyman shook his plump, soggy hand. There was something familiar about him, but it took Wyman a few seconds to remember who he was.

'St John Ashbroke-Sands,' Wyman said slowly. 'It's coming back, now.'

'One of the Whitehall wallahs,' Ashbroke-Sands beamed. 'I didn't think you'd remember. Most flattering. We have met once or twice, a few years ago...'

'Yes. What can I do for you, exactly?'

Ashbroke-Sands sat down and crossed one fat leg over the other.

'You've been doing a spot of travelling lately, haven't you?'

Wyman nodded.

'What of it?'

'Nothing, really. In fact, it's all frightfully silly, if you ask me. Unfortunately, they never do.'

'Who are "they"?'

'Oh, the usual crowd. They insist on the

206

formalities, and who am I to argue–?'

'One moment,' Wyman smiled. 'I know this routine, Mr Ashbroke-Sands. You're trying to win me over by maintaining that this isn't your idea, that you've been asked to do this by some ass of a superior, and that it would be so much easier if we got the wretched thing over with quickly. I don't believe a word of it, and nor do you. Let's just get to the point, shall we? My plane leaves in an hour.'

Ashbroke-Sands nodded sadly at this barbarous departure from custom.

'If you insist,' he sighed. 'We understand you've been looking into this Herbert Feigl business. As you know, the official line is that the poor fellow died accidentally. Just for once, I think the official line is right. You don't agree.'

'Is that a question or a statement?'

Ashbroke-Sands waved his hand wearily.

'It doesn't matter,' he said. 'The whole story is too tiresome for words. I really don't care what you think: it's what you do that counts.'

'And what have I been doing?'

'Let me see; you've been wandering about Yugoslavia, you've been to Austria, and you've been seeing people in London.

You've been going through the WO/202 file at the Public Records Office, and you've visited Major Hampton, formerly of army intelligence.'

'Guilty, my lord. But I didn't know any of that was illegal.'

'It wasn't, it wasn't,' Ashbroke-Sands said quickly. 'My dear chap, no one's *accusing* you of anything. Heaven forbid. But you did also phone one or two former colleagues in the Firm, didn't you?'

'Those were social calls, as you know full well. I presume they were recorded, and you doubtless have the transcripts.'

'Doubtless,' Ashbroke-Sands beamed. 'No one says you've been naughty, I promise you. But some of the chaps think you might be contemplating a bit of naughtiness.'

'Which chaps would these be?'

'The head prefects. Your movements have caused one or two eyebrows to be raised in the common-room, if you catch my drift.'

'I see,' Wyman grinned. 'And you're the poor fellow who has to cane people's bottoms for them. Must be very tedious for you.'

Ashbroke-Sands waved his finger reprovingly.

'No need for that,' he said sternly. 'I just

208

want to remind you of one or two of the rules, in case you've forgotten.'

'Rules?'

'Governing the conduct of former intelligence officers. In case you're tempted to do something silly. Remember: thou shalt not visit countries belonging to the Soviet bloc. Thou shalt not release classified information, or do anything which might result in the disclosure of such information. Thou shalt not have conversations with journalists. Thou shalt not make contact with agents of an enemy power, and if any of them approach thee, thou shalt report such agents to us immediately. Here endeth the lesson.'

'Why are you telling me this?'

'Well, you've ignored at least one of those rules. You might be tempted to ignore the others.'

'What do you mean?' Wyman frowned.

'What!' Ashbroke-Sands exclaimed. 'You're not going to deny that you've been seeing that horrible oik Fulton, are you?'

Wyman threw back his head and laughed loudly, which took Ashbroke-Sands by surprise.

'Joke?'

'Yes,' Wyman chortled. 'Joke. Do you

really suppose I've been handing over bucketfuls of secrets to that ... that ... oh, this is too rich.'

Ashbroke-Sands was not convinced.

'In that case, what were you discussing with him? The cricket score?'

Wyman told Ashbroke-Sands about Fulton's article on Herbie, and the journalist's outlandish theories on the subject.

'I haven't encouraged him,' Wyman said. 'I don't need to. In another age Fulton would have been a travelling story-teller. He has the most lurid imagination I have ever come across.'

'I see,' Ashbroke-Sands muttered. 'So you haven't done anything naughty?'

'Scout's honour,' Wyman laughed.

'Well, we had to check.'

'Of course,' Wyman said understandingly. 'Now, if that's all that was worrying you, I'll be saying goodbye.'

'Right,' Ashbroke-Sands said, as he showed Wyman out. 'It wouldn't be too impertinent to ask how your inquiries are going, would it? Just curious, you understand.'

'As a matter of fact, I've drawn a complete blank.'

'Oh dear.'

'You see, there was only one other person who could have helped me, and he's dead as well. That's why I'm going home.'

'Never mind,' Ashbroke-Sands said. 'But if you decide to resume the search, for whatever reason, take my advice: steer clear of the journalists, eh? They're such smelly proles.'

Wyman nodded solemnly.

'I'll bear it in mind,' he said.

TWENTY-EIGHT

Wyman climbed slowly up the last stairs to his apartment, and dropped his luggage in an untidy heap.

'Hello,' he panted.

Margaret greeted him with a kiss, and picked up his bags.

'You look shattered,' she observed, as they went inside.

'Pulverised,' Wyman nodded. 'But it's all over.'

'Success?'

'Quite the opposite, I'm afraid. There are more loose ends than ever, but I'm damned if I can sort them out. And I'm not sure I really care any more.'

'You've given up?'

'I have to. I've done all I can.'

He noticed a bemused smile on Margaret's face.

'Is something the matter?'

'Are you sure it's all over?' she asked.

'Yes.'

'Quite sure?'

'Of course,' Wyman frowned. 'What are you driving at?'

'In that case,' Margaret said slowly, 'he's come to see you about something else.'

'Who?'

'The man in the front room. His name's Eddie Fulton. Apparently he's a journalist–'

'I know exactly who he is,' Wyman groaned. 'I'm sorry, darling. I thought I'd seen the last of that character. Would you mind if I administer the *coup de grâce?*'

'By all means,' Margaret smiled.

Wyman stepped into the front room and closed the door behind him. Somewhere inside a swirling cloud of cigarette-smoke at the other end of the room, Eddie was half-way through a large glass of Scotch.

'Hello, Eddie,' Wyman said evenly. 'Isn't Rome a little outside your parish? You must have a robust expense account.'

'As a matter of fact, I've taken a few days off.'

'I see,' Wyman said. 'So you don't even have the backing of a newspaper.'

'It doesn't matter,' Eddie shrugged. 'They'll come round to my view soon enough. As soon as I've put the story together, they'll see things my way.'

'Will they, indeed?' Wyman said sceptically. 'You know, I used to think you were merely a childish optimist, but I've changed my mind: you're actually a fanatic. You really believe you've hit the jackpot, don't you?'

'Care to share my winnings?'

'What does that mean?'

Eddie's face tightened, and he spoke rapidly: 'Herbert Feigl is still alive, and hiding – no, don't interrupt, Professor – and you know how to find him. I don't know what he's hiding from, but I know the KGB are part of it.'

'You're deranged,' Wyman breathed.

'No,' Eddie said. 'I want Herbert Feigl's story. You can give it to me. And a newspaper will pay. Simple as that.'

'Cheque book journalism?'

'You could call it that.'

'You're cracked,' Wyman said. 'Absolutely fractured. You admit that no paper will back you, but you think they'll pay me for the details?'

'Yes,' Eddie said. 'The minute you arrange a meeting between Feigl and myself, they'll come running.'

'I see. And why do you think I can find him?'

'What else have you been doing for the last

few weeks? If you thought Feigl died in an accident, you'd have thrown in the towel. But you didn't: you kept on digging, because you knew where to look.'

'But I *have* thrown in the towel,' Wyman groaned. 'You're right: I didn't believe that Herbie died accidentally. I suspect he was murdered, but I don't know why. I've heard one theory on the subject: it isn't satisfactory, but it's better than anything I could produce. That's why I've come home.'

'And that's all there is to it?' Eddie said.

'Correct.'

'Then perhaps you could tell me why I've had a Russian on my tail for the last few days.'

'What?'

'I call him Boris, though I've no idea what his real name is. He follows me around all over the place. I wondered if he was going to follow me all the way here.'

'And did he?'

'No.'

'I'm relieved to hear it.'

'He tailed me to the airport and noted my flight number. When I arrived at Rome airport one of his mates was waiting for me, and *he* followed me here. In fact, if you look out the window, you should see him.'

If Eddie had asked for Wyman's hand in marriage, the effect could not have been more impressive. Wyman tore over to the window, opened it, and peered down on to the Via Porta Pinciana. Down below, Wyman could see a besuited man leaning against a saloon car.

'Is that the man?' he said.

'Yes,' Eddie nodded. 'The car has CD plates and a Soviet embassy sticker on the windscreen. You see, that's when I knew I was on to a winner. My guess is that these blokes are looking for Feigl, and they think one of us can lead them to him.'

'Oh Lord,' Wyman said weakly.

'We've nothing to worry about, Professor.'

'Speak for yourself,' Wyman spluttered. 'You have no idea–'

'They're harmless,' Eddie said nonchalantly. 'I went over to Boris the other day, and we had a little chat. I was rather cheeky, actually, but he didn't do anything about it.'

'You did *what?*'

'Besides, if they decide to get rough, we have the answer, haven't we? That little tale about General Zhdanov's kosher secrets should shut them up. I've checked the lead: his real name's Samuel Gureyvitch, and his brother Semyon lives in Cheshire–'

'Eddie, please listen,' Wyman said earnestly. 'You can't play games with those people. I don't know how you've provoked them, but you must stop it immediately.'

'Oh? And how would I do that?'

'Drop that story and go home.'

'What about Boris?'

'He'll vanish, I promise you.'

Eddie shook his head.

'I don't want him to vanish. As long as Boris hangs around, I know the story's hot.'

There was a knock at the door, and Margaret stepped in.

'Sorry to interrupt,' she said. 'Mr Rawls is here to see you, Michael.'

'Rawls!' Wyman said. 'What on earth does he want?'

'Half an hour of your time,' Rawls called out from the hallway.

Wyman's face was a picture of despair.

'One moment,' he said, and turning to Eddie he added: 'Look, I can't help you, and I wouldn't if I could. Unlike you, I have no burning desire to get involved with KGB hoodlums. There isn't a story here, and even if there were, you aren't the man to deal with it. Do I make myself clear?'

Eddie got to his feet and lit another cigarette.

217

'Perfectly,' he said, as Wyman showed him out. 'But you're wrong. I'm hanging on to this story, and therefore I'll be hanging on to you. Sooner or later you'll lead me to Feigl. Cheers, Professor.'

In the corridor, he brushed past Rawls, who gazed at him curiously.

'If you're selling anything, forget it,' Eddie said to him. 'The Professor isn't buying today.'

'I'll bear that in mind,' Rawls grinned, as Eddie left the apartment. 'Who's your friend?'

'A zealot,' Wyman said wearily. 'A sort of beer-stained Don Quixote. I thought journalists were supposed to be cynical men of the world: I now know better.'

'What does he mean, you'll lead him to Feigl?'

'It means he's a gibbering lunatic,' Wyman sighed. He then explained Eddie's strange obsession with the Feigl story, and his latest suggestion.

'Why is he so sure he's right?' Rawls asked.

'Largely because some idiot at the London *rezidentura* has put a tail on him.'

'No kidding? Well if that's true, he's got a point.'

'Nonsense,' Wyman said. 'The KGB could

have any number of trivial reasons for following him. He's utterly indiscreet, and it would only take one stupid question in the wrong place to arouse their interest.'

'Maybe,' Rawls said. 'But the Russians have been tailing all kinds of people lately for no apparent reason. How's the search going, by the way?'

'I've chucked it in,' Wyman said. 'Gebhard couldn't help me, so I had one last try back in England, and that was equally fruitless. Not sharing your indifference for the "Yugoslav" connection, I explored Herbie's curriculum vitae right back to his war days. I even spoke to one of his old army colleagues, and found out how Herbie knew Milo Lalic.'

Wyman recounted the episode of the prison compound at Stara Fuzina, and why Lalic was thought to be behind it. Rawls listened in noncommittal silence.

'Unfortunately,' Wyman concluded, 'we can't pursue this lead any further, since Lalic is dead. I have no more clues and, to be honest, my heart isn't in it any more.'

Rawls scratched his chin reflectively.

'Pity,' he mused. 'You see, I might have been too hasty back there in Bohinj. I think there's more to this than I suspected.'

'And that's why you've come to see me?'

'Sort of. When I got home from Yugoslavia, I told my people what I'd told you: Lalic was dead and buried, so was Feigl, and we were just left with some tired old piece of Balkan intrigue. They seemed satisfied with that, and they put me on routine secondment to the Paris embassy. I forgot all about it.

'Then Langley started phoning me at strange hours of the day, bugging me with all kinds of stupid questions: clarify this, repeat that, tell us more about Wyman, more about Lalic, and so on. At the end of each call, they tell me to forget it, but that doesn't stop them ringing me back with more questions. It pisses me off.'

'I'm not surprised,' Wyman grinned, as he lit a cigarette. 'What did they want to know about me?'

'They seem particularly worried about your trip to Vienna.'

'Why? You told them what I was up to, didn't you?'

'Sure, I explained why you were seeing Gebhard. That made them very nervous, for some reason.'

Wyman frowned and blew out a perplexed cloud of smoke.

'What does it all mean?'

'I was hoping you'd tell me,' Rawls said. 'I thought if you'd made some progress, maybe we could figure out what the problem is.'

'In that case, you've a wasted journey. As I've explained, I don't want to take this any further. It's all too confusing for words, and I have no idea how to unravel it.'

'Yeah, I understand. As a matter of fact, I didn't come here just to see you. I've got a meeting with Hepburn at the Rome embassy in two hours. But while I was in the neighbourhood, I thought...'

'Sorry, Rawls. I'm out.'

'OK,' Rawls said, and he went to the door. 'But if something happens, or you change your mind, call me. I'll be at the Paris embassy until the end of next month.'

'Very well,' Wyman grinned. 'But don't hold your breath.'

'I won't. But every time I get one of those shit-head phone calls, I'll be blaming you.'

Wyman showed the American out, and sagged with exhaustion as he closed the door. Margaret came up, and put a sympathetic arm around him.

'Now,' she said softly, 'perhaps you'd like to tell me what's been happening.'

AUTUMN

I blossom anew every autumn; the Russian cold is good for my health.

Pushkin *Osen'*

TWENTY-NINE

Rome had cooled down slightly. The oppressive August swelter had given way to the gentler temperatures of September, and one could stroll through the grounds of the Villa Borghese with little risk of sunstroke. On a bright, golden afternoon, Wyman did precisely that, accompanied by his baby daughter.

Catherine had only recently learned to walk, and had not fully mastered the art. Wyman let her practise in a quiet corner of the park, as he sat on a nearby bench and immersed himself in Max Gebhard's second book, *Bureaucracy: the Twentieth Century Plague*.

Wyman found the title irritating, and not just for its pomposity. There were plenty of contenders for the title of 'Twentieth Century Plague': nationalism, nuclear weapons, monetarism and personal stereos, to name but four.

Furthermore, bureaucracy was hardly new to the twentieth century. The Chinese had developed and suffered from their sophisticated bureaucracy over several millenia, and many other nations had been run along similar lines in previous epochs. Nevertheless, Gebhard's point was that this century had created the largest and worst bureaucracies, and suffered the largest and worst disasters in result.

It was probably no coincidence that Gebhard wrote this book in the early 1960s, when, as an MP, he first experienced the full might of Austria's political bureaucracy. However, this topic was an extension of the theme in Gebhard's first work.

While accepting that civil services must exist in all nations, Gebhard argued that closed societies were the 'natural breeding-ground of bureaucracies', since the more a country depended upon laws and central planning, the greater would be the need for people to administer them.

Naturally, Gebhard admitted that such systems also exist in open societies, but he argued that Western bureaucracies were usually inherited from periods when the countries concerned were run as closed societies. Austria, for example, suffered from large and unwieldy bureaucracies, but these were a legacy from the time of the

Hapsburgs. As with many of Gebhard's arguments, Wyman found this account suspiciously neat, but he took the general point.

Gebhard was not simply criticising red tape and pompous officialdom. He sought to show that bureaucracy was responsible for the worst evils of the twentieth century. Bureaucrats, he argued, were not elected and were solely responsible to their immediate superiors. They could therefore be told by rulers to carry out actions which were immoral, illegal, or both.

If these actions were discovered, the bureaucrat would claim he was 'simply obeying orders'. The superior usually claimed he knew nothing about them, or that his orders were misunderstood, and that, after all, he did not physically commit the deed. Thus, the whole notion of personal responsibility ceased to exist, and with it the major obstacle to wicked behaviour. Closed societies, which rejected the notion of personal responsibility, generated bureaucracies and therefore promoted wickedness.

Gebhard's book cited the Nazi policies of extermination as a horrifying example of bureaucracy in a closed society. His point was that the concentration camps should not be seen as an unusual crime, or the product of uniquely perverted politicians. Instead, they were the logical result of a powerful bureaucracy in a closed society.

Wyman found this idea interesting, but he was not wholly convinced.

'It's all a trifle too slick,' he muttered. 'Too easy.'

He found it difficult to relate a flabby paper-pusher like St John Ashbroke-Sands to the men who organised the Holocaust. Something else had to be involved, which Gebhard had failed to consider.

As he examined this point, he felt a slight tug on his trouser-leg. He looked down and saw his daughter gazing up at him inquiringly.

'It's all right, Catherine,' he grinned. 'I usually talk to myself when I'm thinking.'

Then he realised that Catherine was not referring to his musings. A man had sat down beside Wyman, and was looking at him in interest.

'I am sorry to disturb you,' the man said. 'I am here to invite you to accompany me to my superior.'

'Indeed?' Wyman said. 'And who would he be?'

'General Trofim Zhdanov.'

Wyman blinked at him curiously. He was a nondescript young man, in a nondescript suit. He seemed perfectly sincere.

'If this is a joke...'

'No joke,' said the man firmly. 'The General wishes urgently to discuss an important matter of mutual interest.'

'Does he really?' Wyman smiled. 'And he's come all the way to Rome just for a chat with me. I'm highly impressed.'

'He is not in Rome. He is in Moscow. Arrangements have been made for your immediate transportation. You will return tonight.'

'I see,' Wyman said. 'How can I be sure you'll bring me back?'

'The General wishes me to assure you there is no question of a trap. He gives his word on this. I have a letter from him with translation. Both are signed. You may leave these with your wife, if you desire.'

Wyman read the translation and nodded. He knew enough Russian to be sure it matched the original.

'Very well,' he said. 'I get the idea. We'll take Catherine home, and leave at once.'

They stood up, and Wyman took his daughter's hand.

'Off we go,' he said, and turning to the Russian, he added solemnly: 'Take me to your leader.'

THIRTY

Most people are lazy creatures, who want the world to be as simple and undemanding as possible. They prefer to see life's big questions as straightforward problems, requiring clear answers. Others, like Michael Wyman, understand that human beings have made an obscure and difficult world for themselves, and they enjoy its complexity. They maintain that there are no simple solutions: simplicity is just a talisman, which plain men use like a St Christopher medallion when stumbling through murky labyrinths.

There is also a third category, to which Max Gebhard belonged. Like Wyman, he appreciated that the world was a complicated place, and he also relished tackling its conundrums. But unlike the English professor, he believed that there were straightforward solutions to these puzzles, which could be achieved with a little application. He found the process highly stimulating.

His present puzzle was therefore both surprising and disturbing, for it gave him no pleasure at all. A third parcel had arrived for him that morning. Once again, he had discussed it with Karl Weber, and concluded that little could be done about it. But the matter had preyed on his mind all day. Instead of going home to his wife, Gebhard returned to the palace to examine the parcel once more. He told the security guards to send away any callers, and he sat alone in his office, immersed in thought.

The latest parcel also came from Hungary, and it contained another signed copy of his book. Gebhard still assumed it was some kind of attempt to discredit him. His views on Communism were well known, and he had few friends in the Eastern countries. In these days of détente and disarmament, such views were easily mistaken for McCarthyism and paranoia. Gebhard was not a fanatic or a paranoiac: he simply wished to steer his country into safe, though unaccustomed waters. It was a delicate task which could be ruined by the most trivial gaffe, and his opponents knew it. It was safe to assume that a trap had been laid for him.

If Gebhard was correct, these parcels must have been sent by the AVH, Hungary's secret police. In that case, Gebhard wondered, why did the parcels come from different locations in Hungary? The latest one had been sent from Salgótarján, near the Czech frontier. Why would the AVH go to all this trouble? Why not send them all from Budapest? It made little sense. But perhaps this was what the world was expected to think, when Gebhard announced that he was the victim of a plot.

Gebhard sat back in his chair and closed his eyes. Suppose for one moment that the AVH are not behind this, he thought. Suppose I am paranoid, and this has nothing to do with Communist intelligence agencies. In that case, who is responsible, and why? What are they trying to tell me?'

Suddenly, he opened his eyes and stared at the parcel. He remembered now. There was a recent occasion when he had signed several copies of his book. Six copies, to be precise. And on that occasion, he had been asked just to sign his name, with no dedication on the flyleaf.

Gebhard stood up and went over to Karl Weber's office. Weber filed all correspondence relating to Gebhard's appointments and visits: requests, informal invitations, and letters of thanks were stored in two cabinets, labelled 'official' and 'personal'. Gebhard opened the 'personal' cabinet, and found the letter he wanted, which requested a private meeting shortly before the presidential election.

Gebhard took the letter back to his office, and compared it with the label on the parcel. The capital letters 'G', 'M', 'O', 'P' and 'S' were identical on both items. He now knew who the sender was.

The knowledge did not make him feel better. If anything, Gebhard felt worse. The mystery was still there: he still could not understand the purpose of these parcels and the message they were intended to convey, though he began to suspect.

Gebhard went back to Weber's office and put the letter away. He would not tell Weber about his discovery, since there was nothing his secretary could do about it. But a new worry formed in his mind. Presumably, there were three more parcels to come, and Gebhard was prepared for their arrival. But when the sixth parcel had been mailed, and the sender had run out of books, what would he do then?

THIRTY-ONE

Eddie Fulton returned to his flat in north London just after midnight. He was normally oblivious to his environment, but on bad days he noticed all the aspects of his habitat that were best ignored: the dirt, the smell, the disrepair. Today was a bad day. As he climbed the stairs to his third-floor flat, his eyes lingered over the yellowing paintwork, the graffiti on the walls, and the small pools of urine on the landings.

He opened his front door and scooped up a pile of letters. Most of them were demands for money. There were some bills, an acerbic letter from his bank, and a note from his wife's solicitor requiring immediate payment of last month's alimony cheque. He threw them all on a table, poured himself a large Scotch, and sank wearily into an armchair.

He was out of luck, out of ideas, and out of money. The gamble with Wyman had not paid off, and he had no idea of how to proceed. He had expected Boris to be waiting for him when he returned to Heathrow, but he had been disappointed. Presumably the Russians had also given up on him, which meant that he was further than ever from a solution.

That was the infuriating part of it, Eddie thought, as he tossed back the Scotch. He knew he had come close to getting his story. Within inches, in fact. If only he could have persuaded Wyman to talk...

He poured himself another glassful, which he took at a more leisurely pace. No sense in getting pissed, he thought. Too much to think about. Must find something else soon. Something simple and straightforward. Something to pay off these fucking bills.

Of course, the Feigl story would have paid the bills, he thought bitterly. The missing schoolmaster on the run, pursued by the KGB and shielded by an ex-MI6 man. Lovely stuff. And he knew it was true. *It had to be true.* Why else would Wyman scuttle around like a headless chicken? Why else—'

'Bollocks,' he muttered. There was no point in dwelling on a dead story. His chance, if there had been one, was gone. It was now business as usual: hanging around the law courts, sifting through the local papers, phoning the contacts and chatting with colleagues, all in the hope of a few useful crumbs to build a living on. It wasn't very glamorous, but then, neither was Eddie.

After a few more drinks, Eddie fell asleep in his chair. He was awoken two hours later by a rough shake of his arm. He slowly opened his eyes, and gazed blearily at the whisky bottle. It was hovering a few inches away from his mouth, apparently floating in mid-air. As the bottle swam into focus, he realised it was being held by a gloved hand.

He looked up and saw two surprising things. One was a gun, pointed directly at his forehead. The other was the face of its owner.

'Hello,' Eddie mumbled sleepily. 'What are you doing here?'

'Drink,' said the man.

'Help yourself,' Eddie said.

'No. You drink.'

The man pressed the bottle to Eddie's lips, and jammed the gun against his forehead.

'OK, OK,' Eddie said hastily. 'I get the message.'

He took hold of the bottle, and drank a mouthful of Scotch.

'All right? Now perhaps you'd like to–'

'Drink. All of it.'

The gun pressed harder against Eddie's head.

'Oh, come off it,' Eddie said helplessly. 'This isn't orange juice, you know...'

'All of it.'

Eddie took a deep breath, and did as he was told. It was quite easy at first, but gradually his throat began to burn. Before he could empty the bottle, he gave a rasping cough which sent the last dregs dribbling down his chin.

'Christ,' he spluttered.

The other man took the empty bottle out of his hands, put it on the floor, and replaced it with a full one.

'Drink,' he repeated.

Eddie shook his head.

'Fuck off,' he said hoarsely.

The man took the gun away from Eddie's head and pointed it at the carpet at the far end of the room. He squeezed the trigger, but instead of a bang there was only a high-pitched *whoosh*. Eddie took the point.

'Silencer,' he observed.

The man nodded, and returned the gun to Eddie's head.

'Drink,' he commanded.

He put the bottle to his lips and tilted. It was much harder this time: the drink scorched his mouth and lips, and the contents of the first bottle had begun to take effect. The room went out of focus and began to whirl around his head. About halfway through, he felt his grip relax, and the other man took over, steadying the bottle and gradually raising it, until the last drops had burned down Eddie's gullet.

Eddie slumped back and blinked slowly. He rolled his head in an effort to cope with the revolving blur, with no success. As the last of his strength seeped out of his limbs, he was vaguely aware that a third bottle was being jammed against his mouth, and more Scotch was coursing down his throat. Finally, everything went black, and Eddie collapsed.

The man lifted Eddie off the chair and laid him down on the floor, face upwards. A few seconds later, Eddie began to convulse. He made a feeble effort to roll over and vomit, but his head was pinned back firmly against the carpet. He shuddered and retched and struggled to expel the acid welling up in his throat. A small amount bubbled out of his mouth, but most of it seeped up into his nose and down his windpipe and into his lungs. With a long, leaden murmur, Eddie Fulton sagged and died.

THIRTY-TWO

It took four hours to get from Fiumicino Airport to KGB headquarters in Dzerzhinsky Square. They were the fastest four hours of Wyman's life. For most of the flight, he tried to guess what General Zhdanov wanted from him, and how he would respond. Why did the General want to see Wyman in person?

Wyman understood that even the toughest KGB chief had enemies, who might choose to misconstrue an encounter between Zhdanov and a former British Intelligence agent. The General must be reasonably careful. But Wyman was small fry, and there had to be a better explanation for Zhdanov's discreet approach. Presumably it was the subject of the meeting that demanded secrecy: what could that subject be? Not Herbie Feigl, surely. But if it had nothing to do with Herbie's disappearance, what else could it be?

His escort gave him no help with these questions. After reminding Wyman to set his watch forward by two hours, the young officer remained silent through the journey.

At Sheremetyevo Airport, a black limousine was waiting for them on the tarmac. There were no formalities: the escort waved his identity card at the driver, and they were taken directly out onto the main road for the capital.

Wyman had never been to Moscow before, but its outskirts were depressingly familiar. Like most large cities around the world, Moscow is ringed by hundreds of square miles of brutal grey tower-blocks, thrown up to meet the capital's housing crisis.

These problems are not new to Moscow, of course. The concrete forests of the outer zones soon gave way to the solutions of previous generations: the squat, bulky apartments of the Stalin era, with their rust and grime and mouldy brickwork. Finally, as they drew nearer to central Moscow, the bleakness and austerity melted away and was replaced by the ornate, colourful buildings of the pre-revolutionary years, with their domes and spires, pillars and arches, and fussy, human extravagance. The city's nucleus is like a gaudy jewel on a heap of ashes, and Wyman found it oddly comforting: he knew he was on planet Earth again.

By four o'clock they were in Dzerzhinsky Square. As Wyman was led into the mustard-yellow wedding-cake of a building on the north side, a broad, impish grin spread across his face. During thirty years with British Intelligence he had travelled widely and had dealt with many people, but this was the last building and the last organisation he had ever expected to visit as a guest. He realised he was probably the only non-defector ever to have done so.

The escort took him to an office upstairs, knocked on the door, and waved Wyman inside.

'Professor Wyman. Thank you for coming.'

Wyman stared up at a pair of dense, curling eyebrows nearly a foot above him. General Zhdanov was constructed along the same lines as the tower-blocks on Moscow's outskirts. A massive leathery hand wrapped itself around Wyman's, and almost shook his arm out of its socket.

'Pleased to meet you, General,' Wyman gasped.

They both sat down, and Zhdanov got straight to the point. He spoke slowly and deliberately, in surprisingly good English.

'I want to talk about Herbert Feigl,' he

said. 'He was a friend of yours, yes?'

Wyman nodded.

'You have been investigating his disappearance. You have been to Yugoslavia, Austria and London. We have been following your inquiry with sympathy. What are your conclusions?'

'The obvious one,' Wyman said.

'What is that?'

'That Feigl is dead, and you killed him.'

This seemed to take the General by surprise.

'I see,' he muttered. 'Supposing I tell you that he is alive. What do you say now?'

'I'd say you were lying,' Wyman smiled.

Zhdanov seemed disappointed.

'You really think that?' he said plaintively. 'You think I will bring you here, all the way from Rome, just to tell you lies? I thought you were a clever man, Professor. Please be serious. I tell you once more: Feigl is alive. I want your opinion.'

Wyman did not have an opinion. He had convinced himself that Feigl was dead, and it took him a few moments to adjust his thinking to the possibility.

'Very well,' he said at last. 'If Feigl isn't dead, he must be hiding. Who is he hiding from? You, presumably. In which case, I'd be rather silly to help you find him, wouldn't I?'

'So you think he is hiding from us?' Zhdanov mused. 'I understand.'

'Do you deny it?'

Zhdanov ignored the question, and looked down at his hands, like a card-player considering his next move. He closed his eyes and spoke carefully, as if he were trying to remember the exact details of an old story.

'Feigl visited Vienna before he disappeared in Bohinj, yes? You went to Vienna after you visited Bohinj. You were retracing his movements.'

'That's right.'

'That was why you saw the Austrian President. You wanted to know why Feigl visited him. Can you tell me the reason?'

'It was a social call. They were friends.'

Zhdanov looked up in astonishment.

'Friends?' he exclaimed. 'They knew each other?'

'Sort of,' Wyman said. 'You see, Herbie belonged to Freedom of Conscience, the human rights organisation. Gebhard is a patron of FOC, and Herbie had corresponded with him once or twice. He wanted to meet Gebhard and wish him luck in the election.

'But did Feigl ever meet Gebhard before then?'

'I don't think so,' Wyman said. 'What does it matter?'

Zhdanov smiled sourly and looked away.

'The FOC,' he said softly. 'Yes, I know those people. They send me letters. I have even received letters from Gebhard personally.'

'You're not very fond of Gebhard, are you?' Wyman observed.

Zhdanov looked at him sharply.

'What do you mean?' he snapped.

'Only what I've heard,' Wyman said, surprised by the General's vehemence. 'Gebhard makes no secret of his feelings about your government. He seems to be moving away from the traditional Austrian position, and your people don't like it. That's the Party line, isn't it?'

Zhdanov seemed a little embarrassed.

'Yes, yes of course,' he said, grinning sheepishly. 'That is the Party line.'

'What did you think I meant?'

Zhdanov shrugged.

'It is not important,' he said.

'But Gebhard is important,' Wyman said, pressing his point. 'The Austrian general election is coming up, isn't it? You don't want Gebhard's party to win. Has that anything to do with my visit here?'

'I asked you to come here,' Zhdanov said firmly, 'because I want to know about your inquiries about Feigl. You have not given me a specific answer.'

'Are you surprised?' Wyman grinned. 'Most of my career was spent in extracting information from your side of the fence, not vice versa.'

For the first time, General Zhdanov laughed. It was not a delicate laugh; it sounded like an attempt to start a car with a flat battery.

'Just so,' Zhdanov chortled. 'But you agree, I have asked no questions about this.'

'I credit you with more intelligence,' Wyman said.

'Just so, just so,' Zhdanov chuckled. 'So if I ask you nothing about your professional activities, perhaps you can be more frank about your private inquiry.'

'What do you want?'

'Are you still looking for Feigl?'

Wyman gave a reluctant sigh, and threw his hands up in the air.

'No,' he confessed. 'I gave up. I thought he was dead.'

Zhdanov seemed unperturbed by this admission.

'In that case,' he said, 'there is not much else for us to discuss. But if you are thinking of resuming the search, remember we are glad to assist.'

'How?'

The General shrugged.

'We have a large organisation, and great resources. Some of this can be put at your disposal, if necessary.'

'You know General,' Wyman said, 'this conversation is becoming increasingly ironical.'

Zhdanov began to laugh again.

'It is very funny, no? Though I am really being serious.'

'Perhaps,' Wyman said. 'But I'd need to know a lot more before I took up your offer. There would have to be some direct answers to direct questions.'

'Such as?'

'What do you want from Herbert Feigl? Why was Milovan Lalic killed? Why was Nadysev pulled out of the London *rezidentura*? How do all these things connect?'

Zhdanov smiled sarcastically.

'Is that all?'

'No. The CIA are looking for something,

but I don't know what. You're looking for something, but I don't know what. You may be looking for different things, but I doubt it: Lalic is common to both inquiries, and so, I suspect, is Herbie Feigl. If I have to take sides, I'm afraid there's no question of whom I support. Do I have to take sides, General?'

Zhdanov seemed to find this terribly amusing.

'Oh yes,' he bellowed. 'You must support your friends. Which ones, Professor, which ones?'

Wyman frowned.

'I don't think I understand you,' he said.

Zhdanov waved his hand.

'It does not matter, yet,' he said. 'Are those all the questions?'

'They'll do,' Wyman said. 'But there's one more point: why did you put a tail on Eddie Fulton? What on earth can he do for you?'

'Routine,' Zhdanov said reassuringly. 'Just routine. Does it bother you?'

'No, but Fulton bothers me, and you're encouraging him.'

'In that case,' Zhdanov beamed, 'you will be pleased to hear that we have ceased our surveillance. Fulton will no longer be a problem to you.'

'What about the other questions?'

'You will answer them yourself,' Zhdanov said playfully. 'When you have done so, you will contact me.'

'You're very confident about that.'

'Of course, of course. I will give you a special telephone number. A personal number of mine. When you decide to trust me, we will work together.'

'I admire your faith,' Wyman smiled. 'But how do you know I won't go running back to my former employers and tell them all about this meeting? The opportunity to plant a double agent in your office would be irresistible: how do you know I won't give it to them?'

Zhdanov shook with laughter. He slapped his hand down on the desk, and rocked in convulsive mirth.

'Because,' he roared, 'I credit you with more intelligence, Professor Wyman.'

THIRTY-THREE

Wyman stepped outside the Lubyanka and stood quite still for a few moments. With some effort he convinced himself that he was not dreaming, and that he really had concluded a meeting with the head of the KGB.

There was an hour or two to kill before his flight home, and his hosts had offered him a swift guided tour of the city. Wyman had politely declined the offer, preferring to spend the time alone. He was given a tourist map of the city, some copeck pieces to use on public transport, and a brief sermon on the perils of illegal currency exchange. It was agreed that he would return to the Dzerzhinsky Square in three hours, when a car would take him back to the airport.

Wyman had little doubt that his sight-seeing would be watched, but this did not bother him. He simply wanted time to organise his thoughts. There were an awful lot of questions to answer. What was Zhdanov driving at? Did he really expect

Wyman to trust him? He presumably had an ulterior motive, but what could that be? Most importantly, was Herbie still alive?

He groaned disconsolately and lit a cigarette, realising that these questions could not be answered in the three remaining hours. Zhdanov did not expect instant results. He had brought Wyman here to plant a seed, and that was all. The rest was up to Wyman.

He shivered slightly, and turned up his collar. It was not especially chilly, but Moscow was at least twenty degrees cooler than Rome, and he had not yet adjusted. He went across the road to the Metro station, and took a train to the Kalininskaya stop.

The Moscow underground was everything he had read about: red carpets, vaulted ceilings and glittering chandeliers. But he had not read about the pushing, swearing crowds who shove each other in and out of the trains, and occasionally tumble headlong down the steep escalators.

Gebhard would have something to say about all this, Wyman thought with a smile. Politeness? Consideration? You must be joking. In the closed society you obey the law: that's all. If there are no laws about personal matters, you don't bother with manners. Of course, Moscow did not have a monopoly on incivility. Commuters are a rough lot everywhere. But, Wyman reflected, as a small fat woman nonchalantly battered him in the ribs, the Muscovites had turned rudeness into an art-form.

Before he escaped the mêlée in the Kalininskaya station, he noticed a young man in a threadbare overcoat walking a few feet away from him. The same man had been loitering in Dzerzhinsky Square. Wyman smiled wrily. A little obvious, he thought, but then there was no need for subterfuge.

He crossed over the Prospekt Marksa, through the Trinity Tower and into the Kremlin, with the young man hovering loyally behind. He gave himself half an hour to wander around the old fort, to admire its golden-domed cathedrals and palaces, and to examine its newer trappings of power, such as the Palace of Congresses and the Presidium. After this, he returned to the main road and walked along the Kremlin's outer wall, allowing his pursuer plenty of time to note his movements.

Red Square was far bigger than he had imagined – over half a kilometre long. Its late nineteenth-century appearance was carefully preserved, save for the Lenin Mausoleum on the south side. Dozens of groups of tourists, many of them from distant parts of the Soviet Union, were being shown around by Intourist guides.

At the far end, he could see the cluster of multicoloured onion domes above St Basil's cathedral, perhaps Moscow's most famous image. Over on the left was the long pale façade of the *Gosudarstvenny Universal'nyy Magazin,* or 'State Department Store', better known as GUM. A spot of browsing seemed in order, so he went inside.

GUM consists of hundreds of small shops arranged on three storeys along several parallel aisles, covered by vaulted glass roofs. The goods on sale were of sub-Woolworths quality, but this did not deter people from forming long queues to buy them. Russian queues are world-famous, and with good reason. They do not just result from the notorious shortages of goods, but from a mentality which consciously seeks the most elaborate way of performing the simplest tasks.

Thus, GUM's customers do not simply pick the goods they want and pay for them. They must first choose the item; if it is a piece of clothing, they must know the size in advance, for they may not try the garment on. (This is why Russian women tend to hobble along the streets: their shoes seldom fit.) They must then queue for the *kassa,* where they stipulate precisely what they want and pay for it. They are eventually given a ticket, with which they join another long queue to obtain their purchase. Thanks to this remarkable system, it can take an hour to buy three items from three separate shops.

Wyman had already read about this in Gebhard's third book. *The Practice of Soviet Socialism* was the Austrian's most savage diatribe against Russian Communism. It contained a long description of the agonies of Soviety shopping, because Russian queueing and the reasons for it summed up many of Gebhard's complaints about the USSR. The system was designed and run by bureaucrats: it was therefore overmanned and inefficient. And because this was a closed society, no one could complain about it. If there was a check-list of all the things Gebhard detested, the Soviet Union filled it.

Of course, Gebhard had written all this before the new policies of *perestroika* and *glasnost.* But his speech in Vienna had made it perfectly clear what the Austrian thought about 'reorganisation' and 'openness'. The Soviets were faced with a paradox: they wanted to improve their closed society by giving it some features of an open society. But they could not succeed unless they went the whole way, and became genuinely open. This meant allowing political choice, which the authorities would not tolerate. The plan was therefore doomed to failure.

Once again, Wyman was not entirely convinced by Gebhard's view. He agreed that the weary, jostling queues of GUM were intolerable, and probably resulted from the closed system. But once again, he suspected that the subject was more complex than Gebhard thought, and he could not share the Austrian's pessimism about the reform programme.

He went back into Red Square and glanced at his watch. There was not much time left. He lit another cigarette, and began to chuckle at his strange fortune in being brought here at the expense of the KGB, when he felt a peremptory tap on his shoulder. He turned and saw an armed solider gazing sternly at his hand.

'Ni kurit,' said the soldier.

'How do you do,' Wyman replied.

The soldier shook his head.

'*Nilzya kurit!*'

He pointed at Wyman's cigarette.

'No smoking?' Wyman said.

'*Da.* No smoky. Forbidden here.'

He tilted his head towards Lenin's tomb. Wyman nodded understandingly, and crushed out the cigarette with his foot.

'Sorry old chap,' he grinned. 'I forgot this was a place of religious worship.'

The soldier knew enough English to take Wyman's point. He shrugged philosophically and walked away. Wyman turned round and gazed at his pursuer in mild exasperation.

'You could have told me,' he called out.

The young man walked up and looked at him inquiringly.

'English?' he said.

'No,' Wyman chuckled. 'Venezuelan.'

'You have seen me...?'

'Of course I have. A child of five would have spotted you.'

'Then you know what I am here for?'

Wyman nodded.

'So how many?' said the young man.

Wyman blinked in confusion.

'I beg your pardon?'

'Pounds sterling. How many do you want

to change? I give three roubles to the pound.'

'Oh Lord,' Wyman exclaimed. 'You want to change money? Black market, eh? I thought you were from the KGB.'

It was the other man's turn to be surprised.

'KGB?' he breathed.

'Yes,' Wyman said. 'You see, when you saw me in Dzerzhinsky Square I'd just left the Lubyanka. I assumed you were one of their chaps ... hold on a minute!'

The news that Wyman had just been interviewed by the KGB, and was probably being followed by them, had an impressive effect on the young man. He stepped back a few paces, looked about anxiously, and ran away. Wyman watched him with detached amusement.

'Oh very well,' he called out. 'How about two to the pound?'

THIRTY-FOUR

For one week only, the President was meeting his security advisers in the Oval Office, instead of the usual venue in the White House basement. With loud protests and dire warnings, his doctor had persuaded him to take a short break from his gymnastics.

But this did nothing to dampen the President's ardour: his desk was covered in glossy magazines with titles like *Pump, Tension* and *Flex,* whose covers showed shiny, distended gentlemen with bulging biceps, pulsating pectorals and colossal calves. There were also instruction manuals on related topics: *High-Intensity Bodybuilding, Massive Muscles in 10 Weeks,* and *Nutrition for the Ultimate Physique.*

'I've been reading,' said the President, rather unnecessarily.

'Looks very interesting,' Bradwell said.

'Oh, it is. And you know something, George? I've been asking myself for weeks why all this effort hasn't been producing the muscle I want. Something's been wrong, and now I know why.'

'Do you?' Bradwell said guiltily. He had wondered how long it would take the President to guess that his exercise equipment had been doctored.

'Yes,' said the President sternly. 'It's all a question of nutrition. Doesn't matter how much exercise you take. If your nutrition's all wrong, you don't get anywhere.'

'Are you sure this isn't a mistake?' said the Secretary of State anxiously.

'No mistake,' said the CIA Director. 'Klein used to work at the London embassy. He knows Wyman personally.'

'What happened?'

'Apparently Wyman was driven up to the front door in Zhdanov's personal limousine, escorted by one of Zhdanov's bodyguards.'

'That's what I call style,' observed the National Security Adviser.

'But he was back in Rome by midnight.'

'What does it mean?'

'It means a whole new approach,' said the President. 'That's what all the books say. So I've sent away for some mail-order goodies.'

'Goodies? You're not talking about steroids again, are you Mr President?'

'Hell, no George. I'm talking about

Arginine and Lysine capsules. Ornithine and Choline. And best of all, a high protein drink mix. The brand I've sent for has a Net Protein Utilization of ninety-six.'

'That's good?'

'Sure. It means ninety-six per cent of the protein consumed can be converted into muscle mass.'

'Is that a fact?'

'But if he wasn't defecting, what was he doing there? Making small talk?'

'Negotiating,' said the CIA Director. 'My guess is that Zhdanov was trying to squeeze out as much information as Wyman could give him.'

'But Wyman doesn't know anything,' said the Secretary of State.

'Sure, but Zhdanov didn't know that, did he? Jesus, if he's reduced to tailing journalists to get clues, he must be pretty desperate.'

'All right, so he's desperate. How can he use Wyman?'

'The same way we can,' said the CIA Director, 'as a homing device.'

'It makes sense,' nodded the National Security Adviser. 'How do we react?'

'Carefully,' said the CIA Director.

'What have you got in mind?'

'Zinc Gluconate tablets,' said the President. 'Liquid amino acids. And the secret weapon.'

'The secret weapon?' Bradwell said nervously. 'What's that?'

The President replied in a conspiratorial whisper: 'High potency Inosine. According to the book, it's a nucleotide used by Soviet athletes. That's how the sons of bitches keep winning at the Olympics. You know, George, I bet half the Politburo's on this stuff. Well, I won't be left out.'

THIRTY-FIVE

St John Travis de Beaumont Ashbroke-Sands was distressed. Summer had come and gone in London, but by Anglo-Saxon standards Rome was still uncomfortably warm, and there were few things Ashbroke-Sands detested more than what he called 'dago weather', except perhaps the dagos themselves. Rome was full of dust, flies and Italians, and Ashbroke-Sands cared for none of them.

He had arrived from London only two hours ago, and he was already sticky and irritable. His face had turned purple with heat and exasperation. The sweat patches beneath his armpits had crept across his shirt, met beneath his necktie, and were now percolating down his bloated abdomen. His weight precluded swift movement at the best of times; now he was reduced to a sluggish, panting crawl, as he wobbled up the Via Porta Pinciana, occasionally fanning himself with a crumbled copy of that morning's *Telegraph*.

To make matters worse, the natives clearly did not share his discomfort: he noted indignantly that some of them were even wearing sweaters.

Why a civilised Englishman like Wyman should go out of his way to live in such a beastly climate, with its lazy, garrulous inhabitants, baffled Ashbroke-Sands. Fortunately, Wyman's apartment was agreeably cool, and its owner hospitable. This surprised Ashbroke-Sands: he had expected hostility from the old professor, but Wyman was affable and unperturbed. He sat Ashbroke-Sands down with a gin and tonic, and allowed him a few minutes to cool off before asking him what his business was.

'I thought we'd come to an understanding,' Ashbroke-Sands said plaintively. 'I'm sorry to say it, dear boy, but I feel quite let down.'

'By me?'

'Who else?'

'What am I supposed to have done?'

'You've been suffering from another attack of wanderlust,' Ashbroke-Sands said accusingly.

'They say it broadens the mind,' Wyman said blandly.

'They say it's out of bounds,' Ashbroke-

Sands sniffed. 'Trips to Moscow are strictly *verboten,* and you know it.'

'True. It was rather naughty of me.'

'The Joint Intelligence Committee had collective heart failure when it heard. There's even talk of putting out a warrant for your arrest.'

'Is there? How exciting.'

Ashbroke-Sands shook his head in disbelief.

'You take my breath away, you really do. You seem to think it's just a jolly jape, but I promise you the JIC doesn't agree, and nor do the Americans.'

'The Americans?' Wyman said, with interest. 'How do they fit in?'

'It was an American who spotted you wandering around Moscow. A fellow called Klein.'

'I know him,' Wyman said. 'Nice chap. Where did he see me?'

'You were spotted wandering around the Pushkin Museum. Klein rushed off and screamed at his people, and they screamed at us. It really isn't good enough, you know.'

'Simply isn't done,' Wyman agreed.

Ashbroke-Sands took a deep breath.

'Listen, Wyman: if you must go on sightseeing trips, go to Africa. Go to

Australia. Go anywhere, except the bloody Soviet countries. I know you were just taking a holiday, but try to see it from our point of view. What if the KGB spotted you? They might have grabbed you, whipped you off to the Lubyanka, and spent a pleasant afternoon yanking your fingernails out. A lifetime's worth of state secrets forced out in ten easy pulls. Not very agreeable, what?'

'Most unsavoury,' Wyman agreed. 'Care for another drink?'

'Thank you,' Ashbroke-Sands said.

'You know,' Wyman said, as he filled Ashbroke-Sands' glass, 'I'm surprised you haven't accused me of defecting. Even the JIC must have considered that one.'

Ashbroke-Sands frowned.

'It really isn't a laughing matter,' he said crossly. 'You're damned lucky. You've no idea how close you came to getting the same treatment as that oik Fulton.'

'Fulton? What's happened to him?'

'Don't you know? He's been murdered. The official verdict is death by mis-adventure, of course.'

Wyman's smile vanished.

'How did it happen?'

'They forced him to drink epic quantities of booze, and made him choke on his vomit.

Rather a fitting end for a journo, don't you think.'

It was Ashbroke-Sands' turn to be blasé. He seemed to find this story highly amusing. Wyman stared at him grimly.

'Who's responsible?'

'Oh, the KGB, of course. Apparently some thug had been tailing him for quite a while. The stupid bumpkin actually bragged about it to his oppos in El Vino's. Well, much good it did him.'

'Have you any idea why they killed him?'

Ashbroke-Sands shrugged indifferently.

'Who cares? It might teach the rest of those troglodytes to keep out of security matters.'

'Indeed,' Wyman said coldly. 'I admire your compassion.'

'Balls,' Ashbroke-Sands said cheerfully. 'And if Fulton had some excuse for behaving like an ass, you certainly haven't. This is far more serious than you seem to think.'

'Yes,' Wyman said, nodding slowly. 'I think you could be right.'

THIRTY-SIX

'That's the eighth call in two days,' Weber said, as he put the phone down.

'Who was it this time?'

'A TV journalist. He wants to know if it's true that you're receiving anonymous threatening letters.'

Gebhard gave a wry grin.

'I wish I were,' he said. 'At least we'd know exactly what was going on.'

The fourth parcel had arrived that morning. It had come from Banská Stiavnica, a town in Czechoslovakia. It was identical to the other parcels in all respects.

'As things stand,' Weber said, 'there is no real problem. The rumours are all so wide of the mark that we can easily give categorical details. But sooner or later someone will score a direct hit. They'll phrase the question in such a way that we'll either have to tell lies or make some kind of admission. It'll be something like "Has Dr Gebhard been receiving anonymous mail from Communist countries?" and I'll have to answer it. What shall I say?'

Gebhard closed his eyes and thought about it. Then, in practised tones, he said: 'Dr Gebhard receives regular correspondence from the Eastern countries, where he has many friends and supporters. The authorities in these countries would probably disapprove of such correspondence, and would take action against those concerned, were their identities known.

'Naturally, Dr Gebhard appreciates the senders' need for anonymity, and would not wish to expose them to danger by giving their letters unnecessary publicity. He hopes that the press and broadcasting media would share his view.'

'Not bad,' Weber nodded.

'It might even discourage the sender,' Gebhard suggested.

'Either that,' Weber said, 'or it might encourage him to come out into the open.'

Gebhard's face clouded.

'I hadn't thought of that,' he said.

'Are you worried about it?'

'No, of course not,' Gebhard said quickly. 'But I think we should be prepared.'

'What about the Americans?' Weber said. 'Perhaps we should tell them the truth.'

'Why?'

'They'll probably hear about it through their own sources. Better that we should brief them–'

'No,' Gebhard said firmly. 'They could easily misconstrue it. The last thing we need is any suspicion of panic.'

He glanced at his diary.

'I'm seeing two gentlemen from the Pentagon tomorrow. They will want to hear that all is well. I have no intention of disappointing them.'

THIRTY-SEVEN

Edgar Rawls left Rome's US embassy and strolled up the Via Veneto, until he came to one of the gleaming expensive cafés whose tables stretch for over fifty feet up the hill. Most of the patrons were fellow-Americans, who were paying a small fortune to sit in each other's company, drink coffee and feel rich. There were also a few Frenchmen, the occasional Arab, and the odd German. The furthermost tables were empty, save for a rather tatty old English professor of Philosophy, who looked distinctly out of place.

'Welcome to the *nouveau riche*,' Rawls grinned, as he took a seat at Wyman's table. 'I didn't think this was your style.'

'It isn't,' Wyman said. 'But it's a sensible place for you to bump into me. Thank you for coming.'

'Pleasure,' Rawls said. 'I wondered if I was going to hear from you. The Company's buzzing with the story.'

'So I understand,' Wyman said. 'What exactly have you heard?'

'Joe Klein saw you taking snapshots outside the Pushkin Museum. He made inquiries, found out you were there on holiday for a day or two, and sounded the alarm.'

'So you've heard that version too,' Wyman muttered. 'How curious.'

'Why? Isn't it true?'

'Up to a point. I was in Moscow, but only for a few hours. I didn't have a camera, and I went nowhere near the Pushkin Museum.'

Rawls frowned.

'I don't get it.'

'Nor do I,' Wyman said. 'You see, I was there as a guest of General Zhdanov. I was flown to Moscow and taken directly to Dzerzhinsky Square.'

There was a long, stunned silence as Rawls tried to digest the news.

'If this is some kind of joke–'

'It isn't. I don't doubt that Klein saw me in Moscow, but your people have put out a sanitised version of the story. They gave it to the Joint Intelligence Committee in London, who sent a man called Ashbroke-Sands round to reprimand me about holidays in the Eastern bloc. But that isn't what happened, and your senior people know it.'

271

'So what really happened?'

Wyman gave a detailed account of his meeting with General Zhdanov, which left Rawls shaking his head in disbelief.

'This isn't real,' he said.

'It most certainly is,' Wyman retorted. 'And now I'm trying to make sense of it all. Presumably, Herbie Feigl knew something which Zhdanov badly needs.'

'The best kept secret in Europe?'

'Possibly. And your people are after the same thing, whatever it is.'

'How could Feigl know? He was nobody in particular.'

Wyman shrugged.

'It's a fair question, but I think we must just accept it for the time being. The main thing is that the information is highly important, and both sides think I can lead them to it. It's so sensitive that your people will even put out cover stories to protect me from my former employers.'

'But if they're protecting you, why did they tell London about your trip?'

'They had to. Klein doesn't know what's going on, any more than you do. The rumours would have got back to London anyway, so your people leaped in first and made up a cover story for me.'

'This is making me dizzy,' Rawls said.

'Interestingly enough, General Zhdanov seems to take the same furtive line with his own people: that's why he sent Nadysev home, and that's why he saw me in person.'

'Makes sense,' Rawls said.

'But there's more to it,' Wyman went on. 'I got the distinct impression that General Zhdanov is treating this personally.'

'How do you mean?'

'Gebhard cropped up in the conversation, and just for one moment he let his defences slip. I know Gebhard isn't exactly the Kremlin's favourite person, but Zhdanov was surprisingly passionate about him.'

'What's Gebhard got to do with it?'

'I don't know, but he comes into it somewhere. You said yourself that my trip to Vienna bothered a lot of people at your end, but you didn't know why.

'What really baffles me is that Zhdanov thinks I might want to help him. I told him that if there's a conflict between our side and his, I'd always back ours. He laughed and said, "You must support your friends. But which ones?" What on earth could that mean?'

'You don't trust him, do you?'

'Of course not,' Wyman laughed.

'Zhdanov is as trustworthy as the average boa constrictor. I have no desire to share Eddie Fulton's fate.'

'Who?'

'The journalist you saw in my home the other day.'

'The guy with the KGB tail on him?'

'That's right. There was a sting in that particular tail: Eddie was murdered in London that evening. It was very nasty, and quite pointless, as far as I could see. I didn't think Eddie knew anything of any interest.'

'And now you're wondering,' Rawls said. 'I don't blame you. The KGB don't rub people out just for the hell of it.'

'Just so,' Wyman said. 'All I know is that he had two morsels of gossip. A story about Zhdanov, and a code-name he picked up from somewhere. Tango, or Foxtrot, or ... no, that was it: Project Waltz. Any idea what that means?'

Rawls shook his head.

'Search me. But if that's why they killed him, it might be worth finding out.'

'Yes,' Wyman said. 'The Zhdanov story is probably rubbish, but it's easily checkable. It must be Project Waltz. What on earth could that be...?'

He took off his glasses and rubbed his

eyes. He sat in deep concentration for a few minutes, and then took out a note-pad and began scribbling on it.

'I need some information,' he said. 'Your people must have a file on Zhdanov. There's also one on Gebhard. If Zhdanov hates Gebhard as bitterly as I think, I don't believe that Gebhard's human rights work would be the cause. Their paths must have crossed at some point, and the files may tell us where. Also, see if there's anything on Herbie. And lastly, you can see if anyone knows about Project Waltz. It sounds military, so you might ask any friends you have in the Pentagon–'

'Wait a minute,' Rawls protested. 'You want me to pull out classified files and give them to you?'

'Photocopies will do,' Wyman said innocently.

'Jesus, Wyman, what is this? I could get thirty years in the slammer for that. Why should I risk–?'

'I thought you wanted to help,' Wyman said.

'Sure,' Rawls said. 'Legally. Now if you'll take my advice, we'll go down the road to the US embassy and give all this to Hepburn. Make it legitimate.'

'It wouldn't work,' Wyman said. 'You aren't supposed to know about this, remember? Nor is Hepburn. If we tell your superiors, they will spend the next three weeks grilling me about the interior décor at Dzerzhinsky Square, and you'll be posted to somewhere like Tierra del Fuego, where you can't do any harm. Think about it.'

Rawls thought about it, and threw up his hands in resignation.

'All right,' he said miserably. 'I'm supposed to report to Langley next week, anyway. Could be several weeks before I get back here.'

'Not to worry. I need everything you've got on Zhdanov, and I mean everything. Is Bulgakov available?'

'What for?' Rawls said suspiciously.

'I bet he knows a few things about his ex-boss that didn't get into your file.'

'The last time I saw Bulgakov,' Rawls said, 'he made it clear that if I ever called round again, he'd tear my liver out. He's convinced the KGB reprisal squad are looking for him, and he thinks one of us might lead them to him.'

'A standard persecution complex,' Wyman said dismissively. 'Go and have a chat with him.'

'Anything else you want? The Library of Congress, maybe?'

'That will do,' Wyman said. 'For now, at any rate.'s

THIRTY-EIGHT

'I told you not to come back.'

'Yeah, but I thought you were just being polite,' Rawls said.

'I wasn't,' Bulgakov said, closing the door behind them. 'I beg you, Rawls, stop this.'

Rawls gazed curiously at the Russian.

'You know something, Bulgakov? You don't look too good. You're pale. If you want to blend into the scenery around here, you need a sun-tan. Don't you ever go out?'

'I leave the house once a day to get my shopping at the local store. That's all.'

'Jesus! That's no use. You aren't still nervous about that guy from the heavy squad, are you?'

'Drebednev,' Bulgakov said. 'Yes, I still think about him.'

They went upstairs and sat down. The drawing-room was now coated by a grey film of dust. The ashtrays were brimming over with anxious, half-smoked cigarettes; most of them were by the window, where the occupier appeared to spend most of his time. Rawls looked at Bulgakov inquiringly, and the Russian replied with a pained shrug.

'I'm not sure I can stand it any more,' Bulgakov said hoarsely. 'I thought I'd get over it in a month or two, but it only gets worse.'

'Maybe you should move somewhere else,' Rawls suggested.

Bulgakov shook his head miserably.

'What would that achieve? You'd still find me. And if you can trace me, so can they.'

Compassion was not one of Rawls' most outstanding traits, but he could not suppress a twinge of sympathy for Bulgakov. The Russian had once been as hard and polished as a diamond, and Rawls had almost envied him. He now understood his error. These qualities were not intrinsic to Bulgakov, but were acquired from his organisation. The Russian had made the same mistake, and was now suffering from it. Without the KGB, he was neutered and limp. There was an unpleasant moral in all this, which Rawls preferred not to draw.

'You know what I think?' he said cheerfully.

'No, and I don't want to.'

'I think you're going loco because you're

279

alone. Why don't you find yourself a woman?'

Bulgakov stared at Rawls frostily.

'Don't patronise me, Rawls. Just tell me what you've come for.'

Rawls shrugged and gave Bulgakov a slim cardboard folder.

'This,' he said, 'is our file on your ex-boss, Zhdanov. I want you to read it, and if you know anything that's not in there, tell me.'

'May I ask why?'

'Don't,' Rawls advised him. 'It'll only give you a headache.'

Bulgakov nodded and began to read. His only reaction to the file was an occasional frown, or smile of recognition. Fifteen minutes later, he closed the folder and gave it back to Rawls.

'It's not bad,' he said.

'But...?'

'There are two or three weaknesses. Firstly, the general character assessment is superficial. Yes, Zhdanov is volatile, and prone to rages. But he's also shrewd and acute.

'You don't get to his position just by losing your temper. Anyway, most of his tantrums are reserved for bureaucrats and incompetents who generally deserve them. Our system has many such people. Zhdanov is an army man, and he'd like the KGB to be run along military lines.'

'Isn't that how it's meant to be run?'

'Of course. But in practice, it's just a vast clumsy bureaucracy. Most of Zhdanov's time is spent arguing with politicians.'

'About funds?'

'About everything. Also, Zhdanov has to protect himself. Ever since the 27th Congress, the KGB has been on the defensive.'

The Soviet Union's programme of economic and social reforms, or *perestroika,* was ratified by the 27th Party Congress. Although no objections were raised towards the new policies, it was clear that they would find little favour with the KGB.

'Has Zhdanov taken any kind of stand against the reforms?'

'None. His silence is deafening.'

Rawls nodded and made some notes.

'OK,' he said. 'What else?'

'The file begins with Zhdanov's war record, and ignores his early years. This isn't very surprising, because nobody knows much about them. I have heard many stories, but there is no proof...'

'For example?'

'As you know, Zhdanov joined the army as

a private soldier in 1941, when he was eighteen. He signed up in Leningrad, just before the Germans put the city under siege. It was a terrible period, and our people needed all the help they could get. If you enlisted, nobody asked who you were, or where you came from: they just put a gun in your hand.

'Zhdanov was a good soldier. He survived the first winter, which was the hardest part of the siege. After Lake Ladoga froze, they drove supplies into the city across the ice. Zhdanov was put in charge of one of the convoys. He caught the eye of one or two senior people, got promoted, and was transferred to a tank regiment. When the war ended he was a major, with a lot of decorations. He stayed in the army, and by 1953 he was a general.'

'I'm impressed,' Rawls said. 'But what's the story?'

'You don't get promoted that quickly just by being a good soldier,' Bulgakov smiled. 'Not in our army, or anyone else's. Zhdanov was a fanatic. He never took leave. He volunteered for all the dangerous jobs. He took crazy risks.'

'So?'

'No relatives,' Bulgakov said simply. 'Not

even any distant cousins. Of course, everyone lost a relation or two in that war. But there was usually someone to write to. Zhdanov had no one, not even an old school-friend. It was as if they'd all been systematically destroyed. That's why the rumours started.'

'I get it,' Rawls nodded. 'But that's pretty circumstantial, isn't it?'

'Certainly,' Bulgakov agreed. 'I said there was no proof. But that doesn't stop rumours from spreading.'

'Would it make that much difference?'

'Of course,' Bulgakov said. 'The KGB has plenty of trouble from Jewish pressure groups who clamour for exit visas. If it could be shown that Zhdanov is prey to even the tiniest conflict of loyalties...'

Bulgakov made a chopping motion with his hand.

'Do you think it's true?' Rawls asked.

'I've no idea,' Bulgakov said. 'He's also rumoured to be a homosexual, merely because there have been no women in his life. I'm sure *that* isn't true, but it shows you can "prove" anything with negative evidence.'

'How well do you know the guy?'

'He was a friend of my father's,' Bulgakov

said. 'I've met him many times, but we've never had a proper conversation. It's impossible to make small talk with him, and he cares only about his work. To be honest, I found him rather boring.'

Rawls closed his notebook and put away the file.

'I don't know what you're planning,' Bulgakov said, 'but be careful. He's really tough. Most of us think we're like that, but sooner or later we learn the truth.'

'The bigger they are,' Rawls said jauntily.

'I mean it,' Bulgakov said.

'So do I.'

THIRTY-NINE

'Item four,' Kuleshov said. 'The agent Rawls. The latest reports from Washington are not very encouraging, I'm afraid.'

General Zhdanov said nothing. He leaned over the desk, with his chin in his hands and a thoughtful expression on his face. Kuleshov suspected that the General wasn't listening, but he kept this suspicion to himself.

'It appears,' Kuleshov went on, 'that Wyman has reported your meeting to the CIA, and Rawls has simply taken the information back to his superiors. There is no indication that he has taken your hint.'

'As you can see, I have taken out the file on Rawls. He is well known to the First Directorate, thanks to his work in Vietnam, Chile and West Germany. He worked at the US embassy here in Moscow between 1977 and 1980. Of course, he was also responsible for the defection of Major Bulgakov last year...'

Kuleshov noticed a glimmer in the

General's eye, and he paused for comment.

'I was called over to the Foreign Ministry this morning,' Zhdanov said, in a low voice. 'Apparently Gebhard will be visiting Washington one week after the Austrian general election, accompanied by the Foreign Minister. The paperwork will all be ready; it will be just a question of signing it. A *fait accompli*. We don't have much time, Kuleshov.'

Kuleshov was worried. Should he continue with his own report, which he could discuss and defend knowledgeably, or should he reply to the General's remark, which he scarcely understood? He took the safest option.

'Arising from all this,' he said firmly, 'is another matter of passing interest. The men who studied Rawls' movements followed him to an address in Los Angeles. We have reason to believe that Major Bulgakov is living there, though we do need to confirm this. Major Drebednev would like to discuss the matter with you.'

'They've moved more troops into southern Czechoslovakia,' Zhdanov said dreamily. 'As if that's going to stop anything! That bastard Gebhard must be praying for it.'

'Regarding the agent Rawls...'

The General lifted his head and scowled ferociously.

'Rawls?' he barked. 'What about him?'

'Well,' Kuleshov said breathlessly. 'He does appear to have told his masters all about Wyman's visit. We must assume that your initiative has not succeeded.'

'Bollocks,' snorted the General. 'We'll assume nothing of the sort. If Wyman has made Rawls run errands for him, it means he's taken the bait.'

'How can you be sure? Perhaps he just wanted to unburden himself to Rawls and forget about the whole thing. How do you know Rawls hasn't just told his superiors—'

'He probably has,' Zhdanov said. 'But they want Feigl as badly as we do, remember. One of our people at the United Nations saw Rawls burrowing through their library the other day. Who asked him to look there? The CIA have clerks for jobs like that.'

'Very well,' Kuleshov conceded, 'so Wyman asked him. But why do you think only Wyman can find Feigl?'

Zhdanov sighed, and replied with exaggerated patience: 'Wyman knows Feigl, and wants to find him. He's also a professional. But unlike any other professionals, he isn't affiliated. He can get all the information in Britain and America that isn't available to us, but he can also work with us. This means his chances of success are considerably greater than anyone else's. Is that clear enough for you, or would you like me to explain it with diagrams?'

Before Kuleshov could take up the General's offer, there was a knock at the door.

'Who is it?' Zhdanov grunted.

A thin, tall man walked into the room and smiled urbanely at the General.

'Sorry to interrupt you, General, but I'm in something of a hurry. There's a plane in two hours, and I wanted to confirm–'

'What do you want, Drebednev?'

'It's this business about Bulgakov–'

'What the fuck are you talking about?'

Drebednev looking inquiringly at Kuleshov.

'Didn't you explain?'

'I tried,' Kuleshov stammered. 'But the General...'

'Just get to the point,' Zhdanov said.

'Our Washington staff think that Rawls may be in contact with the defector Bulgakov. Major Drebednev would like permission to investigate a certain address in

Los Angeles, where he thinks–'

'Are you sure he's there?' Zhdanov broke in.

'Not entirely,' Drebednev admitted. 'But it was always suspected that Bulgakov may be hiding on the West Coast. With your permission, General...'

'You have it.'

'All the documentation has been prepared...'

Zhdanov waved his hand impatiently.

'Yes, yes. Just get on with it.'

'We could send you an interim situation report if you–'

'Get out!' Zhdanov roared.

Drebednev nodded stiffly and left.

'Where were we?' Zhdanov said. 'Oh yes. Forget about Wyman. If it works, it works. If not, we'll try something else. Have you heard the story about Gebhard's mail?'

Kuleshov blinked curiously at his chief.

'Is this a funny anecdote?'

'No, you turd!' Zhdanov exploded. 'It's a rumour circulating in Vienna. Gebhard is supposed to be receiving anonymous parcels in the post. What are they? Where are they from?'

'I've really no idea,' Kuleshov said meekly.

General Zhdanov suddenly felt a peculiar

urge to perform a Cossack dance on Kuleshov's face. He brought his fists down on the desk and let out a bellow of frustration.

'Oh!' Kuleshov gasped. 'You want me to find out. Very well, General. I'll look into it immediately.'

He gathered his papers and dashed out of the office. Execution without trial was largely a thing of the past in the Soviet Union, but there could always be exceptions to the rule.

FORTY

Anatoli Bulgakov put down his shopping and reached into his pocket for the front-door key. Before he could slide the key into the lock, the door swung open, and Bulgakov found himself gazing at the barrel of a pistol. Its owner was a tall, grey-haired man with a friendly smile and twinkling blue eyes.

'Comrade Bulgakov,' he said pleasantly. 'Welcome home.'

Bulgakov's stomach shrivelled.

'Hello, Drebednev. I've been waiting for you.'

'Of course you have,' Drebednev nodded. 'Would you like to take out your gun? Thank you. Just drop it by my feet. Now, come inside.'

Bulgakov bent down to collect his bag of groceries, but Drebednev shook his head.

'We won't be needing those.'

Bulgakov swept up the bag and threw it at Drebednev's face, swerving sideways to avoid the bullet. He was too slow. A hot skewer ran through his leg, and he fell to the ground.

'Stupid,' Drebednev said mildly.

He picked up the groceries which were scattered across the porch, and tossed them into the hallway. One of Bulgakov's TV dinners caught his eye, and he read its label with amused disgust.

'"MacMurtry's Microwave Macaroni". Is this what you left us for, Bulgakov? A lifetime of this? Quite pathetic.'

Bulgakov did not reply. He rolled on the ground and gritted his teeth in pain and fear.

'Coming inside?' Drebednev said.

Bulgakov shook his head.

'I think my leg's broken.'

'Can't you crawl? We expected you back a lot sooner, you know. Did you take a long walk before you went shopping? Thought so. Never mind; we're still not quite ready.'

Bulgakov slowly stood up on one leg and hopped to the door.

'That's it,' Drebednev said encouragingly. 'Now, up the stairs.'

'You'll have to help me,' Bulgakov panted. 'I'll never be able to—'

'Of course you will,' Drebednev said, closing the door behind them.

Bulgakov's lip curled in disgust.

'I knew you were a sadist, but I didn't think you were petty with it.'

Drebednev looked hurt.

'I'm not a sadist,' he said, with feeling. 'And I'm not petty. I'm merely following the rules. "Wounded examinees must never be given superfluous assistance or medication. Their disability will assist the interrogation."'

'Interrogation!' Bulgakov jeered. 'You're here to kill me, Drebednev. It's the interrogation that's superfluous.'

'Nonsense. You'll tell us everything you told the Americans. You'll tell us exactly what Rawls was after. That's quite relevant. Up you go.'

Bulgakov struggled up the stairs. It took him several minutes, but Drebednev waited until he had reached the landing before joining him.

'Well done,' Drebednev smiled.

Bulgakov crawled into the lounge and on to a chair. Sweat rolled down his face and stung his eyes. The pain worsened, and the room appeared to be doing forty-five r.p.m. around his head.

'Is he all right?' asked a voice.

'He'll be fine,' Drebednev said, as he bound Bulgakov's arms and legs to the chair with leather straps. 'Have you sorted out the lights?'

'I think so. Yuri says he's lost a box of lenses. A blue metal tin.'

'Over by my briefcase, Viktor.'

'Thanks.'

The blurred shapes stopped revolving around Bulgakov's head, and gradually swam into focus. They still made little sense. Two arc lights loomed above him. Cables and boxes were strewn across the floor, leading to a small console on a table. As well as Drebednev, there were two other men setting up various items of equipment. In the centre of the room, a camera stood on a tripod.

'What are you doing?' Bulgakov mumbled.

'You're going to be a film star,' Drebednev grinned. 'That's what most Californians dream of, isn't it?'

Bulgakov glanced around, and saw a couple of open suitcases behind him. Their contents were predictable, if disturbing: pincers, scalpels, syringes, a blow-lamp, wires, crocodile-clips, and a gleaming set of dentist's tools.

'So the old films aren't good enough?' Bulgakov said.

294

'Obviously not,' Drebednev said. 'They weren't good enough to deter you, were they?'

'They weren't even in colour,' Yuri said disdainfully. 'What use is black and white? People expect blood to be red, and quite right too.'

'This time we're doing it properly,' Viktor said, patting the camera. 'Japanese high technology. We've nothing to beat it, I'm sorry to say.'

Drebednev smiled benevolently and put on a pair of rubber surgical gloves.

'Are we ready to begin?'

'Not just yet,' Yuri said. 'I need to check the sound.'

He held a microphone a couple of feet away from Bulgakov's head, as Viktor went to the console and donned a pair of headphones.

'OK,' Viktor said.

'Would you like to say something? Count to ten, if you like.'

Bulgakov gazed at Yuri in disbelief.

'You're mad,' he said.

'No, louder,' Viktor said, shaking his head.

'A quick scream, perhaps,' Yuri suggested. 'Just to give us an idea.'

Bulgakov clenched his teeth in rage.

'Oh dear,' Drebednev sighed. 'Well, how about this?'

He punched Bulgakov's leg, at the spot where the bullet had gone in, and looked up inquiringly at Viktor.

'Not bad,' Viktor said thoughtfully. 'Try something sharper.'

Drebednev jabbed his fingers into Bulgakov's crotch.

'Better,' Viktor nodded. 'I think we'll be fine with the shrieks and screams, but the low visceral moans could be a bit of a problem.'

'You'll have to come in closer with the mike.'

'I suppose so. But I don't want any blood on that microphone,' Viktor said reprovingly. 'The hire company charge us extra for unfair wear and tear.'

'I'll bear it in mind,' Drebednev said solemnly, and turning to Bulgakov, he added: 'Before we start, I'd like to emphasise that we're simply doing our job. There's nothing personal or gratuitous in this.

'You accused me of being a sadist: it's an understandable reaction, but I must confess I found it a little offensive. We are governed by strict rules, you know, and I follow those rules very carefully. Naturally, I want to do my job well. I want to know all about your debrief, and all about Mr Rawls' inquiries. That's all there is to it. I hope you understand.'

'Oh yes,' Bulgakov said wearily.

'Splendid,' Drebednev smiled. 'I'm so glad we could clear that up. Now perhaps we can begin.'

FORTY-ONE

'The latest opinion polls have come in,' Weber said. 'Sixty-eight per cent approve of the OVP's foreign policy.'

'Is that good?' Gebhard smiled.

'Of course it is,' Weber said. 'Don't you agree?'

'This "foreign policy" so far has simply consisted of fine speeches,' Gebhard said. 'Is that what they approve of, or do they agree with the content? Do they want action, or more hot air? Your opinion poll is ambiguous.'

'I see what you mean. Well, you'll have the answer soon enough.'

Weber noticed the unhappy look on the President's face, and smiled encouragingly.

'You're not worried about it, are you?'

'Of course I am, Karl,' Gebhard said. 'I still think we could have been more open about our intentions.'

'Rubbish,' Weber said. 'Everyone knows where you stand. You've made no secret of your–'

'Haven't I?' Gebhard said thoughtfully. 'There's a difference between telling people your position, and explaining precisely where it leads.'

'Pure sophistry,' Weber said. 'But if you're so concerned about honesty, let me be honest with you.'

'Go on,' Gebhard laughed.

'You don't believe a word of what you're saying. You're suffering from last-minute nerves, but you won't admit it. Instead you look for some moral stick to beat yourself with. Just relax, will you? You've done nothing wrong.'

Gebhard grinned ruefully at his secretary.

'Thank you,' he said. 'But I can't share your confidence. Even if we win a clear majority–'

'No ifs about it.'

'–what if the opposition cry foul? They'll say it's a constitutional issue, and demand a referendum.'

'They can demand what they like,' Weber said. 'All the lawyers agree: as long as we're technically neutral, there's no question of a constitutional crisis.'

'I hope you're right,' Gebhard said.

'Of course I am. If you want something to worry about, think of something trivial, like your friend in Czechoslovakia.'

'Who? Oh, him.'

'Parcel number five has just arrived from Brno. The usual contents.'

'Brno? Perhaps number six will come from Prague.'

'Perhaps. What happens then?'

'I don't know,' Gebhard said. 'I've been asking myself that question for some time.'

FORTY-TWO

'What's the matter?' Drebednev said.

'Fuse,' Yuri said, holding up the burnt remains of a plug.

'How fast can you fix it?'

'I'll be a few minutes. The whole plug needs rewiring.'

'Oh dear,' Drebednev said. 'And we were doing so well.'

He looked down anxiously at what remained of Anatoli Bulgakov. The interrogation had proceeded smoothly until its closing stages, when one of the arc lights blew up.

'Can't we finish with just one light?' Drebednev suggested. 'I don't think he'll last much longer.'

'Impossible,' Viktor said emphatically. 'Half of him is in total darkness.'

'It wouldn't do,' Yuri agreed.

'If you insist,' Drebednev said. 'But please be quick.'

He removed his gloves, which were now bright crimson, and reached for his bag. He took out a stethoscope and placed it against Bulgakov's chest.

'Weak,' he said.

Bulgakov was a mess. His flesh was charred, swollen and dribbling. Most of his bones were smashed into fragments. His teeth and fingernails were strewn about the floor in a pool of blood and vomit, along with various other components that Drebednev had removed during their session.

Apart from the fuse, there had only been one small hiccup, involving one of Bulgakov's arteries. Both the microphone and the camera lens had been liberally sprayed, which infuriated Yuri, and caused Viktor to have an artistic tantrum. It took Drebednev several minutes to calm them down.

'How are you planning to end this?' Viktor said.

'There are several alternatives,' Drebednev said. 'We usually finish them off by shooting them in the face. Fairly low-key.'

'Feeble,' Yuri jeered.

'We could use a snub-nosed bullet,' Drebednev suggested. 'They make things spread nicely.'

Viktor was not convinced.

'What else?'

'Something for the cameras,' Yuri urged.

'I've got a small axe,' Drebednev said. 'Maybe we could finish with the handle sticking up out of his skull.'

'Poignant,' Viktor nodded. 'I like it.'

'Too downbeat,' Yuri said. 'We should round things off with a nice dramatic finish. Why don't you just cut his head off?'

'Now that's a good idea,' Viktor said.

'I'm not sure,' Drebednev said, picking up the axe. 'It's too small to lop off his head in one go. I'd have to hack several times. It wouldn't have the impact.'

'Dreary,' Viktor agreed. 'Perhaps we could cheat.'

'How?'

'If you loosened the spine before we started shooting...'

'Good idea,' Drebednev said. 'I've got just the thing: a Gigli saw. I'll cut through the back of the neck, so the head will only be attached at the throat. One stroke with the axe, and you'll have your shot.'

'Great,' Yuri said.

Drebednev examined Bulgakov's heart once again with the stethoscope.

'I think he's gone,' he muttered. 'Yes ... that's it. His heart's stopped.'

'He lasted well,' Viktor observed.

'I've seen better,' Drebednev said.

He pointed at an ashtray in disgust.

'If he wasn't a smoker, we'd have had another thirty minutes out of him, at least. Filthy habit.'

'Not to worry,' Viktor said cheerfully. 'We can still do the take.'

'I suppose so,' Drebednev sighed, as he took out the Gigli saw. 'It simply isn't the same when they're dead. It's so … *artificial.*'

FORTY-THREE

'Yeah,' Rawls said quietly. 'That's Bulgakov.'

He closed the door behind him and patted his brow with a handkerchief. The FBI man studied him warily.

'Are you going to be sick? The John's over there.'

Rawls shook his head.

'I'll be all right,' he said. 'Just tell me the story, Mr...'

'Jack Hammond. Apparently a salesman knocked on the front door this morning. He got no reply, and he noticed some blood on the porch.'

'So why did he phone you?'

'He didn't. He went straight to the police. Some smart cop remembered this address was on our list, and he phoned us.'

'What's your interest?'

'Routine procedure, Mr Rawls. When your people buy someone a safe-house, they let us know. Usually, that is. It's meant to rule out possible embarrassments.'

'Like this, you mean?'

Hammond shrugged.

'It's just a formality,' he said. 'Nobody ever checks them out.'

'So I see,' Rawls said drily. 'Jesus, I need some air.'

They went downstairs and out into the rear garden, where they found a couple of deck-chairs.

'Grass needs cutting,' Hammond observed.

'He didn't go out much. Too scared.'

'You mean he was expecting trouble?'

Rawls smiled bitterly.

'Yeah, and we thought he was paranoid. Looks like we were wrong.'

'So who was he?' Hammond said.

'A defector,' Rawls said flatly.

'You can do better than that.'

'Sure I can,' Rawls agreed. 'But that's all you need.'

'What does that mean?' Hammond said indignantly. 'In case you hadn't noticed, we've got an investigation here.'

'I doubt it,' Rawls said. 'That doctor I saw; has he got a time of death yet?'

'Between thirty and thirty-six hours ago, but that's provisional.'

'In that case, you can forget it. The guy who did this left the country yesterday evening. I guarantee it.'

'You know who the murderer is?'

'His name's Drebednev. You can write to him, care of number two Dzerzhinsky Square, Moscow.'

'Keep talking.'

'He runs a team of reprisal agents. They find KGB defectors and execute them, to discourage other people from getting the same idea. It's supposed to be good for morale.'

Hammond shook his head.

'That wasn't an execution,' he said. 'That was carnage. You saw it. They tore him to pieces. The doctor says he was shot, burned, lacerated, electrocuted...'

'Yeah, yeah,' Rawls said impatiently. 'I get the point. But did you see that big light bulb near the armchair? The plugs and the wires? They filmed it all for the folks back home. It was a propaganda show.'

There was a long silence as Hammond struggled to make sense of this.

'Christ!' he exclaimed finally. 'That has to be the sickest fucking thing I've ever heard of. That's ... that's...'

'That's the way it goes,' Rawls said firmly. 'Bulgakov knew the risks when he defected. He was unlucky.'

'Unlucky?' Hammond said. 'Unlucky? The poor bastard came here to escape that kind of shit, and you let him down, and all you can say is "he was unlucky".'

Rawls nodded calmly.

'That's right. And the best thing you can do is clean this place up and forget it.'

Suddenly Hammond grew angry.

'Jesus, Rawls, what kind of a shit-head are you? You think I'm going to just scrub the floors and go home?'

'That's the general idea.'

'If you think this is going to stop here, you need a new brain. Don't you think the newspapers are going to say something about this?'

'They'll take what we give them,' Rawls said. 'And you'll do the same. Otherwise we'll be doing Drebednev a big favour. Think about it, Hammond.'

Hammond thought about it. The argument was logical, but hardly satisfying.

'I thought we could be hard,' he muttered, 'but what are you guys made of?'

'Barbed wire and acid,' Rawls said sarcastically. 'And if I remember rightly, you Feds aren't averse to shoving your hands down the toilet when it's needed. I didn't say I liked the arrangement, Hammond; I

308

just know when I'm beaten.'

'Just doing your job,' Hammond jeered.

'That's right.'

'And what about this Drebednev charac-ter? He was just doing his job, right?'

Rawls gave a fatalistic shrug.

'Yes,' he said wearily. 'I guess he was.'

WINTER

A sad tale's best for winter:
I have one of sprites and goblins.

Shakespeare *The Winter's Tale*

WINTER

A sad tale's best for winter:
I have one of sprites and goblins.

Shakespeare, *The Winter's Tale*

FORTY-FOUR

'Good man,' Wyman said, as Rawls presented him with a briefcase full of documents.

'You owe me for this,' Rawls said.

'I suppose I do. I see some of these are marked HRA. Highly Restricted Access? Thought so. You must have had some difficulty in smuggling them out.'

'I must have,' Rawls agreed. 'But I'm not sure what good they'll do you.'

He took out Wyman's shopping list and went through it.

'First: Project Waltz. Nobody at the Company has heard of it, so I tried a friend of mine at the State Department. First he said he didn't know what I was talking about, so I told him it might be concerned with Austria. He gave me a funny look and said he wasn't sure, but he thought it smelt like something from the Pentagon.

'So I spoke to someone I knew at the Pentagon. He said it was the name of a confidential memorandum sent in from the

State Department, but he didn't know what it was about. Then he changed the subject.'

'What do you make of that?'

'If it comes from the State Department, it's probably some kind of diplomatic initiative.'

'With military overtones, presumably.'

'Could be,' Rawls said. 'But in that case, why doesn't anyone at Langley know about it?'

'What about the CIA Director?'

Rawls scratched his head in confusion.

'He might know, I guess. But he certainly isn't screaming about it in public. And there was something else. It might be irrelevant, but I'm not sure. After I saw the guy at the Pentagon, I had a drink with an old friend in the arms trade, a guy by the name of Mitchell. He's a kind of broker: sets up deals between manufacturers, governments and so on. He used to be in the army, and with his contacts he gets a lot of trade with the US government.

'It was just a social call, but obviously I asked him how business was doing. He said better than ever: apparently he'd just landed a massive deal with the government for anti-tank weapons. Mitchell expected to make a packet, and he had no complaints, but he couldn't help noticing one funny thing.

'Apparently all these weapons were for export to a European country. This would have made some sense if they were all manufactured in the US, but they weren't. Some were from Germany, others from France. You'd think the weapons would be bought direct from source – all governments have procurement agencies to do exactly that. But no, these guys were only buying through the US.

'Mitchell didn't understand it, but it was OK with him: the commission was excellent. And he said that he was only part of the operation. He was only handling anti-tank weapons, but there were other guys handling different purchases.'

'Most intriguing,' Wyman said. 'And I presume you asked him for the name of that European country.'

'Sure,' Rawls grinned, 'but he wouldn't say. Then I remember this Project Waltz thing, and asked him if it was Austria. He said nothing, but he said it to mean "yes".'

Wyman subsided into thought for a few moments. Then he looked up and smiled.

'Excellent,' he said, clapping his hands. 'I do believe you've cracked it.'

'I have? But none of this makes much

sense. Why the cloak and dagger routine in the State Department? And if the Austrians are shopping for arms–?'

'They aren't,' Wyman broke in. 'At least, not for the time being.'

'You've lost me,' Rawls sighed.

'Gebhard wants closer ties with the Western alliances, doesn't he? He can't join them, of course, because the Austrian constitution prohibits it. But he's made it clear which way he'd like to lean.'

'I still don't get it. Austrian presidents don't create policy. They're just meant to stand around and look good at receptions.'

'Of course. It's Gebhard's party that will implement the policies. At the moment they can't do it because they're stuck in a coalition. All that will change if and when they get a clear majority in the election this month, and that seems quite likely.

'There's been a lot of talk in Austria about a shift to the West, but very little detail. I think your friend Mitchell represents one small item on a big menu. I'm only guessing, of course, but I suspect that US "advisers" will be sent over with these arms.'

'And that's Project Waltz?'

'That's part of it, at least. There could be much more: trade agreements, diplomatic understandings, and heaven knows what else. It will all be implemented by the new government, but Gebhard will sell it to the electorate. No wonder the Russians are so furious.'

'But why the secrecy?' Rawls said. 'Why not just tell everybody about it now?'

Wyman shook his head.

'Think about it,' he said. 'It's a risky policy, and the Austrians traditionally prefer safe options. If the fine details were leaked now, they might scare away enough people to deprive Gebhard's party of a majority. End of Project Waltz.'

'I hate to sound finicky about it,' Rawls said, 'but it seems kind of dishonest.'

Wyman smiled and lit a cigarette.

'It's sharp practice,' he agreed. 'In fact it's quite typical of Gebhard's way of thinking. His books are very clinical and precise, and I'm sure they're quite sincere. But he has a distressing habit of ignoring key facts which might disrupt his pretty conclusions. The sin of omission is Gebhard's hallmark, and he commits it with this policy. The general position is well known, but he's glossed over the details. Anyway, what else did you get?'

'You asked for anything I could find on the war in Yugoslavia. Apparently one or two universities have some material on the subject, but I didn't get time to try them. All I could get was some stuff in the United Nations Library, but most of it's shit.'

'Any references to Herbert Feigl?'

'Yeah, just one. It was one of his war reports.'

'Splendid,' Wyman beamed. 'Now we're getting somewhere.'

'Not so fast,' Rawls cautioned him. 'It's lost. Either someone misfiled it, or they took it out and never returned it. Happens all the time, apparently.

'It was the same story at the National Archives in Washington. When I swiped Gebhard's dossier from Langley, I noticed some reference to the National Archives in the footnotes, so I ordered copies. Some were there, others were missing. Mislaid, they said.'

'How do you mislay a microfilm?' Wyman asked suspiciously.

'I think they mean the original files were mislaid before they were put on film.'

'Is that what they said?'

'Jesus, Wyman! You produce more conspiracy theories than the *Washington Post.*'

'I'm sorry,' Wyman laughed. 'I've got a

nasty suspicious mind.'

'You aren't kidding,' Rawls said. 'Forty years is a long time. I'm surprised they kept any of that stuff.'

'You may be right,' Wyman said, with little conviction. 'So you've got Gebhard's dossier; what about Zhdanov's?'

'Yeah,' Rawls nodded, 'I got his, plus a few extra details that weren't in there. If you want my advice, don't go anywhere near the guy.'

Wyman glanced quizzically at the American.

'Is the dossier so terrible?'

'Not particularly,' Rawls said. 'But his boys reminded me of what happens to people they dislike.'

Wyman frowned.

'Is this a horror story?'

'X-rated,' Rawls said. 'You eaten recently? In that case, let me tell you about Bulgakov.'

FORTY-FIVE

'It's late,' Margaret said, as she put her book down.

'Is it?' Wyman muttered.

'Four o'clock,' she added.

'Indeed,' he said.

Wyman had sunk into his armchair some eight hours before, with Rawls' documents in a neat pile on the coffee-table beside him. Each item was then scanned, annotated, and flung casually on to the carpet like the bones at a medieval banquet. Now the feast was almost over, and the armchair was surrounded by an ocean of paper that lapped at Wyman's feet and threatened to engulf him.

Wyman's forehead creased up into a frown, and he peered at his wife in surprise.

'Did you say it was four o'clock?'

'Two minutes past,' Margaret smiled.

'Good heavens!' he exclaimed. 'Why didn't you say something?'

'I hate to spoil your fun. How's it going?'

'Not too badly,' Wyman said. 'I think I've wrung the last drops of useful information out of all this.'

'And your conclusion...?'

'It's hard to say,' Wyman murmured thoughtfully. 'I've established circumstantial connections between all the key figures in the drama, but I still lack solid evidence for any hypotheses.'

'What's that in plain English?'

Wyman leaned forward and rummaged about in the heap of paper, until he found the dossier he was looking for.

'Firstly, Gebhard. "Born Klagenfurt 1919; took a degree in Law; joined the German army in 1941; served during the invasion of Russia." You will recall that Hitler's invasion consisted of three prongs, aimed at Leningrad, Moscow and Stalingrad respectively.

'Gebhard was a *Leutnant* in an infantry division in *Heeresgruppe Nord,* heading for Leningrad under General Von Leeb. He was wounded in a guerrilla ambush in December 1941, and was sent home to recover. He resumed service in the Balkans from September 1942 until the end of the war, attached to Army Group E.'

'Yugoslavia? Is that your first circumstantial connection?'

Wyman nodded.

'The document says nothing about his work in Yugoslavia, except that he was an *Oberleutnant* serving with the staff of General Alexander Löhr. That could mean anything. No, what really interests me is his earlier spell in Leningrad. That's where Zhdanov comes in.'

He pulled out the KGB chief's dossier.

'The General's early years are surprisingly obscure. It just says "Zhdanov, Trofim Natanovich – born 1922, probably in Leningrad. Exact origins unknown. Joined the Red Army in September 1941 immediately prior to siege of Leningrad." During the early months of the siege, Zhdanov conducted small raiding parties against German supply lines, collected intelligence, took prisoners, and shot collaborators. The Renaissance Man. He was decorated, promoted, and transferred to Moscow in the spring of 1942.'

'So Zhdanov and Gebhard were in the same place at the same time?'

'That's right,' Wyman nodded. 'Gebhard might have been wounded in one of Zhdanov's ambushes. I'm convinced Zhdanov has a personal grudge against Gebhard. If so, it must date back to this period. According to each man's dossier, their paths could never have crossed again.'

'What do they say about their late careers?'

'In Gebhard's case, little I don't know already. Remember, these files are written for the benefit of CIA policy-makers: they're mostly analytical. Gebhard is said to be "essentially lacking in pragmatism", because he spoke out against the CIA's involvement in Chile and one or two episodes in the Vietnam War. They put these childish outbursts down to his inexperience of high office. It doesn't occur to them that he might have some genuine principles.

'Of course, this is all offset by his frequent attacks on the Soviet Union. The Americans heartily approve of that.'

'And Zhdanov?'

'In many ways, Zhdanov is an odd choice for the job of KGB chief. He didn't join the KGB until 1967, when they put him in charge of the Fourth Chief Directorate – the border guards. That's a military job, with little political muscle attached to it. Nevertheless, Andropov liked him, and transferred him to the Second Chief Directorate – Internal Security – in 1970.

'He's a strange, paradoxical character, famed for his coarseness and bad temper, but remarkably acute in political matters. The suggestion here is that the crude, martial exterior is a deliberate camouflage. That sounds oversimplified, but I grant that he's no fool. He certainly knew how to handle me.'

'Where does all this get us?' Margaret asked.

'Good question,' Wyman said. 'We have established the possibility of personal links between Herbie, Gebhard and Zhdanov. We now have to understand what the official connection is, and why the US State Department is involved. The answer is Project Waltz.

'I assume this is an agreement – or proposed agreement – between the United States and Austria. It is the sort of agreement that tends to run counter to Austrian neutrality. That's why the Russians are interested.'

'And Herbie Feigl knows about this?'

Wyman shifted uncomfortably.

'It does sound rather strange, doesn't it? But why else would the Russians want him? And the Americans for that matter? Milo Lalic told the Russians he'd found "the best kept secret in Europe". That must be Project Waltz. Herbie was his source, though

God alone knows how an old schoolmaster could have stumbled across something like that.

'Lalic was trying to set up a deal with the Russians, but it backfired. Why did they kill him? Rawls thought he was trying to swindle the KGB, and they murdered him in reprisal.'

'But you don't agree?'

'No, I don't. You see, Herbie had the goods, but he was an unwilling source. When Lalic tried to involve him in the deal, Herbie ran away to Yugoslavia. The KGB followed him, and so did Lalic. The Russians couldn't find Herbie, but they found Lalic. Now they had identified his source, Lalic was redundant. He was also greedy and obstructive, so they killed him. No, that can't be right...'

He frowned and scratched his head.

'Actually, that doesn't follow,' he murmured.

'But how does all this help you trace Herbie?' Margaret asked.

'I'm not entirely sure,' Wyman admitted. 'If even Zhdanov has drawn a blank, with all the resources he commands, what can I do? The odd thing is that he seems to think I can do something he can't. Ever since our meeting, I've been wondering what that could be.'

He looked down at his notes for guidance, but they were of little help. With a sigh of resignation, he leaned over to drop them on the floor. As he did so, he noticed Gebhard's books, which lay in a heap beside his armchair. Suddenly, his eyes widened, and his jaw dropped stupidly.

'Of course,' he breathed. 'How did I describe it? His hallmark…'

He picked up the top book and gazed curiously at the cover.

'You know,' he added, 'there *is* one thing I can do that Zhdanov can't.'

'Well?' Margaret said impatiently.

'I can have another quiet chat with Max Gebhard.'

FORTY-SIX

'So you're not fully persuaded?' Gebhard smiled.

'Not entirely,' Wyman admitted. 'You offer some excellent arguments, and I agree with much of what you say. But to share your conclusions, I would have to accept *all* the reasoning, and that's the sticking-point.'

Once again, Wyman had secured a meeting with Gebhard at the latter's hotel in the Park Ring. Having poured out a couple of drinks, the President insisted that Wyman tell him what he thought of his books.

'Perhaps you could give me an example of what is troubling you,' Gebhard suggested.

'Certainly,' Wyman said. 'You attack the closed society because it undermines personal responsibility and promotes bureaucracy. You attack bureaucracy because it too undermines personal responsibility. You offer many pertinent, persuasive examples to back up your argument. I don't dispute any of this. But as far as you're concerned, closed societies, bureaucracies and personal immorality form one big package. That's what troubles me.'

'Why?'

'Well, what you call "bureaucratic amorality" also occurs outside bureaucracies. It also crops up in open societies rather a lot. For example, think of the boards of directors who mistreat their workers for profit. They always claim to be acting on behalf of their shareholders. But the shareholders themselves seldom take responsibility for the misbehaviour of their board, especially in very large companies. That's a perfect example of "bureaucratic amorality".

'"Personal responsibility" doesn't seem to exist in these situations, but they happen in the most open societies quite regularly. Your books take no account of that, but they should.'

Gebhard nodded pensively.

'That's a fair point,' he said. 'I do think my arguments would cover that example, but I admit that I haven't dealt with it explicitly.'

'If I may be frank...' Wyman nodded.

'By all means,' Gebhard laughed.

'I think this is the major weakness in your approach. There is a tendency to avoid important facts and details which might ...

cloud the issue. And I suspect this tendency occurs outside your theoretical work.'

'Indeed?' Gebhard said. 'Why do you think that?'

'I fear you were a trifle selective in your account of your meeting with Herbie Feigl.'

Gebhard blinked in surprise.

'Really?'

'Yes,' Wyman said. 'Since our last meeting, a great deal of new information has come into my hands.'

Gebhard pondered this remark carefully, like a chess player considering his next three moves.

'May I ask where you obtained this information?'

'From a variety of sources,' Wyman said. 'To be frank, I lack the precise details. But the overall picture is clear enough.'

'And you are threatening to expose this ... this picture?'

'I'm making no threats, Dr Gebhard. But Herbie Feigl did, didn't he?'

Gebhard nodded slowly.

'To be honest,' Wyman said, 'I don't know where Herbie got the details from. But I'm sure he has them.'

Gebhard frowned in surprise.

'You don't know where he got them from?'

he repeated. 'I thought you were his friend.'

'I am.'

'But you know so little about him that you don't know where he heard this?'

It was Wyman's turn to look uncomfortable.

'Obviously, I don't know him as well as I thought,' he admitted. 'I must confess it's the most baffling feature of this whole business.'

'Quite so,' Gebhard said drily. 'What exactly do you want from me, Professor?'

'I don't know what Herbie sought from you, and I don't care,' Wyman said. 'I just want to find him, and I think you can help.'

'How?'

'I have two questions for you. I'd like straight answers to both. Are you prepared to give them?'

'What are the questions?'

'Firstly, was Herbie's information based on documents?'

Gebhard nodded slowly.

'He has some documents, yes. At least, he claims to have them. He didn't show them to me.'

'Thank you,' Wyman said. 'Secondly, have you had any communication from Herbie since his disappearance?'

Gebhard winced slightly, and reached for his cigarettes. He lit one, and gazed thoughtfully at the lighter.

'Yes,' he said finally.

He stood up and went over to his briefcase. Reluctantly, he drew out a parcel and gave it to Wyman.

'It arrived yesterday,' he said.

Wyman noticed that the parcel was from Prague. He opened it, and found a copy of Gebhard's book inside. The flyleaf carried Gebhard's autograph, and underneath, in a different handwriting, the words 'Make a public admission'.

'I wondered what had become of these,' Wyman said. 'How many has he sent you?'

'All six. This is the last one. It's the first time he's included any kind of message.'

'Were they all from Prague?'

'No,' Gebhard said. 'The first ones came from Hungary.'

'The eye of the storm,' Wyman grinned. 'I'm sure they never thought of looking in their own parish. Why did he send these to you?'

'I've been wondering,' Gebhard said. 'I suppose he wanted to tell me he was still alive. To remind me that he knew. To prick my conscience, I suppose.'

'Didn't it occur to you that it might be a cry for help?'

Gebhard's face screwed up in confusion.

'I don't understand,' he said.

'He's in trouble. A lot of people are looking for him. They want what he knows. If you made that information public, the pressure on him would vanish, wouldn't it? Herbie could come home.'

Wyman pointed to the inscription inside the book.

'That's what it means. You could save him.'

'It's out of the question,' Gebhard said.

'Why? Look, I'm not asking for details: just a press statement in the most general terms to get them off his back. A denial, even. It'll have the same effect.'

Gebhard looked down at the floor, and replied slowly and deliberately, as if he were rehearsing a speech he had just learned.

'From what I understand, Herr Feigl's information is scant and imprecise. It does contain a few grains of truth, but these have been exaggerated and misconstrued. To publicise this information would increase the risk of further misconstruction and wild speculation. The net effect could be quite catastrophic, Professor. You must take my word for this.

'I sympathise deeply with Herr Feigl's predicament, but I regret that there is far more at stake here than the problems of one fugitive man.'

'True,' Wyman said. 'If the Soviets catch him, his problems will be yours.'

'This is pure speculation. I don't believe his information is reliable enough–'

'The Russians don't agree. Nor, I suspect, does the CIA.'

Gebhard shrugged.

'We must take that risk. And in the meantime, Herr Feigl's difficulties are not my responsibility.'

Wyman stared grimly at the Austrian president.

'Spoken like a true bureaucrat,' he said.

FORTY-SEVEN

'You OK, Mr President?'

'Nothing serious, I hope?'

'Sorry to see you like this, Mr President.'

The President acknowledged his advisers' concern with a world-weary smile.

'It's all right, boys. They say it's nothing ... permanent.'

The President's fitness centre had arrived, along with various other palaestric items. There was a Deltoid Press Machine, a Bicep Curling Machine, a Thigh Extension Machine, a Calf Machine, a Hack-Squat Machine, and other equally perilous contraptions whose functions were not entirely clear.

Unfortunately, the President took possession of his new equipment before George Bradwell's mechanics had an opportunity to doctor them. The results were inevitable and painful. The President slipped several discs, and was confined to his bed, with his legs in traction.

Of course, business had to continue. The

President's bed was wheeled into the Oval Office, and his advisers sat round and offered their sympathies, before turning their attention to that day's agenda.

'Right,' said the Secretary of State briskly, 'I see from this memo that Gebhard's been receiving anonymous mail from Hungary and Czechoslovakia. When exactly did we hear about this?'

'Yesterday.'

'Oh yeah? That's a little late, isn't it? Why didn't we hear about this sooner?'

He glanced accusingly at the CIA Director.

'Good point,' said the National Security Adviser. 'I thought we'd bribed his mailman, or something.'

The CIA Director shook his head.

'Parcels are handled separately from ordinary letters. They screen all parcels at the sorting office and send them on a special truck to Gebhard's palace.'

'Hold on a second,' said the President. 'Which Gebhard are we talking about here?'

'The Austrian president.'

'Got it,' nodded the President. 'I thought the name was familiar. Carry on, boys.'

'The important thing,' said the CIA Director, 'is that the parcels are from Feigl.'

How do you know?'

'I can add two and two. Wyman's gone to Prague.'

'Is that a good thing?' asked the Secretary of State.

'Why not?'

'Well, maybe we should have sent one of your people first.'

'Are you kidding?' laughed the CIA Director.

'Joke?'

'Yeah, joke. I send a CIA operative to Prague to find Feigl. He meets Feigl. They're caught by Czech security. Zhdanov gets the documents, and when we claim they're forgeries, Zhdanov produces our agent to prove they're genuine. No thanks, gentlemen.'

The President frowned in bewilderment.

'I'm a little confused here. Who's Zhdanov?'

'The head of the KGB, Mr President.'

'And Wyman?'

'He's British. Used to work in intelligence.'

'No kidding? Is he with us?'

'Not officially. But we're rooting for him.'

'Glad to hear it,' said the President firmly. 'I always liked the Brits.'

336

The National Security Adviser was still not satisfied.

'What if Zhdanov finds Feigl first?'

'It's possible,' admitted the CIA Director. 'But we've been running that risk for weeks. I think it's established that Zhdanov can't do it on his own. Remember, he doesn't know about Prague yet. I say we just leave it to Wyman.'

'You trust that Limey?' said the Secretary of State. 'I think he stinks.'

'I trust him up to a point. He's got no political axe to grind. He just wants to find his buddy.'

'You're breaking my heart,' said the National Security Adviser. 'And even if he finds his bosom pal, how's he going to get him out?'

'Feigl's got forged identity documents. He couldn't have entered those countries any other way. Wyman just has to persuade him that he's safe on our side of the border, and then we can take over. Hunky-dory.'

The President reached out and tapped General Cremona's shoulder.

'Hey, Bud,' he whispered, 'what exactly do we want from this guy Feigl?'

'Feigl is in possession of certain data which jeopardises the integrity of the Waltz initiative, Mr President,' Cremona explained. 'The documentation supplies concrete corroboration of certain scenarios which our opponents have hitherto regarded as purely speculative. Rapid and effective retrieval of this–'

'That does it,' moaned the President.

The advisers all turned to him in surprise. 'Something wrong, Mr President?'

'Yes,' he lamented. 'I don't understand a word of all this. Why don't you guys ever tell me what's going on?'

FORTY-EIGHT

Unlike Moscow, Prague was designed with *Homo sapiens* in mind. Most of its buildings were made on a human scale, and one can walk its streets with reasonable confidence that one is not an ant. The city's problems are not of form, but of substance.

Prague badly needs a coat of paint. Though it is still one of the most beautiful cities in Europe, the Czech capital is grimy and worn down by years of neglect and pollution. The authorities have belatedly acknowledged the problem, and much of the Old Town is now under scaffolding. The medieval cathedrals, baroque palaces, and rococo houses are to be saved for the tourists. But the grey, flaking suburbs, where most people live, will be left to fend for themselves.

Nevertheless, as Wyman's taxi took him into the city centre, he smiled in approval of the cobbled squares, Gothic towers and narrow, porticoed streets. He left the taxi near the Old Town square, paid the driver, and politely refused to sell him any foreign currency. He spent a few minutes admiring the Tyn cathedral and fourteenth-century town hall, where some passers-by invited him to change money, before walking the last few hundred yards to his destination.

Wyman was sure that Herbie was not staying at a hotel. All Prague's hotels are run by Cedok, the state tourist agency, and Herbie would wish to avoid the attentions of any large organisations in the Socialist countries. Nevertheless, he would have to arrange his stay with some official body. He would therefore choose the smallest and least publicised, and one which could organise private accommodation in an obscure part of the city. Pragotour fitted the description perfectly.

This company consists of three girls, two telephones and a prehistoric typewriter in a tiny bar at number 2, Obecniho Domu. The 'office' is usually crammed with foreign students, who are charged ludicrous sums for coffee while they wait for their accommodation to be arranged. For about one third of the cost of a hotel room, they are found rooms in private homes on the city outskirts.

Wyman stepped into the bar and

introduced himself to the girl at the counter.

'I'm looking for a gentleman who booked a place with you recently,' he said, taking out a photograph of Herbie. 'I wonder if you remember him.'

The girl studied the photography carefully, and shook her head.

'I'm sorry,' she said. 'I'll ask the others.'

Another girl recognised Herbie's face, and looked up at Wyman.

'This is Herr Becker, isn't it?'

'That's right,' Wyman said quickly. 'Do you know where he's staying?'

She went to a filing cabinet and riffled through some receipts.

'With the Pitras,' she said, and she wrote down the address for Wyman.

'Take the Metro to the Hradcanska stop,' she explained, 'and change onto an 8, 22 or 23 tram for U Kastanu. It's a couple of minutes' walk from there.'

Wyman thanked her profusely, politely declined to change any currency, and almost danced out of the bar. A few minutes later he was on a Metro train for Hradcanska, the stop just outside Prague castle. The tram journey was quicker than he expected, and within half and hour he was at U Kastanu, a sombre district of colourless houses and drab, dusty shops.

Despite its leaden appearance, this area was home to Prague's more affluent citizens, its professional and managerial classes. Wyman reread the address given him by the girl at Pragotour, and noticed that he was visiting a doctor. Judging by the white hair and wrinkled face of the man who opened the door at number 26, Listopadu, Dr Pitra was retired.

'Good afternoon,' Wyman said. 'I am a friend of Herr Becker, who I believe is staying with you.'

Dr Pitra was mildly suspicious.

'Herr Becker is not here,' he said. 'Perhaps I can help.'

'Perhaps you can,' Wyman smiled. 'My name is Wyman. I am English. I have been looking for Herr Becker on a matter of some urgency. It concerns a mutual friend.'

Wyman could see an elderly woman looking out anxiously from the far end of the hallway. Dr Pitra turned to her and shrugged.

'Please come in,' he said to Wyman.

'Would you like some tea?' asked the woman.

'Yes please,' Wyman said.

The woman retreated to the kitchen, and

Wyman was shown into the living-room.

'Who is this mutual friend?' asked Dr Pitra.

'His name's Feigl,' Wyman said.

Dr Pitra shook his head.

'I've never heard of him. And I'm afraid Herr Becker left here two days ago.'

'Indeed?' Wyman said. 'Do you know where he went?'

'I'm afraid not,' Dr Pitra said apologetically.

'Is he still in Czechoslovakia?'

'I've no idea.'

'He didn't say what he was doing?'

'No.'

'Did he leave a forwarding address?'

Dr Pitra smiled sadly.

'Alas, no.'

Wyman took a deep breath. Dr Pitra was a polite, charming, affable brick wall.

'This is most unfortunate,' Wyman said, but a suspicion was forming in his mind.

'Was Herr Becker expecting any friends to visit him?' he asked.

Dr Pitra gave a melancholy sigh.

'He was not expecting friends,' he said pointedly.

'I understand,' Wyman nodded. 'Has anyone called for him?'

'Not yet. Except yourself, of course.'

Wyman decided on a change of approach.

'It's a pity he didn't leave a forwarding address. If he had, I could have asked you to pass on a message.'

The old woman came into the room with a tray of cups. Each contained a tea-bag and a thin slice of lemon. Without saying a word, she poured hot water into the cups, took one for herself and sat down.

'Of course,' Wyman added, 'it's just possible that Herr Becker may be in touch with you again.'

'Possible,' Dr Pitra agreed, 'but unlikely.'

'Even so, we shouldn't leave anything to chance.'

'Maybe not,' Dr Pitra said.

Wyman picked up his cup, fished out the tea-bag and took a tentative sip. It tasted awful. He tried not to pull a face, but his discomfort was plain. Dr Pitra watched him with interest.

'I was once in England,' he said. 'Many years ago. The English don't like tea this way, do they?'

'It's quite all right,' Wyman said hastily. 'I really don't–'

'They drink strong teas,' Pitra said, ignoring him. 'With milk. It's the Russians who like it without.'

He exchanged glances with the woman, and turned to Wyman.

'As I say, it's unlikely that Herr Becker will be seeing us again. But perhaps you should leave me your message for him.'

Wyman grinned and tore out a page from his diary. He wrote down an address and gave it to Dr Pitra.

'Herr Becker can reach me through this place. It's quite safe. No third parties know about it.'

'Perhaps that's so,' Dr Pitra said drily. 'But how could Herr Becker be sure that you are not a third party?'

'Good point,' Wyman conceded.

He considered this for a moment, and added something to the address. Dr Pitra studied it with interest.

'"*Cogito, ergo discipulus non sum.*" He would understand this?'

Wyman nodded.

'He should. It's a private joke about students.'

'Curious,' Dr Pitra mused. 'Herr Becker didn't strike me as a particularly humorous man.'

'He doesn't have much to laugh about at the moment,' Wyman said. 'Perhaps this will cheer him up.'

The old woman muttered something to Dr Pitra, who nodded in agreement and peered uneasily at Wyman.

'There is one more small thing,' he said.

'Yes?'

'It is perhaps trivial...'

'I'm sure it isn't,' Wyman said eagerly.

Dr Pitra glanced again at the old woman, and in a low voice, he said: 'Perhaps you would like to change some money?'

FORTY-NINE

Wyman returned to the centre of Prague, wondering just how successful his visit had been. Over the years, he had encountered many obscure characters, but Dr Pitra took the price for sheer inscrutability. Herbie might still be in Prague, he might have left. He might have told his landlord who he was, he might not. Dr Pitra might have understood Wyman's request, he might not. There was no way of deciding, which was precisely what Dr Pitra had intended.

One thing was certain: Wyman had no further business in Prague. Even if Herbie was nearby, he would not contact Wyman in Czechoslovakia. Wyman must leave Prague as swiftly as possible.

The next flight was in four hours. Wyman decided to pass another hour in the city centre, spend some of the money he had been required to convert into Czech currency, and then walk down to the Vltava air terminal for a coach to Ruzyne Airport. He strolled down the Celetna, and found himself a table in a noisy, crowded beer-house.

Wyman was not a great beer-drinker, but he was prepared to change his habits in Prague. Czechoslovakia produces some of the world's finest brands, including the Pilsen beers, whose name has been hijacked by inferior foreign products. A large glass of Urquell does not solve all one's problems, but it makes them much easier to bear.

He gulped down his first glass quickly and appreciatively, and ordered another, for a more considered analysis. As an after-thought, he ordered a bowl of goulash and dumpling. The second glass was even better than the first, and the goulash was thick and hot. Wyman barely noticed the man who sat beside him and ordered a glass of water.

'Good food?' the man inquired.

Wyman nodded eagerly.

'Excellent,' he said, through a mouthful of goulash.

The man lit a cigarette and watched the Englishman in quiet amusement.

'How long have you been in Prague?'

'Not long,' Wyman said.

He swallowed another mouthful of beer, and looked thoughtfully at his companion.

'And I'm going today,' he said, 'so I'm

afraid I can't change any currency.'

The man smiled appreciatively, as if Wyman had made a witty remark.

'Not to worry,' he chuckled.

Wyman finished his goulash and pushed the bowl to one side. He emitted a satisfied belch, and glanced at his watch.

'Going soon?' the man asked.

'Quite soon,' Wyman said. 'My flight leaves in three hours.'

The man looked at his own watch, and shook his head.

'No,' he said.

'No?'

'No,' he repeated firmly. 'Your flight leaves in one hour and forty-five minutes.'

Wyman lit a cigarette, and paused to consider this.

'That's cutting it a little fine,' he observed. 'I'm not sure the air-terminal coaches are regular enough.'

'There's a car outside.'

Wyman finished his beer, and called for the bill.

'I'll pay,' said the man.

'Very kind of you,' Wyman said.

'Not at all.'

'Could I phone my wife?' Wyman asked. 'She's expecting me tonight, you see...'

'We have already called her,' said the man. 'We told her you would be home late to-morrow evening.'

'Will I?'

The man replied with a pained expression.

'I beg your pardon,' Wyman said.

FIFTY

Wyman put down his knife and fork, and flirted with the possibility of a third fried egg. The word 'cholesterol' nagged at his thoughts, and he reluctantly abandoned the idea. He poured himself another coffee and gazed contentedly at his surroundings. Leningrad's Astoriya hotel is a sumptuous, pre-revolutionary establishment, which serves sumptuous, pre-revolutionary breakfasts. If life in Communist countries is a continual struggle against drabness, shortages and conformity, the Astoriya is coping admirably. Its cool green lounges, with priceless Tsarist furnishings and immaculate waiters are an elegant gesture of contempt for the twentieth century. If it achieves nothing else, Wyman thought, this business has given me a first-class tour of Eastern Europe.

Wyman had not had time to wander round Leningrad, though the little he had seen the previous evening sharpened his appetite for more. He went to the main lounge, and looked out on to St Isaac's Square, with the huge, ornate cathedral at the far end, over-loaded with pediments and porticoes, statues and gilded cupolas. It seemed too good to miss. Wyman wondered whether to risk a short walk, or wait for his host to arrive. The choice was made for him by a cheerful bellow from the doorway.

'Professor! Good morning! You are well?'

Wyman nodded affably.

'Fine thank you, General,' he said. 'You are also well, I trust?'

'Of course, of course,' Zhdanov said. 'How do you like your hotel? It is very splendid, I think.'

'I think so too,' Wyman smiled. 'Thank you for arranging my stay.'

Zhdanov shrugged modestly.

'I thought this would agree with your tastes. The Astoriya has a great reputation.'

He pointed to an old menu, framed on the wall.

'You know, during the war, the Nazis came within twelve miles of Leningrad. They thought they would be here the next day. Hitler ordered his chef to prepare a victory menu, for the next evening in the Astoriya. They never came, and Hitler never got his meal. But we still have the menu.'

'You were here at the time, weren't you?' Wyman said.

'Yes,' Zhdanov nodded. 'I am from this area. Leningrad is my home city. It is very beautiful, yes?'

'What I've seen is fabulous,' Wyman said. 'But that isn't very much.'

'Of course,' Zhdanov said understandingly. 'I will show you more. But first we can talk some business.'

They sank into armchairs at the far end of the lounge, and Zhdanov called over a waiter.

'Cognac,' he said, and glancing at Wyman he added: 'Two?'

'No thank you,' Wyman gasped. 'A little early for me, I'm afraid.'

'I wake at five a.m.,' Zhdanov said. 'It helps to be ahead of everyone else.'

'Just so,' Wyman smiled.

The General sent the waiter away, and rubbed his hands vigorously.

'Now,' he declared. 'You have something for me, yes?'

'Do I?' Wyman said.

'But of course. You have found Feigl, I think.'

'No. But I think I could.'

The General nodded.

'I understand. He is no longer in Prague?'

'You know he isn't,' Wyman said tonelessly. 'If he were, you'd have him by now, and we wouldn't be holding this conversation.'

'Very logical,' Zhdanov laughed. 'But I forget, you are a professor of Logics. Very good, Professor: you can find Feigl; I need Feigl; we should do business together. Logical, yes?'

'Not really,' Wyman said. 'You don't need Feigl. You need his information.'

'True,' Zhdanov admitted.

'This is what baffles me, General. Whatever Feigl has is highly sensitive. You expect me simply to hand it over on a plate. Why?'

'Because Feigl is your friend,' Zhdanov said. 'He is in danger. If I receive this information, he will be safe again. If I do not, he will be killed.'

'You sound remarkably confident about that,' Wyman observed, 'considering you've had no luck in finding him.'

'He will be found,' Zhdanov said simply. 'And he will die. I promise you.'

'And my loyalty to my friend surpasses my loyalty to the West, is that it?'

Zhdanov rolled his eyes wearily.

'The West,' he groaned. 'What is this compost? I expect logics from you, Professor, not propaganda. The West is in no danger; just a few Western political careers. It is not the same thing.'

'No,' Wyman said thoughtfully. 'I suppose it isn't.'

The waiter arrived with the brandy, which the General downed like lemonade.

'Good,' he said, and he ordered another.

'Very well, General,' Wyman said quietly. 'You want to do business, as you put it. Here is my proposal: you will call off your search for Herbert Feigl, and allow me to find him.'

'This sounds reasonable,' Zhdanov said. 'Then you will give me his documents, yes?'

'Then we will negotiate.'

Zhdanov frowned.

'Negotiate?' he repeated. 'Is that all?'

'Yes.'

'This is not business,' Zhdanov growled. 'This guarantees nothing for me.'

'It guarantees that we will negotiate. You have my word on that.'

Zhdanov laughed incredulously.

'I should trust you?'

'You have to,' Wyman said. 'I'm the only person who can find Feigl. Oh yes, I've no doubt you could track him down if you had a couple of years to spare. But you haven't. You need my knowledge.'

Zhdanov's face grew uglier, which was quite an achievement.

'Remember where you are, Professor,' he said. 'I do need your knowledge. I am in an excellent position to get it.'

'Only theoretically,' Wyman smiled. 'You could wield the bright light and the rubber truncheon, I suppose, but I don't think you want that. It would draw attention to you.'

'Attention?' Zhdanov exclaimed. 'From who? The West? No more joking, Professor.'

'No joking, General. Not from the West; from your own people. The Politburo, for example.'

Zhdanov gave a dismissive snort, but it lacked conviction.

'You are not making sense,' he said guardedly. 'My aim is the same as the government's.'

'Not exactly,' Wyman said. 'Your government wants to scupper an agreement between two Western powers. You're after the architect of that agreement. It's your good fortune that both can be achieved by the same means.'

'What is this rubbish?'

'If the agreement is destroyed, Dr Gebhard will go down with it.'

Zhdanov smiled sourly.

'Austrian foreign policy is dictated by the Austrian government. The President is just a national figurehead.'

'That's right,' Wyman agreed. 'Which is why Gebhard can't move until the new government is elected. But it's his policy, isn't it? His signature is written all over it. And as you said yourself, political careers are at stake. I think you have a personal interest in Gebhard's career.'

The General peered at Wyman warily.

'You have a reason for saying this?'

'I think so,' Wyman said, and his voice dropped to a whisper. 'But is this the best place to discuss it, *Tovarishch* Gureyvitch?'

Zhdanov took it calmly. He sat perfectly still, and his eyes narrowed into two tiny slits. For a long time he said nothing, ignoring the second glass of brandy when it was placed in front of him. Finally he nodded, as if he had reached a painful decision.

'Perhaps,' he said, 'you would like me to show you something of the city.'

Wyman picked up his cigarettes and put them in his pocket.

'Why not?' he said.

FIFTY-ONE

They left the Astoriya and walked slowly along the Ulitsa Gertsena, past the former German and Italian embassies, and down on to the Nevskiy Prospekt, Leningrad's main boulevard. The latter is possibly the most famous street in Russia, with over two miles of apartments, shops, monuments, squares and palaces, ranging in style from the baroque and classical of the eighteenth century to the art nouveau of the early twentieth. The canals and rivers which run across it are faintly reminiscent of Amsterdam, but the elaborate designs of the buildings and their uninhibited colours – dazzling blues, greens, yellows and crimsons – are uniquely Russian.

'Beautiful, yes?' Zhdanov said, rather unnecessarily.

'Very,' Wyman smiled. 'It survived the war remarkably well, didn't it?'

'Yes,' Zhdanov said, 'but much was reconstructed also.'

He pointed to a notice painted on to the

walls of one of the buildings.

'This has been kept as a reminder of the siege. It says "Citizens! During artillery bombardment this side of the street is very dangerous". I tell you, Professor, the other side was not much safer.'

'That was the time you joined the army, wasn't it?'

Zhdanov ignored the question, and continued to gaze at the notice.

'They had big guns, with 900-kilo shells. But this was not the biggest danger. There were three and a half million people here, but when the siege began in September we had one month's supply of food. One month!

'Then they were eating dogs and cats, and later soap, paper, tree bark and leather. The women ate their lipstick. Some ate dead humans. The West says we think too much about that war, that it is just history now. But Professor, more people died just in this city than all the English and Americans in all the war. How can we forget?'

'I looked in the records for that period,' Wyman said. 'The Secretary of the Leningrad Party was called Zhdanov. Did you name yourself after him?'

Zhdanov grinned sheepishly.

'He was the most powerful man here. I

never said he was my relative, but nobody would take any risks with me. They asked no questions.'

They walked on, pausing to look at the Kazan cathedral and its great arc of Corinthian columns, modelled on the colonnade of St Peter's in Rome. Although it was bitterly cold, an ice-cream stand on the pavement was doing excellent business.

'How did you encounter Gebhard?' Wyman asked.

The General's face clouded again, and he gazed uncomfortably into space.

'We have never met,' he said. 'I think I would kill him if we met.'

They sat down on a bench by the cathedral, and Zhdanov struggled to collect his thoughts.

'I have read his books,' he said. 'All of them. I could not believe they were by him. Poison. Lies. And his letters to me!'

'Asking for the release of dissidents?'

Zhdanov nodded grimly.

'For *humanitarian* reasons. I wanted to write to him, to remind him of everything. Of course, I could not.'

'Precisely what happened?'

Zhdanov waved in the direction of the cathedral.

'I come from a village to the west of this city. Forty, forty-five kilometres. There were some Jews there. Not many: most were transported east in the time of the Tsar. My family stayed, with others.

'When the Germans came in 1941, their army was under General von Leeb. Twenty-nine divisions. Later, more came from the south. They were mostly professionals: fast Panzer divisions, and so on. But in July, Hitler sent in the SS *Einsatzgruppe,* the action squads. These were different. They were here just to liquidate citizens. Mostly Jews, but also others.

'I was in this city when the Germans came to my village. A *Wehrmacht* infantry unit. Gebhard was in charge of this. The SS came two days later. They showed him their orders to kill all the people. Gebhard took away his own men so they did not see.'

'How did you find out it was Gebhard?'

'He had some prisoners, who heard this. These men escaped, and one later told me.'

'And the SS killed your family?'

'All. Father, mother, three sisters, brother.'

'Not all of them,' Wyman said quietly. 'Your brother escaped. He's in England now. That's how I know.'

Zhdanov stared hard at Wyman.

361

'Semyon lives? Why has he never…?'

His voice tailed off, for he knew the answer to his own question.

'I'm still puzzled,' Wyman said. 'Your family was killed by the SS, not Gebhard. Why do you blame him?'

'He did nothing,' Zhdanov said. 'He knew this was criminal, but he went away. Then, many years later, he writes about conscience. He says laws and orders are not enough, the hypocrite…'

At last Wyman understood. Zhdanov's rage was born of pain, and impervious to time and reason.

'It may sound pretty feeble,' Wyman said, 'but Gebhard was a young man. Most people would have done the same.'

'Most people are not respected thinkers,' Zhdanov hissed. 'Most people are not national leaders.'

Wyman smiled sadly.

'Most people aren't leaders of the KGB, and look at what *they're* responsible for. What about Bulgakov? Do you deny knowledge of that piece of savagery?'

Zhdanov was unimpressed.

'Bulgakov was not an innocent.'

Wyman stared at the General in disbelief. 'They tortured him to death,' he said faintly. 'Slowly, viciously, and they filmed the lot, *pour encourager les autres.*'

'Yes,' Zhdanov said stubbornly. 'It is our rule. He knew this. I did not invent this policy…'

He shook his head in irritation, and swore angrily in Russian.

'And what about Eddie Fulton?' Wyman persisted. 'He was an innocent. Why murder him? What could that achieve?'

'Fulton?' Zhdanov barked. 'Fulton? What are you talking about?'

'What could you gain from his death?'

Zhdanov smiled unpleasantly.

'Nothing,' he said.

Wyman frowned in bewilderment.

'But in that case, why did you have him killed?'

Zhdanov leaned back on the seat and gazed merrily at the Englishman.

'We did not kill him,' he said.

FIFTY-TWO

Winter had come to Bohinj. Beneath a milky sky, the lake had grown livid and opaque. A sharp, stiff air had settled upon the valley, stripping the mountains of their verdure and bleaching them with snow. Only the conifers lent any colour to the landscape, and that too was weak and leaden.

Wyman's cheeks tingled with cold as he tramped slowly along the path beside the lake. His memories of this route were not fond ones, and the going was even harder this time. The path was lost beneath the snow, and the deep gullies which ran through it had filled up, giving a perilous illusion of evenness.

It took him a long time to reach the woodcutter's hut, and when he arrived he was sagging with exhaustion. Despite the cold, his face shone with sweat, and he was quite breathless. For several minutes he leaned against the door of the hut, gasping loudly and cursing his declining years.

'You're out of condition,' said a voice behind him.

Wyman slowly turned round to see a short, bald man with pale blue eyes, a wispy moustache and an automatic pistol.

'I'm too old for this sort of thing,' Wyman panted, 'and so are you, Herbie. What's the gun for?'

'Are you alone?'

Wyman nodded.

'Good.'

Feigl put the gun inside his coat and shook Wyman's hand.

'Thank you,' he said.

Wyman grinned, and looked up and down at the fugitive schoolmaster.

'You've lost a lot of weight,' he said enviously. 'Are you well?'

'I'm alive,' Feigl said drily.

'You've led them a merry dance, you know. Half the time they thought you'd been killed, and the rest of the time they wondered where you were.'

Feigl smiled appreciatively.

'Cretins,' he said. 'But what about you, Michael? Did you think I was dead?'

'For a while,' Wyman admitted. 'Then I found out that Gebhard's books were missing from your hotel. It seemed curious, but someone might have stolen them. Later I discovered how desperate the Russians were to find you. A gentleman called Zhdanov insisted you were alive and offered me every assistance in tracking you down. At first I thought it was some sort of trick, to make me reveal the information they sought from you.

'But then I remembered Lalic. There was no satisfactory explanation for his death. The Americans found his body, and they assumed the KGB were responsible. But Lalic was looking for you, and the Russians wouldn't kill him until he'd led them to their quarry. You must have done it.'

Feigl grinned ruefully.

'I should have buried him,' he sighed. 'It all happened so fast. I just panicked and ran away.'

He lit a cigarette and flicked the spent match into the snow.

'Originally,' he said, 'I planned to hide up here. I had spare clothes, and false papers I'd had made in Vienna. I thought everything would blow over quickly, and it was just a question of spending a few nights up in the mountains hiding from the search-parties.

'Unfortunately, Lalic found me a few days

later. He knew this area as well as I did, from the war, and he guessed where I was. He said they were all here looking for me: Americans, Russians, all prepared to kill me for this.'

He patted a bulge in his coat.

'Lalic said they were after him too. We'd both die if we didn't hand over the documents. The fool was still convinced he could bargain for some money. I told him he was an imbecile, and he got angry. He threatened to tell them where I was. We had a fight, and he tried to pull a gun out. I got it first and shot him.'

'And then you ran.'

'Immediately,' Feigl said. 'I've been running ever since. And each day I expected to die.'

He looked away and shrugged, and Wyman felt a sudden pang of pity for this small, lonely man.

'It's finished,' Wyman said softly.

Feigl glanced at him sharply.

'Is it?' he said.

'I think so. The Austrian elections are at the end of next week. Gebhard will visit Washington a few days later, and a formal declaration will be signed. After that it won't matter.'

Feigl frowned.

'Are you sure?' he said. 'These documents...'

'Could scupper that agreement. That's what the Russians want. But they'll be too late.'

Feigl seemed confused.

'Is that all? But ... but Gebhard...'

'Gebhard is worried about his agreement. I think he sees it as his life's work. Once it's gone though, he won't care what happens.'

Feigl's eyes bulged in amazement.

'He won't care,' he repeated. 'My God. The sheer cynicism...'

Wyman shrugged sympathetically.

'It's a cynical business, Herbie. The best thing to do is forget it and go home. You can do that now. Look, why don't we get something to eat? It must be a while since you ate in a restaurant.'

'A month or two,' Herbie agreed.

FIFTY-THREE

They climbed down to the lake and followed the path towards the eastern shore. Despite Feigl's long familiarity with this route, they still moved no faster than when Wyman had come out alone. At first Wyman supposed that Herbie was moving slowly in deference to his exhaustion, but he began to have his doubts. As they moved out of the woods and into more open land, these suspicions were confirmed. Feigl slowed down, and looked ahead apprehensively. For the last five hundred yards, the path ran through a bare, gently sloping field.

'We're quite exposed,' he muttered. 'They can see us from the mountain, the woods, everywhere. And we're perfectly silhouetted against the snow.'

'Old habits die hard, eh?' Wyman observed.

'Feigls die hard,' Herbie snapped.

They stopped, and Wyman looked upwards in exasperation.

'It really is quite safe,' he insisted. 'The

Russians aren't looking for you any longer. I've seen to that.'

'And the Americans?'

'They aren't a problem. The Americans know me, and they know what I'm doing. Obviously, they're not exactly delighted with you. You can't just snaffle the details of something as sensitive as Project Waltz, and then expect them to love you for it. I'm still baffled by how you got hold of...'

His voice trailed off, as he noticed a curious expression on Feigl's face.

'Project Waltz?' Herbie said. 'What do you mean?'

'Your documents,' Wyman said. 'I presume they contain details of the proposed agreement.'

Herbie smiled uneasily.

'I don't know what you're talking about,' he said, 'but I think you've made some sort of mistake.'

He unbuttoned his coat and drew out a thick wad of papers. Wyman took them and glanced at the first. It was printed in Serbo-Croat.

'Look at the second one,' Herbie suggested. 'That's the English translation.'

The second item, a carbon-copy numbered FBROI 25572a, was much smaller, and presumably it represented only part of the Yugoslav document. Nevertheless, Wyman found it most surprising.

'"Submission to the Yugoslav War Crimes Commission, September 1946, from Lieutenant Herbert Feigl RA." What on earth…?'

'Page twelve contains the key item,' Herbie added.

The paragraphs in question were ringed in pencil.

'"While I never encountered *Oberleutnant* Gebhard personally",' Wyman read out, '"I became well acquainted with his work. His unit was responsible for the massacre at Cazin in 1944, whose aftermath I witnessed twenty-four hours later.

'"Gebhard was held prisoner at a compound at Stara Fuzina, Slovenia, early in 1945, while I was in the Bohinj area. Unfortunately, he escaped before I had an opportunity to interrogate him. Nevertheless, his rank was undisputed, and he is formally responsible for several well-known atrocities in Bosnia, Montenegro and elsewhere. Certain witnesses, cited in the appendix, can also prove his physical involvement in a number of these incidents.

'"As an *Abwehroffizier* with 03 status, his duties included *Gefangenvernehmung*, ie interrogation of prisoners (including civilian captives), *Sonderaufgaben,* or 'special tasks', including torture and murder of civilians, reprisal raids, etc" ... Lord!'

Wyman read the rest in silence. Suddenly a great many things made sense. His last conversation with Gebhard had been conducted entirely at cross purposes: Wyman had requested the early announcement of Project Waltz; Gebhard had refused to reveal the most unpleasant episode of his career. And Zhdanov sought more than just the downfall of an old scapegoat: he wanted the justification for more than forty years of obsessive hatred.

'I'd forgotten all about it,' Herbie said. 'It was Lalic who remembered. He and Gebhard were both prisoners at Stara Fuzina. When Gebhard stood for the Presidency, Lalic couldn't believe his ears. He knew Gebhard was named in this report, and he went to Belgrade to get a copy. Page twelve had been removed from all editions.

'He knew it had been sent as evidence to the United Nations War Crimes Commission, but their copy was apparently not available. The same went for the US National Archives, which keeps copies of the captured German war documents.

Everywhere he tried, these documents were lost, mutilated or "unavailable". There had been a meticulous cleaning-up operation. Then Lalic remembered me. He came to the school and made all kinds of crazy offers for my copy. He said we could negotiate a fabulous deal with the Russians. I said "no", but he wouldn't go away. Then strange people appeared in the village, asking questions about me and my movements.'

'And that was when you decided to run?'

'Sort of,' Herbie said. 'You see, Lalic made it clear that no one would help me. For some reason the Americans wanted to protect Gebhard, and they would destroy any evidence at the first opportunity. So it was no use asking for police protection, or anything like that.

'I was due to come here for my annual holiday, but I decided to confront Gebhard first. I used the pretext of Freedom of Conscience, and took along some of his books for him to sign. I told him I was going to publicise the information, because this was the only way I could protect myself. I told him he should withdraw from the election campaign to minimise the embarrassment, and make a full confession.'

'How did he react?'

'He said the allegations were untrue, and he could prove it. But the scandal would damage him anyway, and he couldn't afford that. He said there was a vital international agreement in the pipeline, and only he could see it through. He must have been talking about Project Waltz, or whatever you call it. However false, these allegations could destroy the agreement. If it was simply a matter of his personal reputation, he would have no fears, but something far more important was at stake. It was all sickeningly noble.'

Herbie smiled bitterly.

'Then he turned nasty. He said he would use every means to prevent publication of the document. No Austrian newspaper would touch it, I could be sure of that. Foreign papers could be stopped easily: I had no idea of the interests involved here, he said.

'Finally, he smiled and became Mr Nice again. He said it would all blow over, and I shouldn't worry about the Russians. He changed the subject, and talked about Freedom of Conscience, signed his books, and showed me out, as if nothing had happened. Then I knew I must run and hide.'

Wyman folded up the papers and gave

them back to Herbie.

'I don't think he was wholly dishonest,' he said. 'He really does believe in that agreement, and it's quite true that it can't happen without him. Of course that's no consolation for–'

He was interrupted by a sharp crack from about twenty feet away. Herbie shuddered and pitched forward, dropping the papers on to the snow. Wyman caught him, and let him sink slowly to the ground. He could hear running footsteps, and he looked up to see a man coming towards him, gun in hand.

'Rawls!' Wyman yelled. 'For God's sake, stop it!'

Rawls ignored him, and looked down at the ground. Herbie lay on his back, moaning quietly. A large pool of blood was spreading on the snow under his head. Without pausing, Rawls aimed his gun at Herbie's face and squeezed the trigger three times.

There was a long, long silence, as Wyman stood frozen with shock, and Rawls calmly gathered the blood-splattered papers from the ground.

'Why?' Wyman said finally.

'Orders,' Rawls said briskly. 'Sorry.'

'But there was no need...'

'There was. Feigl was a walking disaster-area. Even without the papers, he could still cause all kinds of hassle.'

'Like Eddie Fulton,' Wyman said. 'You killed him as well, didn't you?'

Rawls nodded.

'For different reasons. The guy was an ass-hole. Mouth like a symphony orchestra.'

'What about me?' Wyman said. 'I also know too much.'

'No,' Rawls said. 'You aren't Fulton. You know how to keep your trap shut. And you aren't Feigl, either. You weren't here in the war. You don't know all the dirty little details.'

'Herbie was a decent man,' Wyman breathed. 'And you've murdered him to save that scoundrel in Vienna.'

'No,' Rawls repeated. 'We did it to save the Waltz agreement. That's what counts. Even if it's signed and sealed, how can we go through with it if all this shit comes out? The Jewish lobby would get deeply pissed off if we had anything to do with a suspected war criminal, right?'

He put the documents into his pocket and studied the body on the ground.

'What do you reckon he weighs? Two hundred pounds? I could use a hand burying him.'

376

Wyman did not reply, but his expression made it clear that his shock was rapidly turning to anger.

'OK, OK,' Rawls said hastily. 'I'll do it myself. Sorry I asked.'

He took off Herbie's heavy coat and walking-boots to lighten the load, and threw them to one side.

'At least you can get rid of those for me,' he said, slinging Herbie's body over his shoulder in a fireman's lift. 'Jesus! This guy weighs.'

Using the side of his shoe, he kicked fresh snow across the blood patches, until nothing could be seen. Then he turned and gazed apologetically at Wyman.

'Look, I'm sorry. Really, I am. You've got every right to feel bad. But it's ... it's...'

'Nothing personal?'

'Yeah,' Rawls said lamely. 'Goodbye, Wyman.'

He turned round again, and walked away towards the woods. Wyman picked up Herbie's coat and boots. He felt oddly numb and light-headed, and with complete detachment he noticed his hands were trembling violently. Now, he reflected, I think I know how people go insane.

EPILOGUE

'Jesus wept!' Frank Schofield exclaimed. 'In cold blood? Just like that?'

'Just like that,' Wyman said.

It was past one o'clock in the Foreign Press Club, and the two men had consumed a respectable number of grappas. The waiter had long since abandoned his efforts to evict his garrulous patrons, and had fallen asleep behind the bar. Schofield sighed heavily and nodded.

'Well Mike, I admit it: I'm impressed. It's one fuck of a story. But as things stand, I don't see how I could use it. Without the documentary proof—'

'One moment,' Wyman broke in. 'I haven't finished yet.'

He opened the file on the table and produced some papers. Schofield gave them a quick glance, and stared at Wyman.

'Is all this what I think it is?'

Wyman nodded.

'Jesus wept!' Schofield repeated. 'But how did you...?'

Wyman looked down at his glass, and spoke in a halting whisper.

'I was in a very – odd, yes, odd state. On reflection, I think it was sheer rage. I've never been so furious in all my life. Not just with Rawls, but Gebhard, Zhdanov, the lot of them. Even Ashbroke-Sands. All these bloody prefects and functionaries.'

The grappa was taking its toll of Wyman. His eyes resembled two beetroots, and he swayed gently in his chair.

'Rawls threw away Herbie's coat. He didn't know there was a gun in it. I took it out and followed him into the woods. When I got to within ten feet of him, I called out his name. I wanted him to turn and see me first.'

Schofield's jaw fell open.

'You shot him?'

'Yes. He didn't have time to move. Herbie was still draped over his shoulder, like a rag doll. As I fired, he looked at me with total astonishment. He really hadn't the faintest idea why I was killing him.'

'Are you kidding? He just murdered your friend…'

'Ah,' Wyman said bitterly, 'but that was for a *reason*. It makes all the difference, you see. I was supposed to understand that. After all,

I was one of the boys myself, once. Anything's allowed, provided there's a reason. A rule, an order, a purpose. It's the gratuitous that's unthinkable. The spontaneous. The irrational. The *human*.'

He belched and waved at the files.

'It's all there,' he said. 'Gebhard may have Europe sewn up, but things are different in the United States. At least, I bloody well hope they are. Someone will print them.'

Schofield leafed through the documents and pursed his lips.

'Yeah, I guess someone will. You just want me to give them this, or the whole story?'

'Start with the documents,' Wyman said. 'If things get sticky, we'll take it from there.'

'If?' Schofield exclaimed. 'If? You aren't expecting an easy ride, are you?'

Wyman shrugged.

'We'll see.'

Schofield put the papers back in the file, and emitted a low whistle.

'Hot shit,' he observed. 'That guy will fight this all the way. He'll deny it, he'll call it a forgery, he'll do everything to discredit it.'

'Let him. It's true.'

'So what?' Schofield said cynically. 'Truth

isn't always plausible. I mean, who the fuck is going to believe that an elected Western leader is a war criminal? These things just don't happen.'

The publishers hope that this book has given you enjoyable reading. Large Print Books are especially designed to be as easy to see and hold as possible. If you wish a complete list of our books please ask at your local library or write directly to:

Dales Large Print Books
Magna House, Long Preston,
Skipton, North Yorkshire.
BD23 4ND

This Large Print Book for the partially sighted, who cannot read normal print, is published under the auspices of

THE ULVERSCROFT FOUNDATION

THE ULVERSCROFT FOUNDATION

... we hope that you have enjoyed this Large Print Book. Please think for a moment about those people who have worse eyesight problems than you ... and are unable to even read or enjoy Large Print, without great difficulty.

You can help them by sending a donation, large or small to:

**The Ulverscroft Foundation,
1, The Green, Bradgate Road,
Anstey, Leicestershire, LE7 7FU,
England.**
or request a copy of our brochure for more details.

The Foundation will use all your help to assist those people who are handicapped by various sight problems and need special attention.

Thank you very much for your help.